I0652627

SPUN YARNS UNWOUND: VOL. 1

SCIENCE FICTION FOR ALL AGES

DEBBIE MUMFORD
DEB LOGAN

WDM
Publishing

SCIENCE FICTION FOR ALL AGES

This volume of Spun Yarns Unwound contains science fiction stories written by WDM Publishing's authors.

Deb Logan typically writes contemporary fantasy for younger readers, but in these five tales, she ventures into space.

Debbie Mumford has enjoyed reading science fiction since childhood and writes its short form as often as she can find the time.

So sit back, relax, and look into the future with our authors!

COPYRIGHT

SPUN YARNS UNWOUND: VOL. 1
SCIENCE FICTION FOR ALL AGES
Copyright © 2023 by Debbie Mumford
Published by WDM Publishing
Cover and Layout copyright © 2023 by WDM Publishing
Cover design by WDM Publishing
Cover art copyright © NASA/JPL-Caltech/Univ. of Virginia

"Chattermaster"
Copyright © 2020 by Debbie Mumford
Published by WDM Publishing
Cover and Layout copyright © 2020 by WDM Publishing
Cover design by WDM Publishing
Cover art copyright
© NatashaFedorova | Depositphotos.com

"The Case Of The Missing Inarian"
Copyright © 2021 by Debbie Mumford
First published in "2017 Young Explorer's Adventure Guide" by Dreaming Robot Press,
December, 2016
Published by WDM Publishing
Cover and Layout copyright © 2021 by WDM Publishing
Cover design by WDM Publishing
Cover art copyright © CMik3812345 | Dreamstime.com
and © interactimages | Depositphotos.com

"The Case Of The Glittering Hoard"
Copyright © 2021 by Debbie Mumford
First published in "Fiction River: Stolen" by WMG Publishing, August, 2020
Published by WDM Publishing
Cover and Layout copyright © 2021 by WDM Publishing
Cover design by WDM Publishing
Cover art copyright © CMik3812345 | Dreamstime.com
and © interactimages | Depositphotos.com

"The Case Of The Recreational Thief"
Copyright © 2021 by Debbie Mumford
Published by WDM Publishing
Cover and Layout copyright © 2021 by WDM Publishing
Cover design by WDM Publishing
Cover art copyright © CMik3812345 | Dreamstime.com
and © interactimages | Depositphotos.com

"The Case Of The Vanishing Puppy"
Copyright © 2021 by Debbie Mumford
Published by WDM Publishing
Cover and Layout copyright © 2021 by WDM Publishing
Cover design by WDM Publishing
Cover art copyright © CMik3812345 | Dreamstime.com
and © interactimages | Depositphotos.com

"In Search Of A Valentinian"
Copyright © 2022 by Debbie Mumford
Published by WDM Publishing
Cover and Layout copyright © 2022 by WDM Publishing
Cover design by WDM Publishing
Cover art copyright © yupiramos | Depositphotos.com
and © NASA/JPL-Caltech/UCLA

"Izzie"
Copyright © 2019 by Debbie Mumford
Published by WDM Publishing
Cover and Layout copyright © 2019 by WDM Publishing
Cover design by WDM Publishing
Cover art copyright © IuliiaVerstaBO | Depositphotos.com
and © Sergey Khakimullin | Dreamstime.com

"Simon Says"
Copyright © 2023 by Debbie Mumford
Published by WDM Publishing
Cover and Layout copyright © 2023 by WDM Publishing
Cover design by WDM Publishing
Cover art copyright © algolonline | Depositphotos.com and © NASA/JPL-Caltech/UCLA

"New Year"
Copyright © 2019 by Debbie Mumford

Published by WDM Publishing
Cover and Layout copyright © 2019 by WDM Publishing
Cover design by WDM Publishing
Cover art copyright © Sur | Dreamstime.com
and © Tihis | Dreamstime.com

"Spinning"
Copyright © 2019 by Debbie Mumford
Published by WDM Publishing
Cover and Layout copyright © 2019 by WDM Publishing
Cover design by WDM Publishing
Cover art copyright © Dbajurin | Dreamstime.com
and © Keith Tarrier | Dreamstime.com

"Stargazer"
Copyright © 2023 by Debbie Mumford
Published by WDM Publishing
Cover and Layout copyright © 2023 by WDM Publishing
Cover design by WDM Publishing
Cover art copyright © JozefKlopacka | Depositphotos.com

"The Warbirds Of Absaroka"
Copyright © 2018 by Debbie Mumford
Published by WDM Publishing
Cover and Layout copyright © 2018 by WDM Publishing
Cover design by WDM Publishing
Cover art copyright © Algol | Dreamstime.com

"Awakening The Warrior"
Copyright © 2019 by Debbie Mumford
Published by WDM Publishing
Cover and Layout copyright © 2019 by WDM Publishing
Cover design by WDM Publishing
Cover art copyright © innovari| Depositphotos.com

"Incident On The Odyssey"
Copyright © 2019 by Debbie Mumford
Published by WDM Publishing
Cover and Layout copyright © 2019 by WDM Publishing
Cover design by WDM Publishing
Cover art copyright © Veronika Surovtseva | Dreamstime.com

"The Queen's Captive"
Copyright © 2020 by Debbie Mumford
First published in Amazing Monster Tales, February, 2020
Published by WDM Publishing
Cover and Layout copyright © 2020 by WDM Publishing
Cover design by WDM Publishing
Cover art copyright © Luca Oleastri | Depositphotos.com

"The Lost Colony"
Copyright © 2020 by Debbie Mumford
Published by WDM Publishing
Cover and Layout copyright © 2020 by WDM Publishing
Cover design by WDM Publishing
Cover art copyright © Shad.off | Depositphotos.com

"Eremite"
Copyright © 2022 by Debbie Mumford
Published by WDM Publishing
Cover and Layout copyright © 2022 by WDM Publishing
Cover design by WDM Publishing
Cover art copyright © NASA/JPL-Caltech

"Freighter Families In Space"
Copyright © 2022 by Debbie Mumford
First published in Cargo Wars: Boundary Shock Quarterly 015, July, 2021
Published by WDM Publishing
Cover and Layout copyright © 2022 by WDM Publishing
Cover design by WDM Publishing
Cover art copyright © algolonline | Depositphotos.com
and © NASA/JPL-Caltech/UCLA

"Remembrance"
Copyright © 2019 by Debbie Mumford
Published by WDM Publishing
Cover and Layout copyright © 2019 by WDM Publishing
Cover design by WDM Publishing
Cover art copyright © ra2studio| Depositphotos.com

"An Alien Adventure"
Copyright © 2023 by Debbie Mumford
Published by WDM Publishing

Cover and Layout copyright © 2023 by WDM Publishing
Cover design by WDM Publishing
Cover art copyright © Angela_Harburn | Depositphotos.com

This book is licensed for your personal enjoyment only. All rights reserved. This is a work of fiction. All characters and events portrayed in this book are fictional, and any resemblance to real people or incidents is purely coincidental. This book, or parts thereof, may not be reproduced in any form without permission.

FIVE STORIES BY DEB LOGAN

PART I

CHATTERMASTER

DEB LOGAN

AUTHOR OF *THUNDERBIRD*

CHATTERMASTER

A "READ-TO-ME" STORY

B lake loved to talk. He rarely closed his mouth.
He chatted with his parents over protein shakes at break-fast. He gabbed to his friends on the way to the educational unit. He whispered answers to himself when his instructor called on someone else. He even chanted in a sing-song rhythm during recess in the exercise pod.

Sometimes his happy chatter annoyed other people.

"Don't talk with food in your mouth, Blake," Mother said at dinner one night. She spoke distinctly because the ship's galley brimmed with colonists. Most family units ate at six bells.

"But..."

Father held up one finger, preventing his son's reply.

Blake deflated. He'd only wanted to point out his mouth was empty.

"It's dinner time, Blake," said Father. "Get some food in your mouth."

Obediently, Blake bit into the replicated chicken, chewed and swallowed before opening his mouth. Mother spoke first.

"Tomorrow is a big day for you, Blake," she said, pausing to sip recycled water. "Master Farmer Jaden has agreed to test you for a possible apprenticeship."

Blake's mouth gaped, but no words came out. Master Farmer Jaden grew all the food for the Starship *Generations*. Blake's parents worked alongside the great man in the hydroponics gardens.

"You should be honored," said Father. "The Master Farmer rarely tests applicants."

2

Early the next morning Blake marched into the hydroponics pod. The chamber hummed with activity. Rows upon rows of green plants towered above stainless steel troughs. Pumps whirred, circulating nutrient-rich liquid to nourish the plants that fed the ship's occupants. Farmers and apprentices made careful adjustments or harvested ripe fruit.

Blake waved to Mother and Father. They smiled and nodded toward the Master Farmer's office.

At Blake's approach, the office doors whooshed open to reveal the Master Farmer hunched over a computer console. Wispy white hair framed a wrinkled face. Antique glasses perched upon his nose. When he looked up, faded brown eyes measured Blake.

"Good. You're prompt," said the old man. He straightened and strode past Blake out the door. "Walk with me and tell me what you know of gardening, boy."

Blake raced to keep up with the man's long-legged stride. The invitation to talk thrilled him.

"Both my parents are farmers," he said, "so I know lots about plants. This garden is so efficient, it feeds the whole ship. Nothing is wasted."

Blake happily parroted information gained during visits to the garden. He explained how the plants grew in liquid without icky, old-fashioned dirt. Blake gabbled non-stop, barely pausing to breathe.

Master Farmer Jaden stopped outside a chamber on the far side of the hydroponics pod. He raised a hand to stem Blake's chatter. Silver-green silence bloomed.

Blake waited.

The Master Farmer remained still.

Blake fidgeted, but kept quiet.

After what felt like ages, Master Farmer Jaden spoke. "Well, boy, it is clear you have an active mind and can absorb what you are told. Certainly, you communicate well. Both are qualities I will require in my next apprentice."

"That's wonderful, sir," said Blake. "I'd love to be your apprentice. Father always says..."

He trailed off at the old man's raised eyebrow.

Silence ruled again.

Blake squirmed under Master Farmer Jaden's gaze, but kept his lips together.

Finally, the Master Farmer spoke. "I will watch your progress, boy. When you're twelve, if you've learned the value of silence, you'll be my next apprentice.

"Make no mistake; this will be a challenging position. Your parents were born on this ship and have lived their whole lives with hydroponics, but things are changing. My next apprentice will be required to learn the secrets of this chamber."

The old man waved a hand and the chamber doors whooshed open.

Warm moist air greeted Blake as he stepped onto a dark, cushiony surface. An unfamiliar odor teased his nose. He sniffed cautiously and then inhaled deeply.

Master Farmer Jaden nodded. "That smell is dirt. These plants are growing in it. You're standing on it, too."

Blake glanced down. His thin-soled shoes sank into a mushy brown substance.

"Dirt?"

"Yes, dirt." The old man observed Blake's confusion, smiled and laid a hand on his shoulder. "You see, boy, this ship will reach planet-fall during the prime of your life. My next apprentice must learn the art of growing food in dirt. This small chamber has been preserved for generations to train the first planetside farmer.

"What do you think, Blake? Will you be up to the challenge?"

Blake squatted and touched the dirt. He pinched a bit, brought his fingers to his nose and savored the rich, distinctive aroma. Quiet warmth blossomed in his chest; he'd found his calling.

"Yes, sir!" he said. Blake grinned broadly—and closed his mouth.

PART II

THE CINNAMON FILES: CASE ONE

The Case of the Missing Inarian

The Cinnamon Files
Case One

DEB LOGAN

SPACE STATION DETECTIVE

My name is Cinnamon Chou, and I'm a detective.

Okay, I'm a kid, but I'm going to be a detective when I grow up. Just like my dad. For now, I'm practicing on the easy stuff. You know, like lost full-spectrum goggles ("They're perched on top of your head, Master Engineer Wyandotte"), missing red silk slippers ("Got 'em, Mrs. Abrega! When was the last time you cleaned under your bed?"), or my favorite, *The Case of the Missing Inarian*.

What's an Inarian? I'm glad you asked.

An Inarian is a warm-blooded denizen of the planet Inaria. They're cute and cuddly and definitely don't meet the standard of intelligence necessary to classify them as Class I Sapient Beings. Reading through my data links on old Earth biology, I've decided they're pretty similar to hamsters. They make great pets, but they're about as bright as deep space with no stars in sight.

My best friend, Lando Maxon, has an Inarian named Dumpling. When Lando woke up that morning, he discovered that Dumpling had managed to escape from his habitat. Inarians may not be smart, but they can wriggle out of places you'd swear were tightly sealed.

Normally, a Dumpling escape wouldn't merit my intervention as a detective. Lando would just set out a bowl of Dumpling's favorite treats and wait for his pet to get hungry. But today was not a normal day. Today Lando and his family were leaving the space station and returning to Centauri Three, their home planet.

That's one of the real bummers about living on a space station. Sooner or later all of your friends move away.

Of course, the up side is that new friends cycle in constantly.

At least, that's what my mom tells me every time a close friend leaves for a distant star system. Dad says Mom is an optimist. He's right, but so is she. By the time I grow up and take my place in the Universal Star League, I'll have friends in so many star systems I'll need my own database just to keep track of them all.

Back to Dumpling. I was eating breakfast with Mom and Dad when Lando pinged my link. "Lando Maxon," my link announced.

Mom frowned at the link on my wrist. "Not at the table, Cinnamon," she said, using her duty officer voice. "You know the rules."

I swallowed a mouthful of protein-rich, calcium-enhanced syntho-juice, wiped my mouth on a recycled napkin and said, "But Mom, Lando is leaving the station in less than six hours. If I don't answer him, I may not have another chance."

Mom glanced at Dad, who nodded.

"Very well, Cinnamon," she said, "Your father and I will make an exception this time. You are dismissed."

I grabbed a slice of replicated toast, jumped out of my chair, and dashed for the door. I didn't want to give Mom time to reconsider.

Not that she would. Decisions were Mom's life. As a senior officer assigned to the bridge of Space Station Zeta, Mom made hundreds of decisions. She was awesome. Cool and professional, with nerves of steel. Nobody messed with Mom.

She was also beautiful, in a cool and commanding kind of way. Sleek black hair, dark chocolate skin, and eyes as green as all-clear lights. She had a spacer's body, tall and willowy, but tough as nano-enhanced titanium.

Dad, a detective assigned to station security, was a genetic throwback. Despite being born on Cygnus 12, his DNA identified him as ethnic Chinese. He wasn't exactly short, but he wasn't tall and willowy like Mom. Dad had a compact strength, like a compressed spring. And smart. Oh yeah. Dad's brain held onto facts like a super-computer, but with the ability to make intuitive leaps that computers still hadn't mastered.

Me? Dad says I'm the best of both of them. I've got Dad's thought-processing brilliance combined with Mom's decision-making skills. I just need time to develop my intuition and experience to feed my knowledge base.

I'm also a genetic combination. Where Mom is dark-skinned and Dad is gold-hued, I'm ... well, cinnamon skin-toned. That's where I got my name. Dad took one look at me and said, "She's perfect, Maria. Our own little cinnamon sugar cookie."

Fortunately for me, they dropped the cookie reference and left it at Cinnamon. I'm cool with that. Nothing wrong with being named after an old world spice. Cinnamon might have been common back on old Earth, but out here in space, it's exotic. I like being exotic.

Once I escaped our quarters and made it into the corridor, I answered Lando's ping.

"What's up, Lando? Need help packing?"

A tiny 3-D model of my friend hovered above my wrist link. It was hard to tell on such a miniscule face, but I thought he looked worried.

"Kinda ... maybe. Look, it's Dumpling. He escaped again. Only this time I don't have time to wait for him to come out of hiding."

I nodded, thoughts racing. "Plus, I'll bet your quarters haven't been sealed. Not with everyone packing and moving boxes to the landing bay."

"He could be anywhere," Lando agreed.

"I'm on my way." I paused, thinking about my approach to the case. "Does your family have a DNA detector?"

The tiny Lando shrugged. "Maybe, but if we do, it would've been packed long ago. Not exactly a necessity."

"Gotcha," I replied. "I'll ask Dad to borrow his. See you in a few. Cinnamon Chou, over and out."

I ended the link, but before I could return to our quarters, Dad stepped into the corridor.

"Just the person I needed to see," I said, giving him my brightest smile.

Dad cocked an eyebrow, glanced from my dazzling smile to the finger hovering above my link and said, "What do you need, sugar cookie? Or rather, what does Lando need?"

I grimaced. Only Dad could get away with comparing me to an overly sweet pastry. "Lando's Inarian has escaped and he doesn't have time to wait for it to reappear on its own."

Dad nodded. "You're hoping for a DNA detector?"

I upped the wattage on my smile and nodded.

"I don't know, Cinnamon. Those are delicate instruments, easily misread."

My smile morphed into a scowl in a nanosecond. "Really, Dad? You think I'd mistake Inarian DNA for, oh, I don't know, a Tenarian tunnel rat?"

Dad had the grace to drop his gaze. "No. I know you'd use it properly." He sighed, stared at the ceiling for a moment, then nodded. "Follow me, Detective Chou."

My grin returned, and I skipped down the corridor at Dad's heels.

Space station corridors can be very confusing. A person new to the station often thinks they all look alike, but they're wrong. You just have to get used to the subtle clues. Since I've grown up on Space Station Zeta, I'm never lost. I can tell purple sector from blue without even having to resort to the colored chips embedded in the corridor walls and floors. I can tell the sectors by their odors.

Green sector houses hydroponics and smells of nutrients, water and growing plants. Purple sector houses the market district. Purple always smells of hot oil, spices, and too many humans and aliens packed into too little space. Red sector is mechanical engineering. If you think nanobots and computer circuitry don't have distinct odors, then you've never lived on a space station.

And then there's white sector. Medics and remedies; antiseptics and bile; with a stiff overlay of fear. I shivered. I hated even walking past white sector.

But now I followed Dad to my favorite sector: blue. Blue sector is administration, which translates to military since Space Station Zeta is a Universal Star League station. As such the station is under the command and protection of the USL Fleet. Both of my parents are USL officers, so blue sector smells of peace, security, and home.

Not that we lived in blue sector. All living quarters were in the central core — yellow sector. Yellow was further divided into crew and civilian quarters, and then by individual or family, but beyond that our station had no class boundaries. At least not where living quarters were concerned.

Dad paused before the entrance to security, waited for the station to acknowledge his voice and retinal prints, and then strode inside when the entry irised open. I followed quickly. The door would've irised open for me as well, but why wait to be scanned when I could just stick close to Dad?

Everyone but me wore blue and silver USL uniforms. The officers, like Dad, with insignia of rank emblazoned on chest and shoulder, the crew with the simple, stylized USL logo. Everyone saluted when Dad entered, since he was the ranking officer. When he returned their salute, they relaxed and called greetings to me as well.

"Aikens," Dad called, and a young man snapped to attention. "Please find an old DNA detector for Cinnamon. It doesn't need to be state-of-the-art," he continued, "just functional."

"Sir. Yes, sir."

Dad cocked a brow at me. "What are you waiting for, Detective Chou? Follow Aikens, collect your gear, and get out of my office."

I grinned, saluted, and ran to follow Aikens. I found him in the supply closet, rummaging through a box of outdated gear.

"What are you up to today, Cinnamon?" he asked as he rooted through the box. "Why a DNA detector?"

"My friend is cycling off-station today, and his Inarian escaped. I'm hoping to help him track it down before he ships out."

Aikens paused, dislodged a small electronic device, and pulled it free of the box. Thumbing it on, he checked the read-out, then nodded.

"This should do the trick," he said, handing the detector to me. "It's got plenty of juice and is reading properly. Good luck with your search."

"Thanks! This should make it easy." I saluted Aikens, ran back past Dad's office and out into the station corridor. Now to get to Lando's quarters on the double.

I arrived at the Maxon family quarters in yellow sector sweaty and out of breath.

"Hi ... Mrs. Maxon ..." I wheezed. "Is ... Lando ... home?"

Lando's mother gave me a distracted look and waved toward Lando's room. "He's in his room. Searching for Dumpling."

I nodded. "I heard," I said, my breathing settling into a more normal pattern. "I'm here to help."

She turned back to the wardrobe she was inventorying. "I hope you can. We won't be able to delay our departure for an Inarian."

"Understood," I said, already on my way to join my friend. As the door whooshed open and I stepped into Lando's room, he raced forward, grabbed my hand and pulled me to the habitat.

"I think I've found where he got out," he said, pointing to a junction between the main habitat and one of the tubular trails that allowed Dumpling to roam the edges of Lando's room. "That connection is slightly loose. It doesn't look wide enough for escape, but it's the only possibility I've found."

I got down on my hands and knees to examine the evidence. Sure enough, Lando had discovered a half-inch gap between the main habitat and the tube.

Now Inarians are small, but they're not *that* small. Dumpling was at least six inches long, but while he looked like he was as round as he was long, he was actually little more than a walking ball of fluff. I'd seen him squeeze himself flat under his exercise wheel. No idea why he'd done that, but I'd witnessed it with my own two eyes. If he could get into that tiny space, he could ooze out through the loose connection Lando had discovered.

I pulled the DNA detector out of my pocket and turned it on.

"Okay," I said, "this device is our best hope. Look around and find me a bit of his fur or blood, or, well, whatever might have his DNA."

I examined the escape point to see if he might have scraped himself and left a sample behind, but the smooth edges were clear. A whoop of victory told me that Lando had fared better.

"Here, Cinnamon. I found a clump of fur."

I held my breath as we touched the DNA detector's probe to the fur. "Let there be DNA," I whispered. "Let there be DNA." I knew enough about genetics to know that unless a hair has the follicle or root attached, you can't get a DNA reading. I watched the meter's read-out. Nothing.

Carefully, I touched a different bit of the fur with the probe ... and the screen lit. We had a reading!

Lando said, "Yes!" and I exhaled in relief.

"Now what?" he asked.

"Now we follow Dumpling's DNA trail." I worked the dials on the device and locked in the sample reading. Now the screen would only light when matching DNA was detected.

Crawling along Lando's bedroom floor, we followed the trace evidence Dumpling had left behind. The trail led to a very small hole in the wall between Lando's bedroom and the main room of the family's quarters.

I glanced at Lando and saw his shoulders sag. He was thinking the same thing I was ... what if Dumpling found a way to scurry along inside the walls? We'd never be able to track him through the permaplastic.

After a quick discussion of our options, we agreed that Lando would stay in his room beside the hole, while I ran into the main room to see if there was an exit anywhere nearby.

I laid the DNA detector on the floor and tapped the wall, hoping to hear Lando tapping back. There! I was about six feet too far into the room. I moved toward his rappings, pleased to hear the noise getting louder. When I found the right place, I lay down on my stomach and searched the junction of floor and wall.

"Lando!" I shouted into the little hole. "I found it. There's a matching hole on this side."

"Did he come through?" Lando yelled back. "Does the DNA trail continue?"

Rats! Or maybe I should say, Inarians! The detector was several feet away on the floor where I'd left it. I jumped up to retrieve it, just in time to see a loading dock worker push a floating cargo cart into the room. He'd come to collect some of the Maxons' belongings, and he stopped the cart right over the DNA detector.

If he allowed the cart to settle, he'd crush the instrument that was our only hope of finding Dumpling in time!

"No!" I yelled. "Don't settle the cart there. You'll crush my gadget."

The dock worker stared at me, then checked around his feet, clearly confused. He was just about to lower the cart when I pulled a Dumpling and threw myself into the space under the cart. The way too small space to accommodate my bulk.

"What the..." the worker said, and steered the cart into the center of the room, away from my flying feet and fingers. "Are you nuts, kid? This thing could break you in half."

I grabbed the detector and hugged it close to my hammering heart. "I know," I answered, "but it would've pulverized my DNA detector."

Shaking his head at the lunacy of kids, the dock worker settled the cargo cart and began loading it with boxes.

Moving back to the hole in the wall, I sank to the floor, closed my eyes, and allowed myself to simply breathe until Lando joined me.

"Well?" he asked. "Do we have a trail, or don't we?"

I held the detector out to him. "You check," I said. "I'm still recovering from a close encounter."

He cocked his head and gave me a quizzical expression, silently asking for an explanation, but I waved him toward the hole. I'd tell him all about it later, in a cyber-sending if not in person.

Lando bent to the floor and a moment later gave a fist pump. "We have a trail," he cried and crawled off toward the family kitchen.

Thanks to Dad's old DNA detector, we found Dumpling fifteen

minutes later curled up in an empty kitchen cabinet, surrounded by bits of breakfast cereal. The cabinet door was firmly latched, with no cracks big enough for even the flattest Inarian to wriggle through.

Lando and I decided that Dumpling must have already been in the cabinet when Mrs. Maxon gave the kitchen a final once-over and closed the door.

With the over-full Inarian still sleeping off his cereal high, Lando and I set about disassembling his habitat and packing it for the journey. Dumpling would be confined to a small carry-case for the duration, but he seemed blissfully unconcerned.

I walked my best friend and his family to the loading dock. Not the cargo loading dock. The people loading dock. There wasn't much to see, just a little waiting room with a door that led into a tube. It reminded me of Dumpling's tubular trail system, only this tube would carry my best friend in the whole universe to the space ship that would take him from our home on Space Station Zeta to his new home on Centauri Three.

I wasn't sure how many light years would separate us, but it really didn't matter. Too many to bridge with a tubular trail.

The light over the exit turned green, and passengers began to move slowly to the tube.

Mr. and Mrs. Maxon each hugged me and thanked me again for rescuing Dumpling ... and thereby their son. Then they stepped aside so Lando could approach.

"Well," he said, staring at his shoes, "I guess this is it, Cinnamon."

"Yeah," I sighed. "I guess so." I looked at the floor, too, willing the tears not to flow.

"Thanks for being my friend." He touched my hand, and suddenly my arms were around him, hugging him tight.

"You'll always be my friend," I whispered, my throat tight with tears I didn't want to shed. "Light years can't change that."

He nodded and we stepped apart.

"Take care of Dumpling for me," I said. Then a thought struck. "Here. Take this." I thrust the DNA detector into his hands. "It's old and Dad doesn't need it ... and you never know when you might need to track an Inarian."

Lando smiled, brushed the back of his hand across his eyes, and said, "Thanks, Cinnamon. You're the best."

A moment later Lando and his parents disappeared into the tube. I stood there staring at the empty passageway until a blue and silver clad security crewmember closed and locked the door.

I walked away from the dock, heading back to tell Dad what had happened to his DNA detector, when I heard a woman speaking. A woman who sounded like she was trying to be excited but was failing rather spectacularly.

Turning, I saw a tall, willowy blonde woman in the blue and silver of the USL leading a blue-eyed girl with light brown hair pulled into braids. "Don't worry, Sammy. I'm sure we'll be happy here. You'll make friends in no time, and I ... I'll learn my new post quickly. Everything is going to be A-Okay."

She raised her eyes, saw me watching, and gave a little wave. "See, honey? There's a little girl about your age. Maybe she can help us find our quarters."

I straightened my shoulders, pasted on a smile, and walked over to the newcomers. This Sammy person might not be able to replace Lando, but I could definitely help them find their quarters.

After all, Space Station Zeta was my home, and I was a detective. I could find *anything*!

PART III

THE CINNAMON FILES: CASE TWO

The Case of the Glittering Hoard

The Cinnamon Files
Case Two

DEB LOGAN

1

I slipped through the corridors as silent as a holographic image. I wasn't on a case, but a good detective hones her skills so they're ready when she needs them. At least, that's what Dad says, and since he's a real detective and I'm still a kid, I'll take his word for it.

It's not easy to be stealthy on a space station where you've spent your whole life. Even though my soft leather boots made no sound as I passed through purple sector's crowded marketplace, vendors who'd known me since infancy kept smiling and waving, a few even calling me by name.

"Good morning, Cinnamon," said Mr. Zitnik as he arranged fat, round loaves of fresh, crusty bread on the shelves of his stall. Tall and thin as one of Dad's fighting sticks, Mr. Zitnik always had a cookie or a tart ready for me. Today his dark eyes crinkled with suppressed laughter as he offered me a cinnamon sugar cookie.

I managed not to roll my eyes as I waved and said, "Thanks, Mr. Zitnik, but not today. I'm on a case." I wasn't, but the white lie kept me from accepting the cookie and allowing his good-natured teasing about my name. See, my dad actually calls me *Cinnamon Sugar Cookie*. Now, I don't mind Dad referring to me as an overly sweet pastry, but I draw the line at casual acquaintances making the reference.

It all goes back to my birth. My mom, senior bridge officer for Space Station Zeta, has beautiful dark chocolate skin, while my dad, the station's chief security officer, is an utterly gorgeous golden hue. Since I'm a combination of the two, my skin tone is a spicy shade of cinnamon. That's where I got my name. Dad took one look at me and said, "She's perfect, Maria. Our own little cinnamon sugar cookie."

"Ahh," Mr. Zitnik said, replacing the cookie on its tray. "I wouldn't want to interfere with official business. Good hunting, little one."

I melted into the morning crowd making a mental note to use a disguise if I ever really needed to follow someone. Too many people knew me too well. I'd just managed to perfect my stealthy gait when my wrist link pinged. Several shoppers glanced my direction.

Mental note number two: silence your wrist link when tailing a suspect.

I gave up on stealth and strode boldly toward Trigger's Exotic Creature Emporium as I activated my wrist link. A tiny 3-D version of my best friend Sammy appeared above the link.

"Where are you?" she asked, minuscule fists on itty-bitty hips. "I've been here for ages!"

"Don't exaggerate," I said, picking up my pace. "I'm only a couple of minutes late."

"Fine. I was early," she admitted, "but you're still late."

"Almost there," I said and deactivated the connection. Sammy's tiny form winked out of existence. I swung around a decorative planter of Andolian fern trees, stepped up behind Sammy, and tapped her shoulder.

"Surprise! I'm here."

She jumped and whirled at the same time—a move I'm sure her Kendo instructor would've been proud of—and glared at me. "Why can't you ever just walk into my field of vision and say 'hello' like a normal person?"

I shrugged. "Where's the fun in that?"

Her glare morphed into a grudging grin and she grabbed my arm. "Come on. Mom said I could have a pet for my birthday and I want to check out the puppies."

This time I didn't bother to suppress an eye-roll. Puppies? Of all the exotic critters available at Trigger's, Sammy wanted to play with plain old Earth-normal puppies? My best friend had no imagination, no sense of adventure.

While Sammy cooed over the various breeds of available puppies, I examined the emporium's more unusual offerings. I smiled wistfully at a display of fluffy little Inarians. My previous best friend, Lando Maxon, had owned one of the hamster-like creatures. I still missed Lando, but his family had departed the space station the same day Sammy and her mom had arrived.

I hoped Sammy wouldn't choose an Inarian.

I wandered over to a large glass-fronted container built into the side wall of the emporium. Two lizard-like creatures lounged on permaplastic branches and watched me with hooded amber eyes. I glanced at the information panel and discovered that they were Fornaxian dragons.

"Stunning, aren't they?"

I looked to my left and saw that Micah Trigger, the emporium's owner, had joined me.

"Would you like to meet one?"

I eyed the creatures doubtfully. About the size of a small Earth dog, the dragons weren't remotely cute or cuddly. Sure, the green one had shiny, almost emerald scales that complimented its amber eyes, but the black one looked surly, as though I were giving offense by looking at it.

"I don't know," I said. "They don't look very friendly."

Mr. Trigger smiled. "If they wouldn't make good companions, I wouldn't have them in stock. They just need to get to know you."

Sammy joined us and gazed wide-eyed at the creatures. "What are those? I've never seen anything like them."

"Fornaxian dragons," answered Mr. Trigger. "Named after a mythological Earth creature. I was supposed to receive three, but something went wrong. When the crate was delivered to the shop, there were only these two."

"Do they fly," I asked.

Sammy looked at me like I was nuts, but Mr. Trigger smiled.

"Very perceptive, Cinnamon. Most people don't notice their wings until they unfurl them. They're very effectively camouflaged," he said. "Yes, they can fly."

"Wow," said Sammy. "Do they breathe fire too?"

Mr. Trigger laughed. "No. That would put them into an untradeable class. No fire, but they do like to hoard shiny objects. Another reason their discoverers called them dragons."

I pulled Sammy away from the dragons. They were really interesting, but Mom had made it clear that she didn't think I was ready for the responsibility of a pet. I didn't want to risk getting too attached.

"I thought you wanted to play with the puppies," I reminded Sammy. "You know, pick out your birthday present?"

Mr. Trigger brightened. "Oh? Which breed can I show you? Do you want a large dog or small?"

While Mr. Trigger gave Sammy the details of several dog breeds, I continued my circuit of the store. Along with the exotics like Inarians and Fornaxians, the emporium offered kittens, aquariums of fish from several solar systems, and more birds than I had names for.

By the time I completed my inspection, Sammy had settled on a little black and tan ball of fluff. Mr. Trigger lifted the puppy from its cage and carried it to a meeting area—a section of the main room with waist-high walls where customers could interact with potential pets of the non-flying variety.

Sammy knelt inside the enclosure while I stood just outside, leaning on the half-wall that separated us. The puppy bounced and tumbled over her, wriggling and licking and generally expressing its joy in her attention.

"Isn't he perfect, Cinnamon?"

I had to admit, the little furball was adorable. "What kind is it?" I asked. "How big will it get?"

"Mr. Trigger said he's a sheltie. He's very smart and won't get too big for our quarters. I think I'll name him Fred."

"Fred? Really?"

Sammy nodded happily and rubbed Fred's belly while he attempted to lick every inch of her exposed skin.

I closed my eyes. Fred. Truly, Sammy had no imagination, no sense of style.

Mr. Trigger brought out several other puppies, but Sammy refused to relinquish Fred. Clearly, she had made her choice. Before we left the emporium, Sammy contacted her mom via wrist link and Mr. Trigger was authorized the hold the puppy until the adults could finalize the arrangements.

2

That night at dinner I told Mom and Dad all about our adventure in the pet store. "Can you believe it?" I finished. "Out of all the amazing creatures in the emporium, Sammy chose a puppy. An Earth-normal puppy!"

I stabbed the last bite of synth-chicken and popped it in my mouth. When I finished chewing, I continued, "And guess what she named it?"

Mom and Dad exchanged amused glances before responding. "No idea," Mom said. "Don't keep us in suspense," said Dad.

I took a deep breath and announced, "She named him Fred."

Mom blinked. "Fred?"

Dad laughed. "Nothing wrong with that. Fred's a good solid name."

I threw my hands up in despair. "Yeah. Solid. Stable. *Normal*. Why couldn't she give it a more adventurous name?"

"What would you name a dog?" Mom asked.

I considered the question, but before I could answer, Dad's wrist link flashed red.

"Sorry, Maria," he said before Mom could object to links at the table. "This is code red, I have to take it."

Mom nodded. "We were finished anyway. Cinnamon, help me clear the table, please."

Sammy and Fred were relegated to the back of my mind as I lingered in the eating nook trying to accidentally overhear Dad's conversation. Mom was wise to my tricks though. "Cinnamon, on task, please."

"Yes, ma'am," I answered, stifling both a sigh *and* an eye-roll.

Mom and I were just finishing up when Dad joined us in the kitchen. He kissed Mom's cheek and ruffled my short dark hair. "I've got to go to the market sector," he said, slipping into his blue and silver USL uniform jacket. "There's been a rash of thefts. Mostly inexpensive jewelry and small metallic objects, but a few valuable items are missing as well. I want to examine the affected shops as quickly as possible."

Mom nodded, but I spoke up. "Can I come with you?"

"I don't know, Sugar Cookie," he said, a slight frown creasing his brow. "This is official business; an active crime scene."

"I promise I'll stay out of the way," I said quickly. "I won't be any bother." I crossed my fingers behind my back and held my breath while he considered.

Dad glanced at Mom. "What do you think, Maria?"

"Up to you, Li. The chances of you actually encountering the thief are negligible, so she'll be in no danger. The only question is whether or not she'll interfere with your work."

"I won't," I said, trying to keep my voice from rising to a shrill squeal.

Mom gave me her famous remain-quiet-if-you-know-what's-good-for-you glare, and I zipped my lips.

Dad eyed me thoughtfully. After what felt like an eternity while I stood still (despite nerves that made me want to bounce off the walls), kept my mouth shut (SO hard when I wanted to beg for this opportunity to learn about real detective work), and tried to look mature and responsible (I was twelve years old, after all!), Dad nodded. "All right, Cinnamon. You may come. But," he pointed a finger at me and gave me his best commanding officer expression, "you will obey my every command immediately and without question. Is that understood?"

"Sir! Yes, sir," I responded with a crisp salute.

"Very well. Follow me, Detective-in-training Chou."

I stifled a squeal, beamed at Mom, and followed Dad into the corridor.

Space station corridors can be very confusing. A person new to the station often thinks they all look alike, but they're wrong. You just have to get used to the subtle clues. Since I've grown up on Space Station Zeta, I'm never lost. I can tell purple sector from blue without even having to resort to the colored chips embedded in the corridor walls and floors. I can tell the sectors by their odors.

Green sector houses hydroponics and smells of nutrients, water and growing plants. Red sector is mechanical engineering. If you think nanobots and computer circuitry don't have distinct odors, then you've never lived on a space station. Blue sector is administration, which translates to military since Space Station Zeta is a Universal Star League station. As such the station is under the command and protection of the USL Fleet. Both of my parents are USL officers, so blue sector smells of peace, security, and home.

Not that we lived in blue sector. All living quarters were in the central core—yellow sector. Yellow was further divided into crew and civilian quarters, and then by individual or family, but beyond that our station had no class boundaries. At least not where living quarters were concerned.

And then there's white sector. Medics and remedies; antiseptics and bile; with a stiff overlay of fear. I hated even walking past white sector.

But now I followed Dad to purple sector, the market district. Purple always smells of hot oil, spices, and too many humans and aliens packed into too little space—even now, when many of Space Station Zeta's inhabitants had returned to their quarters for the dinner hour.

I practiced my stealth mode as I followed Dad from shop to shop, trying to stay close, be unobtrusive, and soak up as much of Dad's investigative technique as possible. We examined display cases, noted unusual patterns of destruction, and searched for entry and exit points.

All of the affected shops were empty at the time of the theft, the owners having locked up for the three-hour break between afternoon and evening commerce that most of the market sector observed. I stepped carefully across what looked like an old Earth tree branch that had been knocked to the floor by the thief and stopped beside Dad.

"And you're sure you locked the doors when you left?" Dad asked the proprietor.

"Yes, sir. I ran through my usual closing routine. The doors were locked, and as you can see we don't have any windows other than the front display, and it's in tact."

Dad nodded and I followed his gaze as he studied the small shop. Bits of jewelry littered the terra cotta colored permaplastic floor along with the decorative branch. The enclosed glass cases were undisturbed, though items had been swept from their tops. A manikin standing sentinel near the door was missing its wig (which rested on the floor at its feet like a small, furry pet), but its clothing still hung in meticulously arranged folds.

When Dad turned his attention to the ceiling, I saw his eyes narrow. That's when I noticed the air vent. The screen covering dangled from the duct at a precarious angle.

"How long has that vent cover been damaged?" Dad asked the owner, pointing to the eighteen-inch opening near the ceiling.

"What? We don't have..." his words sputtered to a halt as he saw the damaged vent. Frowning, he said, "I'm sure that was fine when I left the shop."

"Aikens," Dad called, and a young man dressed in USL blue and silver and wearing a security badge snapped to attention. "Yes, sir?" he said.

"Make a quick tour of the other affected shops. Notice if others have damaged air vents," he said, pointing upward.

"Right away, sir!" Aikens turned and strode from the shop.

The owner watched Aikens' departure and then turned to Dad. "Surely you don't think the thief used the vent," he said. "It's too small. Why, even your daughter would be too big for such an opening, plus, the culprit would need to fly to leave by the same opening."

I didn't hear Dad's reply; I'd stopped listening. I stared at the gaping vent and imagined a pair of amber eyes staring back at me. Mr. Trigger's words from earlier in the day echoed in my memory, *Fornaxian dragons ... I was supposed to receive three, but something went wrong. When the crate was delivered to the shop, there were only these two.*

I tugged on Dad's jacket sleeve.

"Not now, Cinnamon," he said as Aikens stopped in front of him.

"But Dad..." He silenced me with hand movement.

"Report, Aikens."

Aikens straightened and said, "Sir, each shop has a damaged air vent. All appear to have been pushed outward from inside the vent."

Dad nodded, gazing thoughtfully at the vent. I tugged on his sleeve again.

"What part of 'not now' do you not understand, Detective-in-training Chou?"

I squared my shoulders and met his gaze boldly. "Sir, I have pertinent information to report."

Dad lifted an eyebrow, but said, "Very well. Report, Chou."

"Sir, when Sammy and I visited Trigger's Exotic Creature Emporium, Mr. Trigger mentioned a discrepancy in his inventory." I paused and Dad nodded for me to continue. "He had expected three Fornaxian dragons, but only two were delivered."

"I see, and do these dragons fly and breathe fire?"

"No sir, they do not breathe fire," I said, then hurried to add, "but they do fly and Mr. Trigger reports that they like to hoard shiny objects." That's when my excitement got the better of me and I dropped my detective-in-training act. "Isn't everything that's missing shiny? And a good-sized flying lizard-y creature would be able to come and go through the vents! I'm right, aren't I, Dad? Someone on the loading dock lost one of the dragons and it escaped into the air vents."

Dad nodded. "That's a plausible theory, Cinnamon. Thank you for the information. We'll investigate the possibility, but right now, it's time for you to go home. Aikens!"

My shoulders dropped. "You mean I don't get to see this through to the end?"

Dad crouched down to my eye level. "This isn't a punishment, Sugar Cookie. I think you've probably just solved the mystery, but it's getting late and I'm going to be moving all over the station following this lead. You need your sleep. I'll let you know what happens in the morning." He straightened, tousled my hair, and turned to Aikens. "Please escort my daughter back to our quarters, then report to me in the cargo bay."

Aikens smiled at me. "It will be my pleasure, sir."

The next morning at breakfast, Dad told Mom all about how I'd cracked the case for him. Mom listened thoughtfully and when Dad finished his report, smiled.

"Well done, Cinnamon. I'm very proud of you and I'm sure Dad is as well."

I swallowed a mouthful of protein-rich, calcium-enhanced syntho-juice, wiped my mouth on a recycled napkin and said, "Thanks, Mom. Dad, did they catch the dragon yet?"

"No, but we found its hoard by sending the cleaning robot through the ducts and caught a glimpse of the red devil. Mr. Trigger has arranged a nice display of glittering jewelry to tempt it into an enclosure. All the merchants donated their shiniest pieces to the trap —Mr. Trigger assured them that nothing would be damaged—and they've removed anything else that might interest a dragon from their shelves for the day. We expect to have the perp in custody by evening."

I giggled. "I don't envy the kid who ends up with that creature for a pet."

Dad raised an eyebrow. "Truly? Mr. Trigger said he'd be delighted to place the unexpected dragon in your custody," he said, "as long as you promise to take good care of it and teach it not to steal."

My eyes widened and I stared at Dad, then Mom, then back to Dad. "Really? You'd let me have a Fornaxian dragon?"

Mom smiled. "I think you've proven yourself responsible enough for a pet."

"You don't have to accept," Dad said. "But if you want this little red devil, it's yours."

I thought of the other two dragons, the gleaming scales of the emerald one and the surly glare of the black one. What would the red one be like? Obviously intelligent. Definitely exotic. Just the kind of pet I'd always dreamed of.

No solid, stable, *normal* pet for me. No sir. Cinnamon Chou, space station detective, needed a pet with spunk and imagination. Now I just needed to find a suitably adventurous name for dragon who was about to become a reformed thief!

PART IV

THE CINNAMON FILES: CASE THREE

The Case of the Recreational Thief

The Cinnamon Files
—Case Three—

DEB LOGAN

1

The door to my bedroom irised open with a nearly inaudible *whoosh*, and I stepped inside clutching Dad's gift to my chest. I couldn't believe my luck! My very first grown-up, never-owned-by-anyone-else tablet, complete with security features encoded to my thumbprint and DNA.

Not even Mom or Dad would be able to access this tablet without my permission. How cool was that?

I hopped up onto my built-in bunk, settled the tablet on my knees, opened my very first folder, and titled it: *The Case Files of Cinnamon Chou, Space Station Detective*.

A happy sigh escaped my lips. I might still be a kid, but I had big dreams. I was going to be a Universal Star League detective, just like my dad. By the time I was old enough to attend the USL Academy, I intended to have a sizable number of cases documented in my files.

That's how I'd gotten this tablet. I'd prepared my case, presented my argument (referencing my Academy aspirations), and Mom and Dad had agreed to my request.

"All right, Sugar Cookie," Dad said—he was the only living being (human *or* alien) who was allowed to refer to me as the overly sweet pastry responsible for my name. The story goes that the first instant he saw me, he told my mother that my combination of her ebony complexion and his gold-toned coloration reminded him of an old-fashioned cinnamon sugar cookie.

Parents.

What can you do with them?

Anyway, Dad said, "All right, Sugar Cookie. You've made your case. We'll get you a secure tablet...on one condition."

I held my breath to keep from screaming in delight and waited for him to elaborate.

He glanced at Mom, received a minuscule nod, and said, "Like any commanding officer, your mother and I reserve the right to review your files." He lifted an eyebrow and waited for my response.

I considered for a mere heartbeat before nodding. "Sir, yes sir," I said, giving him a crisp USL salute. "As a junior detective under your command, my files will be open for your inspection." I paused, licked my lips, and countered. "But only when requested in advance and reviewed in my presence."

Mom and Dad exchanged glances. Mom, as senior USL officer present, nodded. "That is acceptable, Junior Detective Chou. You will have your tablet within the week. Dismissed."

I pumped my fist, squealed and ran to hug them. First Dad, then Mom; then, in an excess of exuberance, both at once. "Thank you! This is going to be so awesome!"

Dad tousled my hair, and Mom grinned. "You did a great job building your case, Cinnamon. We can't wait to see the case files you write."

Secure in my bedroom, I created my first file: *The Case of the Missing Inarian*.

A broad beam of sadness swept through my heart and tears misted my vision. That had been my best friend Lando Maxon's last day on Space Station Zeta, and I still missed him terribly. Writing up that case would be a bittersweet reminder of a great friend.

I glanced across the room to the habitat Dad and I had built for my very first pet, a handsome red Fornaxian dragon I'd named

Raphael. Rafe, a reformed thief, would be the focus of my second file: *The Case of the Glittering Hoard*.

When I finished transferring my hand written case notes to my new tablet, I pulled on the special sheath glove Dad had designed for me, opened Rafe's habitat, and invited him onto my forearm. The glove protected my skin (and my tunic) from Rafe's claws. Dad said it served a similar purpose to protective gear used by his ancient ancestors, the eagle hunters of a place on Earth known as Mongolia.

Rafe eyed my extended arm for a moment before deciding to take me up on the invitation to leave his habitat. He unfurled his ruby-red wings and flew from one of his perches to my arm. I managed to take his weight without bobbling; I was definitely getting stronger. Rafe was easily the size of a small Earth dog, one of those described as "lap dogs." He was red scaled, with a barbed tail that was nearly as long as his body.

When he first came to me, his expression was haughty and aloof, like he was doing me a favor by making eye contact. Now that we'd been together for a few months he actually seemed to like me, even chirping and purring and nuzzling my cheek when he perched on my arm or shoulder.

Of course, his good mood was probably ninety-percent due to the amazing habitat Dad had created. Rafe's "cage" easily took up half of my bedroom. It rose from floor to ceiling, included multiple permaplastic perches that reminded me of tree limbs, and had a small pond on the floor for both drinking and bathing.

I was responsible for keeping his habitat clean, and believe me, it was a chore—especially cleaning that pond. But I was lucky... Fornaxian dragons are very clean animals. Rafe used one specific corner of his habitat as a toilet, and as long as I kept that area well supplied with faux-cedar chips, scooping out the refuse was a breeze.

Stepping out of the habitat with Rafe on my arm, I strode from my bedroom to our living room.

"I'm taking Rafe to the recreation area," I called to my parents. "We'll be back before dinner."

"Have fun," Mom said, looking up from the novel she was reading on her tablet.

"Don't forget to work on his training exercises," Dad said.

I grinned and palmed the door open. "Don't worry. Rafe and I are getting really good at working together. We're a good team!"

2

The recreation area was actually a large park at the center of yellow sector. All living quarters were located at the central core of Space Station Zeta and were designated as yellow sector. The area was divided into crew and civilian quarters, and then by individual or family units, but beyond that our station had no class distinctions. At least not where living quarters were concerned.

The ground in the recreation area was artificial turf. That springy green stuff that's supposed to mimic old Earth grass. Since I've never experienced the original plant life, I can't say how closely the turf matched its model, but it worked for me. We had game fields (soccer, baseball, and galactic jumpball), trees (like the ever present Andolian fern trees), and lots of open space where kids like me could run and jump and play made-up games.

Rafe and I headed straight for the middle of the open space. I gave him the "fly free" sign, and he launched from my arm, soaring into the high-ceilinged "sky." He circled the field three times before heading over to the Andolian ferns and landing on a sturdy branch. Once stationary, he began grooming himself, flicking his long tongue over every scale on his body. I was still amazed that he could actually groom the top of his head and the back of his neck... talk about limber. When he finished, his scales gleamed like faceted gems in the clear, simulated sunlight.

Rabbie, a boy in my educational unit, jogged up to me.

"Hey, Cinnamon, wanna play jumpball?" he asked. "Or are you too busy admiring your dragon?"

I glanced sideways at him. "Who else is playing?"

He nodded toward a knot of kids a few yards away. "We've got Ginger and Liu and Aaron and Jase. Sammy said she'd come back as soon as she took Fred home."

Before I could stop myself, I rolled my eyes, exasperated by the name my best friend on the whole station had given her Earth-normal puppy.

"What?" asked Rabbie.

"Fred," I said. "Have you ever heard a stupider name for a puppy?"

He glanced down and shrugged. "I dunno. He's her dog. She can call him what she wants."

"Yeah. I know. But seriously... Fred? Surely Sammy could've come up with something a little more interesting."

"It's just a name, *Cinnamon*," he said, giving my name just a little too much emphasis.

We joined the other kids and played a quick game of jumpball, while Rafe circled the field chittering and screaming his encouragement.

At least *I* knew it was encouragement.

The other kids seemed to find a dragon flying over their heads worrisome. Even though Sammy hadn't returned, I called Rafe back to my wrist when the first game ended and headed home.

"See you tomorrow," I yelled to my friends, who waved back, looking just a bit too relieved at our departure.

But the next day, my world fell apart.

3
___

Before class even started Sammy stormed up to me, fists on hips and eyes sparkling with anger. "Why do you have to be so mean about Fred?" she asked.

I'd never seen her so angry, and I didn't have a clue what she was talking about. I mean, aside from his ridiculous name, Fred was an adorable little black and tan ball of fluff. Who could be mean to a little guy whose only aim in life was to wriggle and lick you and beg for belly rubs?

"I'm not mean to Fred," I said, feeling hurt and confused. "I think Fred is sweet."

"Not *to* Fred," she said, exasperation clear in her voice, "*about* him. His name."

She paused, glaring at me. Probably waiting for me to defend myself. I decided silence was my best defense.

"Rabbie told me what you said," she clarified. Then, with a smug little grin, added, "He also said he thought it was pretty rich for someone named *Cinnamon*, whose dad calls her *Sugar Cookie*, to be making fun of anyone else's name."

I glanced around, found Rabbie, and stabbed him with a glare.

Turning my attention back to Sammy, I said, in my best calm-and-collected voice, "Look, he's your puppy, but even you have to admit that Fred is a goofy name for a dog."

Sammy's eyes narrowed and she turned redder than I'd ever imagined my pale-skinned, blonde friend could manage. "You're a fine one to talk. You named that stupid dragon Ralph."

My temper flared. "Did not! His name is Rafe, and it's short for Raphael. Which you know perfectly well."

"Ralph!" she taunted. "And everyone knows..." she paused for dramatic effect, "...Ralph is a thief!"

I'd never wanted to punch anyone in the face as much as I did right then. My thoughts smoldered and my fists clenched, but I turned around and walked away. Mom and Dad would be proud... but that didn't make me feel any better.

My best friend in the whole space station had just betrayed me.

I hated her!

The rest of the day, we stayed as far away from each other as possible. Our teacher, Mrs. Sheffield, looked at us with bemused concern, but didn't insist on us working together. Which was unusual. Normally, Sammy and I were inseparable.

But not today. Today, we were mortal enemies.

After school, I stormed into my bedroom, released Rafe from his habitat, and plopped onto my back on my bed. Rafe circled the room a couple of times before landing on the bed beside me. Crooning, he stretched out between my arm and my side and rested his head on my shoulder.

Ruby red love with gleaming amber eyes.

His crooning changed to a purr... which soothed my frazzled nerves.

I stroked his long, lean body, feeling content for the first time since my fight with Sammy.

"What do I need her for when I've got you?" I smiled, a little sadly, and closed my eyes. "You're the only friend I need."

I knew in my heart that wasn't true, but saying it made me feel better.

4

The next day at school, things got even worse!

Groups of chattering kids suddenly fell silent when I approached, their gazes following me as I walked from room to room.

What? I wanted to yell. What have I done now?

But I didn't.

By lunchtime, I'd reached my limit. I marched over to the table where Rabbie and Ginger and Liu were sitting with Sammy. "What's going on?" I demanded. "Why is everyone treating me like I have an infectious disease?"

Rabbie glanced around the table for support, then stood and faced me. "Haven't you heard? Stuff has been going missing from the recreation area."

I narrowed my eyes, my gaze flitting from him to the others sitting at the table and back again. "What kind of stuff?"

Sammy caught my gaze and held it. "Shiny stuff," she said meaningfully.

"And you think..." I stopped. I didn't want to say it out loud.

Sammy nodded. "Ralph. Everyone knows he was caught red-pawed stealing shiny jewelry in the purple sector."

"He didn't do it," I cried. "I mean, yes, he was guilty of the market sector robberies, but that was before I adopted him. He's reformed now. He hasn't stolen anything since he came to live with us."

"That you know of," Rabbie said, so smugly that I wanted to punch him.

Wow. That was the second time in two days I'd felt like punching one of my friends!

I controlled my anger... and my worry... and turned around and left.

Did I even have any friends anymore?

Feeling more than a little nauseous, I excused myself for the rest of the day and ran home. As it was the middle of the day and both my parents were on duty, Rafe was my only confidant. I released him from his habitat and he flew beside me as I paced through the rooms of our living quarters.

"Think, Cinnamon," I told myself. "Think. You know Rafe's not guilty. How are you going to prove it?"

I raced to my room, my dragon shadowing my movements, and grabbed my new tablet. The answer was obvious. I had to solve the case! Opening a new file, I titled it *The Case of the Recreational Thief* and began to type out my thoughts.

I was a detective. The daughter of an excellent detective. I could do this.

But first, I needed to gather evidence. I needed to visit the scene of the crime.

5

The recreational area was deserted in the middle of the day. All the school age kids were busy with lessons and the littles were undoubtedly napping. Adults were either on duty, at their jobs, or sleeping in preparation for their next shift. Rafe and I had the place to ourselves.

I placed my new tablet carefully on a picnic table and plopped onto the bench. Scanning the area, I allowed my thoughts to simmer.

I doubted the thief was human... or one of the sapient alien species who inhabited Space Station Zeta. The missing items weren't valuable enough for even a child to steal.

But they were all shiny... and small. Things that caught and refracted the light, but were small enough for a Fornaxian dragon to carry away.

Not that he did. Because he didn't.

A stylus. A faceted glass marble. A chocolate bar with a shiny wrapper.

Things of too little value to be of concern to my dad's security force. I was the only detective interested enough to take on the case... and my motivation wasn't the recovery of stolen property, it was clearing my dragon's good name.

Rafe flew around the recreation area, circling the open space and flitting from tree to tree in the forested part, while I puzzled over the culprit's identity.

If it wasn't one of the human or alien *people*, then it must be a creature. Since the space station didn't have wild animals like the squirrels and chipmunks or even rats of Earth, any critter living in the park would have to be feral. A pet that had gotten loose, very likely when its owners cycled off station.

That could've easily happened to my friend Lando's Inarian. The small, hamster-like creature had escaped from its cage the morning Lando and his family were leaving the station. If I hadn't helped him find the little furball, Dumpling could've been left behind. But I couldn't see an Inarian surviving in the wild, let alone stealing non-food objects.

I reviewed a mental list of station pets.

Dogs; not likely.

Cats; probably smart enough, but with no motive that I could see.

Fish; uhm... no.

Dragons; definitely capable and prone to hoarding shiny objects, but since the only ones on station were my Rafe and the two that remained in *Trigger's Exotic Creature Emporium*, I ruled them out.

Birds.

I frowned, glancing at the sky. Birds had a lot in common with my dragon. They could fly. Some species were very smart; some could even talk. They were inquisitive, and were perfectly capable of picking up a small, shiny object if it caught their interest. And they were frequently brought aboard as pets.

I cocked my head and studied the Andolian fern tree forest. Could the thief be living wild in those trees?

Whistling for Rafe, I designed a two-fold trap. I didn't know how much Standard Rafe understood, but I knew he was smart, and I knew he understood more of what I told him than my parents would believe. When he landed on the picnic table beside my tablet, I explained our dilemma.

"So," I finished, "I want you to fly through the forest and look for a nest, one with a hoard of shiny objects. Stuff you might like if I didn't give you lots of nice things for your very own."

Rafe cocked his head and closed his amber eyes very slowly. When he opened them again, he bounced his head once before leaping into flight.

Great. Trap one was in motion.

Digging around in the pocket of my tunic, I pulled out an inexpensive bracelet that sparkled in the sunlight and a small mirror with a gilt handle. I ran to a picnic table well away from the one where my tablet rested and placed the mirror on it in full sight. The bracelet ended up in the middle of the jumpball field where it sparkled nicely.

Returning to the picnic table I'd claimed as my base of operations, I glanced back and forth from the mirror to the bracelet. Trap two was baited and ready.

I soon wished I'd just put out one shiny object. My eyes got tired of shifting from one site to the other. If I wasn't careful, I'd have nothing but a nasty headache to show for my efforts.

Just then a scream sounded from the trees. A Fornaxian dragon scream.

I jumped to my feet and was about to run to the forest when two creatures burst from the greenery; a good-sized bird with glossy purple-black feathers and a bright yellow-orange patch near its head was being chased through the air by my ruby red dragon!

"Help," the bird screamed. "Help me!"

6

Dad and Mr. Trigger came to the rescue. The *Creature Emporium* owner brought a large cage and, with a little help from Rafe, managed to capture the unhappy bird.

The cage represented safety to the bird who'd most likely been hand raised, and being chased by a ruby red dragon provided the terror that made the safety of the cage seem very appealing.

When Rafe landed on my arm, I transferred him to my shoulder, where he crooned happily and nuzzled my neck.

"It's a myna," Mr. Trigger explained. "I don't sell them, so this one must have been brought aboard as a pet."

"Well," said Dad, "since no one has reported a missing bird, his owners must have lost him when cycling off station."

Mr. Trigger nodded. "Very likely." He turned to me. "You say you heard him speak, Cinnamon?"

I grinned. "Yep. When Rafe chased him out of the trees he was screaming, 'Help me!'"

"Good to know," Mr. Trigger said. "That'll make him easier to place with a new family. Why was Rafe chasing him?"

I stroked my dragon's scales. "I asked him to find a nest with shiny things in it," I explained. "He probably found this bird examining its hoard and brought him to me."

Dad looked skeptical. "Don't you think you're giving Rafe a little too much credit, Sugar Cookie?"

I frowned. I really needed to talk to Dad about calling me that in public, but Rafe chirped indignantly at the slight, so I concentrated on him.

"He's smarter than you give him credit for, Dad. I bet he could take us to that nest right now, if I asked."

Rafe chirped his agreement.

Dad swept an arm toward the forest. "Let's see if he can do it."

After nuzzling my neck one more time, Rafe leapt into flight. Dad and Mr. Trigger and I followed. Rafe landed about fifteen feet up in a fern tree beside a nest of twigs and leaves. He cocked his head at us and then kicked the nest to the ground.

Shiny objects rained down on us along with the remains of the nest.

"Well," said Dad, raking through the debris with gloved fingers, "I guess that answers both questions; Rafe found the thief, and he's smarter than I thought." He turned a brilliant smile on me. "He definitely understood you, Sugar Cookie."

7

It didn't take long for the story of Rafe's apprehension of the recreational thief to filter through yellow sector. My ruby red dragon was a hero, his earlier thievery forgiven, if not forgotten.

That very afternoon Rafe and I ran into Sammy and Fred in the park's open space. After an uncomfortable instant we both said, "I'm sorry," at the same time.

Laughing, I held out my hand.

Sammy accepted it and we shook.

"I'm sorry I accused Rafe of stealing those things," she said.

I nodded. "And I'm sorry for making fun of Fred's name." I knelt down and the puppy wriggled over to me, turning belly up so I could rub his soft underside. Which I did. Happily.

Glancing up at Sammy, I said, "He's the cutest puppy on the station, and if you say his name is Fred, then that's fine by me. Fred's a good solid name for an adorable furball."

Sammy grinned and pointed at Rafe, who was circling the open space and showing off his rolls and flips. "Rafe is amazing," she said. "I only called him Ralph because I was mad at you. I know his name is Raphael, and Rafe is a great nickname."

Standing, I met her gaze. "Friends?"

She nodded. "Always."

We hugged each other while Rafe chittered happily and Fred wriggled in delight.

Pets (even highly intelligent Fornaxian dragons) are great, but best friends are better!

PART V

THE CINNAMON FILES: CASE FOUR

The Case of the Vanishing Puppy

The Cinnamon Files
- Case Four -

DEB LOGAN

I sat at the table in our dining alcove across from Dad, my precious tablet clutched tightly to my chest. My heart beat rapidly, but I maintained a carefully neutral expression. Dad leaned forward, his hands resting on the permaplastic surface of the table. Mom stood off to one side, feet slightly spread in her ready-for-anything stance, hands clasped behind her back.

"Detective-in-training Chou," Mom said, "in accordance with our agreement you will unlock your tablet and surrender it for inspection."

"Sir, yes sir!" I responded. Pressing my thumb to the activation screen, I licked my lips and handed my tablet to Dad. "As you can see, sir, my case files are correctly labeled and saved appropriately."

Dad swiped the screen, smiled, and glanced at me, one eyebrow raised. "*The Case Files of Cinnamon Chou, Space Station Detective.* Really? That's a very ambitious title, Sugar Cookie."

My face heated, but I held my gaze steady and managed not to roll my eyes. Parents. They're incorrigible. No matter how many times I asked Dad not to call me *Sugar Cookie*, he persisted. His excuse? Force of habit.

"You've always taught me that I can do anything," I said. I wanted to shrug my shoulders, but controlled the impulse. "I intend to be a detective. Just like you, Dad."

Mom moved to stand behind Dad and studied the tablet over his shoulder.

"Very nicely arranged, Cinnamon," she said. "Your reports appear concise and to the point."

Dad nodded, swiped back to my home screen, and handed the tablet back to me. "I agree. You're doing a great job recording your case files." He paused for a moment, watching me thumb my tablet into dormancy. "Would you like to have a report template? One that my detectives use?"

My eyes widened. A real, live case report template? Just like the detectives on Dad's security team used? Wow! Like I was going to pass up that opportunity!

"That would be awesome, Dad," I said, barely managing not to squeal. When I couldn't contain my excitement, I bounced up from my chair, hugging my tablet to my chest and danced a little jig. "I'm going to be so far ahead of my class at the academy," I said, grinning happily. "I can hardly wait!"

Mom laughed. "Well, I can," she said. "You have years here on Space Station Zeta before you can apply for the USL Academy. Don't go wishing your childhood away."

"I know," I said, twirling around the dining alcove, "but I'm going to make the best use of my time." I stopped twirling before I got too dizzy to stand and raced to hug Dad. "Besides, detecting is in my blood. *Cinnamon Chou, Space Station Detective*. It's who I am!"

The USL Academy. That's where I was headed and everyone knew it. Mom and Dad were both Universal Star League officers. Mom commanded Space Station Zeta, Dad was the ranking security officer, and I was their only offspring. The academy was my destiny.

Dad stood, hugged me back, and ruffled my sleek black hair. "I'll see that you get that template right away, Sugar Cookie."

There it was again, the nickname that refused to die. Now, I don't really mind Dad referring to me as an overly sweet pastry, but I draw the line at casual acquaintances using the name, and when Dad called me that in public, other station inhabitants, both human and alien, seemed to think they could refer to me that way too.

Honestly! I appreciate the fact that Dad has called me his sugar cookie since he first set eyes on me mere moments after my birth, but I'm not a baby anymore. I'm twelve Earth-standard years old, and just because my skin tone, the perfect combination of Mom's ebony complexion and Dad's gold-toned coloration (a throwback to his heritage from the ancient Earth region known as China), reminded him of an old-fashioned cinnamon sugar cookie is no reason to call me that in public.

But, what can a detective-in-training do? Put up with it, that's what. Because Dad is the best dad in the universe and I couldn't imagine loving anyone more. Except of course Mom. I loved her equally as well as Dad.

Let's face it, nicknames aside, I was one lucky girl. Great parents. An awesome pet— how many kids do you know who can claim a Fornaxian dragon as their own?— and an ever expanding universe of friends.

My wrist link pinged and announced, "Samantha Lindstrom." I grimaced. Sammy really needed to change her link settings. She hated being called Samantha almost as much as I disliked anyone but Dad calling me Sugar Cookie.

I waved to Mom and Dad and rushed down the hall to my room. The door irised open with a nearly inaudible *whoosh*, and I answered my link as I stepped inside, the door irising closed behind me.

"Hey, Sammy. What's up?"

A tiny 3-D model of my friend appeared above the link on my wrist, her eyes wide and swimming with tears.

"Emergency, Cinnamon," she wailed. "Fred has disappeared! We were playing in the recreation area, and… and…" She paused, swiped tears from her face with a hand, and took a deep gulp of air. "He vanished, Cinnamon. Fred just vanished!"

Now Sammy may not be a detective-in-training like me, but she is the daughter of a USL officer. Sammy doesn't lie and she doesn't distort the facts. If she said her puppy had vanished, then Fred had vanished. At least, he'd wriggled completely out of her sight. But before I could make an informed decision, I needed cold, hard facts. And to get those, I needed two things: a calm best friend and the opportunity to study the scene of the crime... er, incident... er, disappearance.

"Calm down, Sammy, and tell me what happened."

"Calm down?" she said, her voice rising into the squeaking range as she scowled at my image. "How can you expect me to calm down? Fred just vanished! My puppy is missing!" She paused again, took another gulp of air, and said in a more normal tone, "Besides, I already told you what happened. We were playing in the recreation area and... and... he disappeared."

Fine. Every good detective knows that witness statements can be unreliable. I needed to move on to option #2: investigate the scene of the... disappearance.

"Don't worry, Sammy. Rafe and I are on the case. Stay where you are and we'll be right there. Where are you, exactly?"

"The picnic table next to the jumpball court," she said quickly. "Hurry, Cinnamon. He could be hurt and I'm sure he's scared."

"We're on the way," I assured her and closed the link.

I grabbed the special sheath glove and the padded vest Dad had designed for me, pulled them on, and opened the door to Rafe's habitat. My Fornaxian dragon cocked his head and stared at me with beady amber eyes. He gave a little chirp, as if asking what we were doing.

"Fred's in trouble," I told him, gesturing for him to come to my gloved forearm. "We're going to meet Sammy in the recreation area."

He bobbed his head, ruffled his wings and glided from his permaplastic perch to land lightly on my glove. Well, *lightly* might be stretching the truth. Rafe (Raphael if you want to get formal) was about the size of a small earth dog with ruby red scales, a barbed tail that was nearly as long as his body, and seriously wicked claws. The sheath glove and padded vest with reinforced shoulders protected me from his claws, but I'd really had to work to build up my muscles so that I could hold my arm steady when he landed on the glove.

Transferring him to my shoulder, I waited for him to get settled before leaving my room and hurrying to the door to the corridor.

Mom glanced up from the table where she and Dad were going over some paperwork. "Where are you and Rafe off to, Cinnamon?"

I didn't even pause, just called over my shoulder, "We're meeting Sammy and Fred at the recreation area." At least, I sure hoped we'd be seeing Fred too!

Mom nodded. "Have fun, but be home in plenty of time for dinner."

"Will do," I said and slid through the opening iris into the corridor.

Some people think that space station corridors are confusing, but not me. I grew up on Space Station Zeta and I could navigate its corridors with my eyes closed. Yes, the corridors were color coded: blue for administration; red for engineering; green for hydroponics; white for medical; and purple for the market district; but each section also had its own, unique odors. I could follow my nose to any place I needed to go. But today wasn't even a challenge. Rafe and I wouldn't even need to leave the last and arguably most important sector: yellow— the central core that housed the space station's living quarters, educational units, and recreational areas.

I slowed from a jog to a brisk walk as we entered the large park at the center of yellow sector. The ground underfoot changed from permaplastic flooring to artificial turf, a springy green surface that supposedly mimicked the grass of old Earth. Glancing from the forest of Andolian fern trees that ringed the park to the game fields for soccer and baseball, my gaze came to rest on one of the picnic tables beside the galactic jumpball court. A small figure huddled on the bench, looking miserable and lonely.

Sammy.

Without Fred.

3

I hurried over to join Sammy at the picnic table. My friend looked up when I sat down beside her and tried to smile, but her lips trembled. Her blue eyes were swollen from crying, and her light brown hair was escaping from its usual neat braids.

"Don't worry," I said, giving her arm a squeeze. "We'll find him."

Rafe hopped from my shoulder to the picnic table and nuzzled Sammy's cheek, crooning softly.

"See? Rafe agrees. Everything will be fine."

This time Sammy's smile succeeded. She reached up and stroked Rafe's muzzle, then nodded at me.

"Okay," I said. "Walk us through it. What happened? Tell us everything you can remember."

Sammy nodded, took a deep breath, and stood up. "Right. We were over here," she said, walking to an open area a few feet away. "I was throwing his favorite yellow ball and he was chasing it and bringing it back to me."

I nodded and squinted me eyes. I could almost see the scene. Sammy tossing the bouncy yellow ball and Fred running to catch it and bring it back. Fred was an absolutely adorable little furball. Black and tan and wriggly, the Earth-normal puppy adored belly rubs and playing fetch. I liked the little ball of fluff, but even Sammy would agree that he wasn't exactly what you'd call smart. Not like Rafe, who understood Standard almost as well as I did.

But Sammy hadn't been looking for intelligence in her pet, she'd wanted cuddly, and Fred excelled at cuddles. Rafe? Not so much. When he'd first come to me, Rafe had been... well, *haughty* and *aloof* are probably the best words, but we'd grown on each other and now we were excellent friends. But no one would ever accuse my dragon of being cuddly.

"Where's the ball now?" I asked.

"That's the thing," Sammy said, "I don't know. The last time I threw it, it hit that big rock over there and bounced into the trees. Fred followed it. I heard him yelp, ran to check on him, and couldn't find him." Her eyes widened and her voice got kind of screechy. "He disappeared, Cinnamon. Vanished! Without a trace!"

I grabbed my friend and hugged her. "It's okay, Sammy. We're going to find him."

"But Cinnamon," she cried, her tears transferring from her cheek to mine, "you don't understand. He yelped! He's hurt and scared and I can't find him!"

"Hush now, Sammy. We're going to find him." I patted her back for a minute, then stepped out of our hug. "Why don't you go over there and lie down in the grass. The sunshine will warm you up. Rafe and I will look for Fred."

Now, Sammy and I both know that there isn't any grass or sunshine in the recreational area, any more than there are rocks, but she nodded and flopped into the pretend grass anyway. In reality, the recreation area consists of artificial turf, great lighting programs, and permaplastic boulders for the littlest kids to climb around on. The only living things in the recreational area, besides people and pets, were the Andolian fern trees, and those were grown in hydroponic solutions, their roots traveling deep beneath the permaplastic deck plating into reservoirs maintained by engineering and a special hydroponics team.

Once Sammy was settled, I motioned for Rafe to follow me into the forest. First we stopped by the boulder Sammy had indicated, made a guess as to where the ball had bounced and stepped into the shadows under the fern trees. I glanced up at Rafe— he'd landed on a branch just above my head— and said, "Fly around. See if you can spot Fred or his yellow ball. If you find anything, come get me."

Rafe bobbed his head once and launched into flight.

Great. Air support was on the job. Now for a close inspection of the ground. Noting the trees around me, I imagined a grid overlaying the artificial turf and began a careful inspection of the tree trunks and the turf. It was boring work. The blades of turf didn't bend or break the way living plants might. It just sprang back into shape after being stepped on. I had no way of knowing if Fred had raced over a particular spot as he chased his ball. And even though the fern trees were alive, they'd all been planted at the same time, had received the same nutrients and light, and had grown in very similar patterns.

The Andolian fern tree forest wasn't giving me the clues I needed.

I stopped, hands on hips, then turned and marched back to where Sammy rested in the grass.

When I stood over her, I said, "We need more people."

She shaded her eyes and stared up at me. "Why?"

"We need a line of people to walk from the edge of the open space through the forest watching for clues."

"What kind of clues?"

I threw my hands in the air. "I don't know, but by myself I can't tell where I've been and what I've already looked at." I pointed at the trees. "Everything in there looks the same."

She sat up. "Okay. I see what you're saying. That's why I couldn't find him. I couldn't tell where he'd gone."

I nodded. "But we know about where he went in, and we know he wasn't out of sight long before he yelped, so we shouldn't need too many people."

"Let's call Rabbie and Ginger. I'm sure they'll help."

"Right, and Liu and Aaron and Jase will come... as long as their parents don't have plans for them."

4

Sammy and I got busy with our links and a few minutes later our friends rushed into the park to help us search for Fred.

Rafe perched on my shoulder as I outlined the plan. He hadn't found any sign of the missing puppy either.

"So," I said as I wrapped up the briefing, "Rafe will fly low, using his keen sense of smell as well as his eyes, so don't be surprised if he goes past you. Trust me, he won't do more than brush you with a wingtip."

All seven of us lined up near the rock that had deflected Sammy's ball toss. With our arms outstretched, we positioned ourselves so that our fingertips just barely touched. At my command, we dropped our arms and stepped forward into the trees.

"Remember," I called, "if you see anything suspicious, shout and everyone will stop until I examine the clue."

"Got it." "Right." Will do," called my friends.

I'd only gone about ten paces when Rabbie yelled. "I think Rafe's found something!"

"Everyone stop and hold you places," I said as I raced to find Rabbie and Rafe. I found Rabbie first. He pointed to the base of a fern tree where Rafe sat staring at the ground, his tail barb beating the artificial turf in agitation.

I crept up to my dragon and stroked his shoulder. "What is it, Rafe? What did you find?"

He cocked his head and then bobbed his muzzled toward the spot he'd been observing. I leaned around the base of the fern tree and gasped. Rafe had found a hole in the artificial turf and deck plating. A hole big enough to swallow a puppy whole!

I edged closer to the hole and gazed into its depths. There, about five feet below me was the vat of hydroponic solution that fed the fern tree, and swimming around in the liquid was one very unhappy, very tired puppy!

"Rabbie," I called. "Get Sammy. Bring everyone else. We've found Fred!"

Reaching for my dragon, I stroked his shoulder again. "Well done, Rafe. You solved the mystery. Let's call Dad."

Dad answered my link immediately. "What is it, Sugar Cookie?"

I suppressed a grimace and said, "I need help, Dad. I'm in the recreational area with my friends and we've found a dangerous hole. Sammy's puppy fell through and is in one of the hydroponic tanks. He's swimming, but he's getting tired and we can't reach him."

"Stay where you are, Detective-in-Training Chou. Help is on the way." Dad closed the link and I breathed a sigh of relief.

"Don't worry, Fred," I called to the waterlogged pup. "Dad will rescue you."

Footsteps rushed to my side and soon I was surrounded by friends. Sammy was so relieved to see Fred, she cried and laughed at the same time. I frowned and stared at the edge of the hole. What had caused the opening? Was the edge stable? Possibly not.

"Listen everyone," I said loudly to get their attention. "I think we need to move away from the hole. The edge could give way."

"Right," agreed Rabbie. "I didn't think there could be a hole like that in the deck plating. Let's all move back." He turned to me. "You called security, didn't you?"

I nodded. "Dad said help is on the way, but until they get here, we need to be careful."

Everyone moved away from the hole and back toward the permaplastic boulder. Everyone except Sammy.

"No," she said, her eyes blazing. "I'm not leaving him. He's tired and wet and unhappy. He'll think I'm deserting him."

I nodded. "I understand, but don't kneel like that. At least lay flat so your weight is spread out more evenly."

"Okay. Maybe you'd better call Rafe away."

Rafe cocked his head, glanced from Sammy to me, then spread his wings and flew to a branch a few trees away, but still within sight of Sammy and the hole.

"Good enough," I said and gave him a nod.

The rest of us milled around the boulder while keeping an anxious eye on Sammy.

After a few nervous minutes, Sammy scrambled away from the hole and ran to join us, grinning broadly.

"A hydroponics worker showed up, scooped Fred out of the solution, and waved at me," she said happily. "He said he'd wash Fred off, blow his fur dry, and then bring him up to me."

She grabbed me and hugged me, bouncing up and down the whole time. "Thank you, Cinnamon! ThankyouThankyouThankyou!"

When I managed to disentangle myself, I grinned and said, "You're welcome, but it was a team effort," and gestured to all five of our other friends. "Rabbie and Ginger and Liu and Aaron and Jase came as soon as we asked." I beamed at each of them. "We couldn't have done it without you."

EPILOGUE

The next day, Sammy and I met our five friends at the recreational area for a picnic lunch. Rafe and Fred played chase in the open area, with Fred running and barking while Rafe flew back and forth, zipping down to brush Fred's fur with his tail barb or a wingtip. I'd given Rafe strict instructions to stay away from the trees, and to make sure Fred did the same.

The other kids and I scarfed down synth-chicken sandwiches, hydroponic apples, and soy-based cookies while we watched the engineers and construction team moving back and forth from the place where we knew the hole was to their equipment in a cordoned off section of the open space.

"What do you think made that hole?" Rabbie asked between mouthfuls of sandwich. "I mean, if the permaplastic plating can give way, we could all end up in space."

I shivered at the thought, but repeated what Dad had told me that morning. "Don't worry, Rabbie. Space Station Zeta has the best engineering team in the galaxy. Whatever the problem is, we've discovered it early, thanks to Fred. Engineering will figure it out, and if they can't, the best USL minds in the universe are just an ansible call away. No one is getting spaced."

Ginger nodded. "My mom is an engineer. She said the same thing. Space Station Zeta is safe."

Liu poked Sammy. "Who knows, maybe Commander Chou will give Fred a medal for alerting us to danger."

Sammy grinned. "That would be awesome, but I'm just glad to have my puppy back." She paused and made eye contact with each of us in turn. "And to have the best friends in the whole wide universe!"

We all gave a cheer and thumped our fists on the picnic table. I cleared my throat to get their attention and said, "Thanks, everyone, for helping me solve *The Case of the Vanishing Puppy*."

They all groaned, but Sammy laughed, shook her head, and said, "Trust Cinnamon to turn Fred's adventure into one of her case files!"

15 STORIES BY DEBBIE MUMFORD

PART I

IN SEARCH OF A VALENTINIAN

IN SEARCH OF A
VALENTINIAN

A DEEP SPACE
SHORT STORY

DEBBIE MUMFORD

1

Rafe DaNaal strode into the board room of the *Futura Prime* and nodded to the men and women who rose in acknowledgement of his arrival. The captain and executive officer of the luxury liner—the flagship of Rafe's commercial fleet—wore full dress uniforms, while the other individuals sparkled in a rainbow of corporate finery. Rafe controlled the spurt of irritation at the fashion-slavery of his upper management. By the Black! The men were bedecked in more frills and spangles than the women, and the females were too lavishly decorated for his tastes.

He nodded curtly, motioned to the plush synth-leather chairs surrounding the crystalline table. "Be seated." After smoothing his own well-cut but clean-lined black jacket, he rested his clasped hands on the back of the command chair.

"Captain Joran, report."

Futura Prime's captain rose, clasped his hands behind his fusion-rod-straight back and stared past Rafe's right shoulder. "Sir. We have disengaged the Icarus drive and returned to normal space. We expect to be in orbit around Valentine I in approximately two standard days."

Rafe drew in a deep breath, and immediately regretted it. The combination of repulsively sweet fragrances worn by his corporate underlings was enough to choke a proverbial horse. He'd breathe more shallowly from here on out, or risk losing his typical breakfast of tea, toast, and a single soft-boiled egg.

Blackness! What he wouldn't give to be living a few centuries back when board rooms were filled with cigar smoke and the fumes of expensive liquor. His pre-space ancestors hadn't known how good they had it. No Interplanetary Council. No aliens mucking up their economy. No time wasted traveling between distant stars. Just clean and simple commerce. Everything a man needed on a single planet. Yes. Those were the days. Too bad they ended two hundred years before Rafe's birth.

"Thank you, Captain," he said, fighting his gag reflex and willing his eyes not to water. "Savoy, where do we stand on the negotiations?"

The least offensively dressed woman rose and faced him. Her buttercup yellow skinsuit left nothing to the imagination regarding the curves and planes of her small frame—he could even see the indentation of her naval—but at least she wasn't decked out in a three dimensional model of the Valentinian solar system like the man to her right.

She cleared her throat and Rafe focused on the sleek coils of her elaborately coiffed dark hair. "The negotiations have been tedious, sir. Since no one has yet discovered an adult of the Valentinian species, no one is certain with whom we should be negotiating."

"The IC hasn't made a ruling on this yet?" Rafe asked, his voice sharp. "I thought the ruling was imminent before we left Centauri."

Savoy inclined her head, causing Rafe to wonder just how those coils of hair maintained their structural integrity. He yanked his wandering attention back to her words.

"So thought we all, sir. Yet, when communications were reestablished after the I-drive was suspended, I found that nothing had changed."

"The status quo stands?"

"It does, sir. Valentine I remains a protectorate of the Interplanetary Council until such time as an adult Valentinian can be discovered."

Rafe motioned the woman to sit, then paced around the table, his booted feet silent against the rubberized coating of the board room's decking. By the Black, he couldn't believe his council contacts had failed so miserably. He'd been assured that by the time he arrived in the Valentine system, the planet would be open for trade. Rafe DaNaal was famous for initiating commerce with alien species. His people might be peacocks, but they were the best at recognizing and exploiting lucrative opportunities. And Valentine I promised to be an opportunity-rich world.

He stopped, his gaze zeroing in on Savoy. "Will we be allowed access to the planet?"

"We are in negotiations."

"Make it happen," he ordered. "At the very least I want to observe the Valentinians first hand. Perhaps our interplanetary sociologists will be able to make a case for the cherubs being adults. Perhaps there isn't a truly intelligent species for the IC to protect."

Savoy glanced nervously at her fellows before licking her lips and replying, "It shall be done, Mr. DaNaal."

2

Two standard days later, Rafe DaNaal met his first Valentinian cherub.

Rafe shook his head, amazed that an alien creature could so closely resemble the stereotypical Cupid of Earth's commercial heritage. That resemblance, of course, was the reason for the planetary and system designation of Valentine. Someone in exploration and cartography should be executed for that decision. Not that Rafe had an opinion.

The cherub floated at Rafe's eye-level, little golden wings beating rapidly to hold his pudgy, infant-like body aloft. Soft golden curls surrounded a wide-eyed, apple-cheeked face. Why, the infantile creature was even swaddled in a snowy-white drape that covered what Rafe assumed were its genitals. The only thing lacking to complete the Cupidic image was a tiny bow and arrow.

Thankfully, the cherub was unarmed.

Rafe extended his hand toward the small being. It smiled and pointed a chubby finger at him. When their index fingers touched, time stopped.

Literally.

A gleaming, crystalline structure unfolded from the point of contact and expanded until it encompassed Rafe and the cherub. Rafe tried to withdraw his hand, to move beyond the reach of the rapidly building cocoon, but he was immobilized. His finger fused to that of the cherub.

Panic seized Rafe. His heart beat wildly, its roar against his eardrums deafening him. His breath came in shallow gasps, and perspiration sheened his face and neck.

This couldn't be happening. Not to him. Not to the great Rafe DaNaal. Where were his bodyguards? How could an alien who was the picture of innocence abduct him and hold him hostage? For that must be what this was about. Surely it was no accident that the curly-mopped cherub chose to freeze Rafe DaNaal in whatever the hell this was.

He glanced about, certain that his people would find a way to break into the chrysalis, but they were gone. Rafe and the cherub hung suspended in space, surrounded by the velvet blackness of endless night. Tiny pinpricks of light glistened around them, reminders that in the far reaches of the universe, planets revolved around suns, moons around planets.

Rafe's heart rate regulated. Panic wouldn't remedy this situation. He was doomed. A dead man floating in space with an inarticulate alien. Might as well relax and enjoy the view for whatever moments remained to him.

Resignation brought peace and its calm allowed him to review his life. It had been a good one. His regrets were few. He should have bonded with Annalise. He enjoyed her sexually, appreciated her quick and agile mind, enjoyed their animated discussions. He treasured their moments together. Did that constitute love? He supposed it did.

What had he expected? A bolt from the blue?

Wry laughter pushed past his lips. Here he was, floating in space in a chrysalis created by Cupid, contemplating the vagaries of love. How much more prosaic could a man get?

You are an interesting creature.

The thought whispered through Rafe's mind. He frowned and

turned his attention to the cherubic infant still attached to his outstretched index finger.

"Did you say something?"

I did, though I am not the... what did you call it? Ah, yes... the cherub you are frowning at.

"You're not? Then what are you? More importantly, *where* are you?"

I surround you. The cherub is merely my physical manifestation on your plane of existence.

Rafe's frown deepened. "Your physical manifestation? The cherubs aren't immature members of your species?"

A sound Rafe couldn't classify, but interpreted as laughter swept through his mind. *No indeed. Our species as you call it has no need of a larval stage. We exist. We extrude extensions in various planes to interact with more... limited... creatures. Your kind has approached slowly, with great care. You are the first to afford us with an opportunity for contact.*

Rafe couldn't help comparing the innocent-looking cherub with the type of lure used by an arboreal lifeform on Vegas IV. The creature was invisible to the human eye, but sported an appendage that resembled a particularly delicious edible fruit. When the unwary touched the fruit, they were trapped by a gluey excretion and, unable to escape, consumed by a creature they couldn't even see.

Needless to say, Vegas IV was not a popular tourist destination.

Still, Rafe had made a killing on exports from that market once he and his team had found a way to safely harvest the actual fruit that the creature so effectively imitated.

And even with his knowledge of the predators of Vegas IV, Rafe had still fallen prey to the cherub.

Interesting, the Valentinian remarked. *Your thoughts turn immediately to predator and prey. You assume I will cause your destruction.*

"Is my assumption incorrect?" Rafe glanced around himself. "You have brought me to a place that is hostile to life, but have not explained your purpose in doing so. I have no escape; no way to exist except by your benevolence. Are you a benevolent creature?"

Benevolence? Ah, I see the concept in your mind. I am neither benevo-

lent nor... what is the other, the antithetical concept? Ah, yes. There it is... merciless. I simply am.

Rafe considered. Feeling that he had nothing to lose, he pushed. "And your purpose in extracting me from the planet and bringing me here?"

A quieter version of what Rafe still thought of as laughter—a chuckle, perhaps?—sighed through his brain. *Information, of course. Knowledge of your species. Obtaining such information, requires communication. Or long periods of observation. Since opportunities for observation have been minimal and your presented yourself as a willing candidate, I opted for direct communication.*

"And direct communication required my abduction?"

Silence filled the crystalline cocoon and echoed through the infinity of space beyond its faceted planes. Rafe hung motionless, still connected by his fingertip to the cherub that had been used to lure him to his fate.

Abduction was not intended. You are free to go.

Before Rafe could even absorb the meaning of the creature's words, the crystalline structure retracted, folded in upon itself, and he found himself staggering under his own weight, the gravity of Valentine I having reasserted itself upon his physique.

The cherub withdrew its touch, but as it did so, Rafe heard a final thought echo through his brain, *No harm was intended. We will study this problem and find another way.*

And then Rafe was alone in his mind while his body was surrounded by his bodyguards, Interplanetary Council scientists and security officers, and underlings in his employ. He was whisked into a shuttle, transported back to *Futura Prime*, and placed immediately into medical quarantine while the scientists and security officers argued about how best to handle the extraordinary events that had taken place on the planet's surface.

No one listened to Rafe, which he found distasteful in the extreme.

3

Rafe tolerated quarantine. For a day. He'd endured the decontamination chamber. Had dressed in the flimsy white jumpsuit of sterile synth-fabric, though he detested the feel of the scratchy material against his skin. But when yet another medic approached him with a pressure syringe, his patience snapped.

"I am not a lab rat," he said through gritted teeth. All things considered, he thought his tone remarkably calm and cool. "I have been poked and prodded enough. You have sufficient samples of my bodily fluids. I demand to be released."

"I haven't the authority..." the medic began, but Rafe raised a hand to forestall the excuse.

"Then find someone who does." When the medic simply stood there with his mouth hanging open, Rafe snapped out a single word. "Now!" The man turned and ran, the entry barely having time to *whoosh* open before him.

Rafe jumped down from the examination table and strode to a communication panel above the narrow white counter that ran the length of the med bay. Slapping his palm against it for authorization, he barked an order. "This is DaNaal. Get me Savoy." When his staffer's face appeared on the view screen, a wave of relief mixed with impatience nearly swamped him.

"Mr. DaNaal. It's good to see you, sir."

"Get me some decent clothes, Savoy, and get me out of here."

"But sir..."

"No excuses, Savoy, just get it done. I need clothes, a real meal, and a meeting with IC's top security officer, scientist, and yourself. And I want it now."

"I'll see to it, sir."

An hour later Rafe DaNaal was feeling a great deal more like himself. He'd eaten a light meal of green salad (hydroponically grown), grilled chicken (real meat, not the synthetic substitute), and a mixed berry cobbler (made from the freshest ingredients available aboard the *Futura Prime*). Now, dressed again in one of his signature black suits, he sat in his board room and surveyed the men and women he'd called together.

Savoy, recognizing her employer's mood, was dressed sensibly in a charcoal gray jumpsuit with no outlandish adornments. Her black hair was pulled back from her face in a simple, but effective, knot at the base of her skull. The style emphasized her dark, almond shaped eyes. Rafe approved the conservative look.

Major Edwards, of the Interplanetary Council Security Force, was a formidable looking woman. Steel gray hair cut so short it stood on end in brush-like bristle. Ice blue eyes, that observed Rafe with a shrewd expression. Her pea-green uniform with its crisp creases and straight edges suited her box-like build.

Dr. Takimoto, the senior exogeneticist assigned to Valentine I, had the reputation of being one of the IC's top scientists. The man was tall, thin, and wore the white lab coat that had been the uniform of a scientist for the centuries now. His hair was still black, but its line was receding, giving the impression that his cranium was larger than the average man's. Perhaps it was. Dr. Takimoto's intelligence quotient was undeniably above average. A brain that size might require more space than was usual.

Major Edwards spoke first, undoubtedly hoping to take control of the meeting, despite the fact that Rafe had called them together.

"If you're feeling up to it, Mr. DaNaal, I'd like a first-hand report of what happened on the surface."

Rafe inclined his head. "I'm sure you would, Major, but as I am not under your command and you are in fact aboard my ship, I'll ask the questions."

The major's lips thinned to a mere line and her nostrils flared, but she made no further comment.

"Dr. Takimoto," Rafe continued, his gaze dismissing the major and landing on the scientist, "what can you tell me about the cherubs? Has their activity changed since my... interaction with the one?"

The man met and held Rafe's gaze. "As a matter of fact, yes. Before the incident, the cherubs appeared to mill around in random patterns. They gave no appearance of communication or interaction with each other, and their movements followed no discernable pattern."

"And now?" Rafe asked, leaning forward in his chair.

"Now all movement has stopped. The cherubs arranged themselves in a concentric helix soon after your return and have remained in that pattern since." He frowned and lifted his hands. "It's as if they are frozen in place."

Rafe nodded. Despite his earlier refusal to report to Major Edwards, he gave the three a succinct version of what he had learned during his conversation with the Valentinian.

"So the cherubs are not infantile versions of the inhabitants of this planet?" Major Edwards asked. The confusion evident on her face forced Rafe to place a hand over his mouth and fake a cough to cover the laugh that threatened the gravity of the situation.

"Fascinating," Dr. Takimoto said. "An extension or extrusion of their being into another plane of existence. Were you able to ascertain why they would wish to make such an effort?"

Rafe nodded. "I was... and I intend to return to surface in order to exploit that knowledge."

"What?" the other three burst out in simultaneous indignation.

"Sir!" Savoy's voice rang out above the others'. "You can't put yourself in that kind of peril?"

"And who should I place in jeopardy, Savoy? You?"

Major Edwards jumped to her feet. "No one. This is an IC security issue and I will not have you, a civilian, making first contact with an unknown alien species."

This time Rafe didn't bother to hide his laugh, and at the sound, the other three subsided.

"I'm sorry, Major, but your argument is moot. Civilian or not, I have already made first contact with a Valentinian." He glared at each of the others in turn, waiting until Edwards resumed her seat before continuing. "Furthermore, I am the best equipped to negotiate. Not only is the creature already accustomed to the structure of my mind, but I've built a considerable financial empire on my ability to find common ground, mutual benefit if you will, with other alien species."

He stood, walked around the table, and leaned forward hands braced against its solid surface and stared down the security officer, the scientist, and his own subordinate. "I am, quite literally, the closest thing you have to a subject matter expert."

"Very well," said Dr. Takimoto.

Savoy inclined her head. "As you wish, Mr. DaNaal."

But Major Edwards scowled and shook her head. "How will you even know which cherub to approach? How can you know you'll be dealing with the same creature?"

Rafe shrugged and moved to the door. "I won't, but as they know who I am, I have faith that they'll put forward the proper individual." He paused, a small frown creasing his brow. "Assuming that all those cherubs even represent individuals. They could be a collective."

And with that parting thought, he strode from the room.

4

Rafe DaNaal strode across the compound that housed both the IC security team and its contingent of scientists. The labs and living quarters—barracks for the security teams, small residential units for the scientists—were well-equipped and squared away. Pristine white buildings set in a regulated quadrant, with little in the way of local flora to distinguish this compound from hundreds of others on multiple other worlds across the galaxy. Savoy scurried in his wake while Takimoto pressed forward, a worried expression on his face, and Edwards marched at his side, her lips thin and her eyes sparking with indignation.

When they reached a rise where they could see the complex pattern of frozen cherubs stretching into the distance, Rafe halted, turned to his companions, and said, "Remember, no matter what happens, do not interfere."

Savoy lowered her head for a moment, then straightened her shoulders and met his gaze directly. "But, Rafe, you could be killed. You can't expect me to stand by and watch you die without even attempting to save you."

Rafe studied his aide, surprised by her gall. No one questioned a direct order from Rafe DaNaal. No one. Not publicly. Not if they expected to remain in his employ. But something in Savoy's gaze touched him. She cared for him, was genuinely concerned for his safety.

He gave a slight nod and said, "Yes, Savoy. I can. You will not interfere." He smiled and lowered his voice, speaking for her alone, "And I will not die, Annalise. Trust me. I know what I'm doing."

A blush stained her cheeks and, lowering her gaze, she stepped back. He'd embarrassed her by using her given name. He never called her Annalise in public. Given names were private, and only to be used in intimate circumstances. He hoped he was correct, that he would live to further explore her feelings. Both of their feelings.

Nodding to his companions, Rafe strode toward the cherubs... and was met by a single entity, its finger outstretched.

Rafe extended his own hand, touched the cherub's finger, expecting to be transported to the crystal cocoon. Nothing happened. His feet remained firmly planted on the soil of Valentine I. He frowned, confused. Rafe DaNaal disliked confusion. He turned his head to glance back at his companions...

...and a voice exploded in his mind.

You returned!

"Yes, and you didn't abduct me. Explain, and if possible, please modify your sending."

My sending?

"The force of your thoughts," Rafe gasped. "The intensity is painful. Extremely."

A moment passed. And then another. Rafe wondered if the cherub would withdraw. If he had offended the entity.

No offense was taken. Pain was not the intention. Is this more acceptable?

Rafe nodded and relief cleared the frown from his face. "Much. Thank you. Why are we still on the planet surface?"

We studied the problem. My coterie deduced that if all others held the pattern, I would be able to communicate with you on this plane. We did not anticipate the problem of intensity. Is this form of communication acceptable to you?

"It is. I thank you for your accommodation. Please extend my gratitude to your... coterie."

We are pleased with your return. We wish to learn more of your species, of this plane of existence. You are the first who has been willing to communicate with us.

"My species is also anxious to learn of you. Your ability to cross planes is new to us. Is your coterie comfortable? Can they maintain this pattern? Is our timeframe of limited duration?"

We can maintain.

"Then let us begin."

5

Rafe and the Valentinian took it slowly that first day. Both were pleased that accommodations had been made and communication achieved. Neither worried that the other would fail to return to what Rafe thought of as the negotiation table.

By the end of the second day, Dr. Takimoto and two of his fellow scientists had been paired with other coterie members. The Valentinians discovered the balance necessary for their concentric helix pattern to allow multiple strands of communication. Information was exchanged and additional scientists and their assistants buzzed with excitement as they recorded the formulas and computations Dr. Takimoto and his associates provided.

Rafe was well pleased with the team's efforts and with his own contributions. Eventually, though, he realized it was time to move on.

"I thank you, Valentine Maximus, for allowing me the opportunity to communicate with you." Rafe sat in a folding camp chair, his hand extended to the cherub who never failed to join him.

I see in your mind the intention to leave this planet.

Rafe inclined his head. "I have many and varied responsibilities. It is time for me to attend to them."

Will you return?

"Eventually. I have enjoyed our interaction too much to terminate it completely." He paused and gestured to a conservatively clad young man. At least, Javon Singh's black skinsuit with deep blue overblouse was conservative by the fashion conscious members of Rafe's upper management. "If you will allow, I would like to introduce you to an associate." The young man hurried forward and positioned himself just behind Rafe's right shoulder.

Valentine Maximus held silent. Rafe wondered if his associate would be rejected. Rafe and Savoy had studied the backgrounds of all DaNaal personnel aboard the *Futura Prime* and had selected Singh for the position. He was young, but he was steady, reliable, and detail-oriented. If accepted, he would be an excellent conduit between Rafe and Valentine Maximus.

Ask your protégé to place his hand on your shoulder. I will allow him to join our communication.

Rafe relayed the information and Singh complied.

Are you at ease in this link, Javon Singh?

Singh started, and Rafe realized he could read the man's reaction through their link. Valentine Maximus's usage of his name had startled him.

"I am, sir." Singh said, and Rafe was pleased at the steadiness of the young man's voice.

I am also comfortable, Maximus replied. *And pleased with your selection. I will communicate with Singh in your absence, Rafe DaNaal.*

"Thank you, Valentine Maximus," Rafe said, inclining his head. "I will be pleased to maintain contact with you through Mr. Singh."

And I with you.

With that Maximus's cherub withdrew and Rafe and Javon Singh were left alone.

Singh turned to Rafe, his eyes shining. "Sir. Thank you for this opportunity. That was amazing. I felt... I don't know what I felt, but I know there is so much to learn and I'm humbled to be part of this great experiment."

Rafe stood. Studied the young man, and extended his hand. "I have great faith in you, Singh. I know you'll do well."

Singh shook Rafe's hand, opened his mouth to speak, but Rafe forestalled him.

"You'll do well, Singh, but if it becomes too much, make sure you report that as well." He laid his other hand over the one he already clasped. "Having an alien presence in your mind can be... unsettling. Don't be afraid to ask for help."

"Sir," Singh said, his face still aglow with wonder. "I won't let you down. You or the Valentinian."

Rafe gave the young man's hand a final squeeze. "I have no doubt."

And with that, Rafe DaNaal crossed the IC compound to return to his ship. The situation on Valentine I was under control. It was time to follow his destiny to its next destination... wherever that might be.

PART II

IZZIE

DEBBIE MUMFORD

BESTSELLING AUTHOR OF *SORCHA'S HEART*

Izzie

A Very Short Story of the Future

IZZIE

My new friend and her husband lived in a well-to-do neighborhood. A twinge of envy stabbed my soul as I strolled up the flower-lined walk to Emily's perfectly groomed front porch. I made a mental note never to invite her to my third-floor walk-up.

She opened the front door at my first hesitant knock and welcomed me into her home. My sense of inferiority vanished. Her living room looked like it had suffered a minor explosion.

"Please excuse the mess," she said with a pretty blush. "My own personal mini-tornado makes sure I never have a neat room."

As she spoke a small boy ran squealing through the room chasing a large gray and white cat. The animal loped easily, almost lazily, before the child, reminding me of the mechanical rabbit I'd seen luring greyhounds in a race on a historical vid.

"He certainly seems happy," I said, unable to keep from smiling as the little fellow disappeared around a corner.

Emily laughed and waved me into a comfortable overstuffed chair. "Kevin's a bundle of energy, and the light of my life. I swear, before we got Izzie, I struggled to get anything done while he was awake. Three is such an energetic age."

"Izzie?"

She gestured toward the doorway where Kevin had disappeared. "The cat. She's been an absolute life-saver."

Before I could comment, Kevin reappeared. This time he walked slowly into the room, burdened as he was with the cat. Stretched out, Izzie nearly matched Kevin's height. He held her beneath her front legs, her back tight against his chest. They made a comical picture as they marched into the room. Kevin's face glowed with pride; clearly, he thought he was carrying the cat. In truth, Izzie's back feet connected firmly with the carpet and she walked calmly between his straddling legs. I'd never imagined a cat would tolerate that kind of behavior.

"Kevin! Put Izzie down this instant." Emily started to rise, but Kevin complied. "That's a good boy. Now, tell Izzie 'sorry.'"

"Thorry, Ithie," Kevin lisped.

I'd expected the cat to streak from the room or at least take refuge under the couch, but Izzie merely puddled at Kevin's feet and began to groom her disarranged fur. When the toddler collapsed beside her, she laid a possessive paw across his leg.

"Yes," Emily said, turning her attention back to me, "Izzie is the best investment we ever made. Of course, she cost nearly as much as this house, but it's not like we intend for Kevin to be an only child." Color stained her cheeks again, and she lowered her eyes demurely.

Understanding dawned. "Wouldn't it have been simpler to hire a nanny?" I asked.

She glanced across the room to where Kevin was running a toy train in circles around the cat before meeting my eyes. "Nannies are so hard to come by these days," she said, "and besides, I don't want to compete with another woman for my own child's affection. Izzie's just a cat."

Just a cat, I thought. *Right.*

Now that I'd seen Izzie in action, I prayed that Jason and I would be able to afford one of the genetically-enhanced miracles when our turn came to start a family. My visit with Emily had certainly been eye-opening.

PART III

SIMON SAYS

SIMON SAYS

A DEEP SPACE
SHORT STORY

DEBBIE MUMFORD

1

Captain Simon Jeffords commanded the *Glacial Floe*. Well, commanded might be a bit of a stretch seeing as he was the only human aboard the compact little ice hauler. Still, *Floe* was his, from stem to stern.

He glanced around the command station where he sat in the deck's one and only plasteel chair. Upright at the moment, though the angle would change when the ship pulled multiple Gs to yank a loosened ice floe from its gravitational field. Four multi-dimensional comm screens displayed *Floe's* position in space. He seldom did more than glance at the port and starboard views, preferring the fore and aft screens.

After all, fore gave him a view of where he was headed—especially important in asteroid fields where most ice floes were found—and aft allowed him to be sure whatever he was hauling was following in good order.

He nodded. *Floe's* command center was a slick little unit. Not state-of-the-art, of course. No ice hauler could afford all the latest bells and whistles, but *Floe* hummed right along, and he was proud to be her captain.

He stood, intending to slide down the ladder to the galley. He'd made enough off that last haul to load his syntho-chef with some prime ingredients, and he had a hankering for steak and eggs. Just the thought of red meat—yeah, yeah, *synthesized* red meat, but meat nonetheless—made his mouth water and his nostrils flare.

The stop at the mining colony on Corona Prime had been a good one. He'd sold the ice he'd been hauling for more credits than he'd seen in a year, resupplied at reasonable rates, and still had enough to buy a few luxuries. Like beyond-the-basic syntho-chef ingredients. This next ice hunt was going to be far more comfortable than the last one. He'd been eating syntho-protein mush for a month and was running on fumes when he'd docked at Corona Prime.

Before he made it to the ladder, a melodious female voice interrupted his dreams of steak and eggs.

"Simon, we have a guest."

He frowned. "Don't call me *Simon*. It's *Captain Jeffords* to you, Flo." He paused, grabbed the rails of the ladder, and glanced toward the command center. "And what do you mean we have a guest? There's no one on this ship but me."

"I'm sorry to disagree, Simon, but there's a young female sitting in the storage compartment next to the aft air lock."

"Don't call me *Simon*," he growled as he slid down the ladder and strode aft.

"I'm sorry, Simon, but name protocols are hard-wired into my programming."

"Your programmers were idiots," he muttered, fully aware that the ship's sensors would pick up his comments no matter how quietly he uttered them.

"My programmers felt that use of the given name would make humans more comfortable with AI. Artificial intelligence still worries some of your species."

"Well, I'm not worried, Flo, and I'd be much more comfortable if you'd call me Captain Jeffords."

"Your comfort is my first priority, Simon," the ship responded, her musical voice sounding as innocent and guileless as a newborn lamb.

Not that Simon had ever encountered a lamb, newborn or otherwise.

He stopped, fisted his hands on his hips to keep from shaking them at the disembodied voice, and took a deep breath. He wanted to shout. He wanted to rant at the top of his lungs. But he knew from experience that yelling at his ship's AI wouldn't produce the desired results.

"Flo," he said in as reasonable a tone as he could manage, "why are you just now telling me about this stow-away? Why didn't you inform me while we were still docked at Corona Prime?"

"You ordered me to maintain silence, Simon. You said you needed to concentrate." The AI waited a beat before adding, "I always obey your orders, Simon."

He narrowly avoided rolling his eyes, but gave in to the impulse to throw his hands in the air. "Fine," he said. "Since you're always obedient to my orders, I *order* you to address me as Captain Jeffords."

"I'm so sorry, Simon," the ship intoned sweetly, "but as I've already explained, name protocols are hard-wired into my program. Now, would you like to meet our guest?"

"She's not a guest, Flo. She's a stow-away, and if she gives me any trouble, I'll be forced to space her."

"Of course, Simon. You're the captain."

"Now she remembers," he muttered as he made his way to the storage compartment next to the aft air lock.

Arriving at the compartment door, he paused to straighten his serviceable dark blue tunic and run his hands through his bowl-cut dark hair. He hadn't had a woman on his ship in a long time and, stow-away or not, he wanted to look presentable.

Presentable, but not welcoming.

He was the captain. She was a stow-away.

He needed to make sure she knew who was in charge here. Arranging his features in his best no-nonsense, command expression, he palmed the door open.

With a distinctive *whoosh* and a puff of slightly pungent air, the door disappeared into the bulkhead. Leaving him staring at a freckle-faced little girl of no more than eight. A cloud of curly red hair surrounded a dirty face with the widest gray-green eyes he'd ever seen. Her rust colored tunic and leggings were threadbare and none too clean and the toes of her shoes sported holes he could stick a finger through. She didn't exactly look like she was starving—no bloated belly that he could see, but she certainly wasn't well fed. And the odor wafting from her was distinctly unpleasant.

The child needed a bath and a good meal. Preferably in that order.

He thought of his coveted steak and eggs and sighed. He had enough for two, but...

"Flo," he snapped, "I thought you said there was a young woman in this compartment."

"Excuse me, Simon. I believe I told you our guest was a young female. I can replay our conversation, if you like."

He bit his lip to avoid screaming. "That won't be necessary."

"This is Alia, Simon. She's female, seven years old, and an orphan."

"And how do you know all that?"

"I asked her, Simon," the AI replied smoothly.

"You asked her," he muttered. "You couldn't be bothered to tell me she was aboard, but you had time for a little chat with a stow-away."

"You didn't order me to silence everywhere, Simon. Only in your presence. I am capable of carrying on multiple conversations simultaneously, and I had to ask her name in order to comply with my name protocol."

The little girl chose that moment to climb to her feet and examine Simon as though she were the captain and he was the stow-away.

"Who are you?" she asked, crossing stick-thin arms over her little chest.

"I'm Captain Jeffords, and you're a stow-away."

"Why does Flo call you Simon?"

"Because her programming is defective.

"My programming is not defective," Flo said, but without the indignant tone a human would have used. "My name protocol requires that I address humans by their given name. This is Simon Jeffords, Alia. He is my captain."

He stared at the ceiling. "There," he said. "You know all the proper words, Flo. Kindly put them in the correct order and address me as *Captain Jeffords*."

"I'm sorry, Simon," the AI said, and managed to infuse her words with a tiny semblance of regret, "but my programming won't allow that designation."

"I'm having your circuits torn out as soon as I can afford to replace them."

Alia cocked her head and frowned. "Are you sure you're the captain? Arguing with your AI isn't smart, and a captain has to be smart."

He stared at the child in disbelief. The pint-sized ragamuffin had just insulted him.

"Believe it or don't," he growled. "I'm in charge and you're a problem. Come with me."

He strode down the corridor, not bothering to see if the child followed. The *Glacial Floe* wasn't a large ship, so it didn't take long to reach the crew quarters. Fortunately the *Floe* was equipped with two private sleeping rooms as well as a bunk room that could accommodate six.

He led Alia to the unused private room. The door *whooshed* open when he palmed the security plate. "You can stay here for now," he told the little girl. "Flo, set the palm plate for Alia. Give her access to the head, the galley, and the exercise area. My quarters are off limits as is the command deck."

"Of course, Simon."

Alia wandered around the small sleeping room, trailing her fingers—undoubtedly *dirty* fingers—across the bed, the small desk, and peering into the narrow wardrobe.

"This is all for me?" she squeaked. Turning those big, gray-green eyes on Simon, she said, "I've never had my own room before."

He fisted his hands behind his back and forced his expression to remain stern, but his heart melted a little at her words. She was just a little girl. And she'd obviously had it tough.

He nodded. "All yours until we reach a port where I can turn you over to the authorities."

"Oh," she said quietly, and turned back to investigate the built-in drawers beside the wardrobe.

"Flo, explain the procedure for showering to Alia and see if you can direct her to something clean to wear." He frowned, then said to the child, "You can shower by yourself, can't you? I mean, you won't need help or anything?"

She turned around and stared at him, then put her hands on her hips and glared. "Of course I can shower by myself. I'm not a baby, you know."

He cleared his throat to cover a sigh of relief. "Right. Not a baby. Fine."

He turned to leave, but hesitated in the doorway. "Get cleaned up, then come to the galley. I'll show you how to work the syntho-chef."

2

Captain Simon Jeffords would never have characterized himself as lonely. He simply worked alone—and liked his solitude.

But having Alia aboard changed everything.

Before he knew it, the little stow-away had wormed her way into his heart, becoming a necessary part of his existence. He listened for her laughter as he searched the comm unit for asteroid belts with tell-tale signs of ice bearing rock. He cocked his head to catch the cadences of her chatter as she carried on long conversations with Flo. And he looked forward to their daily shared meals. He didn't even begrudge her the prime rations he would usually have hoarded for himself.

Alia opened his world and thawed his heart. He wanted nothing but the best for the child.

Using what he'd learned of her life on Corona Prime, he searched all the data banks he could access for traces of her extended family.

And found nothing.

Capturing a large ice floe, he searched the star maps for a port that would not only provide optimal revenue, but would also have a stable enough governing body to have a system to care for a child.

A special child.

A delightful child.

A child who deserved a chance at a decent life. With a good family who would not just care for her basic needs, but would love and cherish her.

He finally settled on hauling his ice, and his stow-away, to Space Station Zeta. He wouldn't get top dollar for the ice, but with the Universal Star League in charge, he knew Alia would receive the best care.

He set his course, leaned back in the command chair, and allowed an unaccustomed sadness to roll over him. The *Glacial Floe* was going to feel incredibly empty when Alia was no longer aboard.

"Why are we going to Space Station Zeta, Simon?"

"To sell our ice, of course." He'd given up arguing with the ship's AI over his name. Alia's comment about his intelligence had hit home. Just one of the many changes the child had caused him to make.

And, truth be told, he was happier for those changes.

"Are you feeling well, Simon?" Flo asked, her musical voice tinged with just a hint of concern. "You've always said selling to the USL left too many credits on the table."

He sighed and closed his eyes. "It's different this time. There are other concerns than just profit."

"You mean like me?" Alia's childish voice echoed up the ladder from where she waited on the floor below the command deck.

Simon's head suddenly throbbed. He rubbed his temples in a vain attempt to ease the pressure and bit his lip to contain another sigh. When neither action afforded him relief, he stood and made his way down the ladder.

Kneeling beside the child, he met her clear-eyed gaze and nodded. "Yes. I mean like you. The USL will have a system in place to care for you. They'll find a family for you."

She cocked her head, but didn't break eye contact. "But I already have a family."

He shifted to sit cross-legged on the floor and pulled her into his lap.

"I'm sorry, kiddo, but your parents are dead and I haven't found any trace of other family. Maybe the USL will have better luck.

She squirmed around until she could see his face. "I know that," she said, her voice reminding him of her indignant proclamation at their first meeting that she wasn't a baby. "I don't mean them. I mean you and Flo. You're my family now."

Simon stared at her. A tiny waif of a girl, wearing one of his oldest tunics as a dress, belted with a length of copper tubing and with the sleeves rolled to allow her to use her hands, had just claimed him as family.

Worse yet, she'd included his ship's AI in the statement.

"Alia," he said quietly, locking his gaze to hers. "Flo isn't real. She's a computer program. And I don't know anything about taking care of a little girl."

A look of stubborn determination creased her forehead and settled in her eyes. "Flo is too real. She talks to me and teaches me and helps me when I need it. That's more than people did for me on Corona Prime."

Her gaze softened and she placed a hand on his cheek. "And you know lots. You don't even argue with Flo anymore." She paused, giving him a mischievous grin before continuing. "You just need to buy me some real clothes. After you sell the ice, of course."

An unexpected warmth settled in his chest. "You'd really like to stay on the *Glacial Floe?*" he asked, not daring to believe he might be able to keep her, that she might be willing to take a chance on a confirmed bachelor with no clue about child-rearing.

Alia nodded, and his heart swelled.

Flo chimed in. "Then everything is settled. Alia will stay. Simon will be her father and I will be her mother. And we'll find a more profitable place to sell our ice."

Simon glanced at the ceiling. "Our ice? It's *my* ice, Flo. And you're not Alia's mother. You're a computer program."

"Semantics, Simon. Alia knows who we are."

Alia chose that moment to throw her arms around Simon's neck and squeeze with more strength than he'd believed her little arms contained. He found himself wrapping her tiny body in a bear hug, and relishing the act.

He couldn't remember the last time he'd hugged anyone, let alone a child.

"I know exactly who we are," Alia said, and the joy in her voice brought tears to his eyes. "We're a family!"

PART IV

NEW YEAR

DEBBIE MUMFORD

BESTSELLING AUTHOR OF *SORCHA'S HEART*

NEW YEAR

How could she face a year without her daughter?

SPUN YARNS
A Short Story

1

New Year's Eve. Tomorrow would be a new year. A year without her in it. A year I'd have to face without her in my life. How could such a year exist? It couldn't. Not in my lifetime.

Parent's aren't supposed to outlive their children.

I puttered around her workspace in the laboratory, picking up one object after another. The large room was empty, my footsteps echoed against white tile floors, bounced off sparkling windows and featureless white walls. I was alone, as I had been since her death. Who else would be in the lab on New Year's Eve? Who but a daughterless mother seeking some remnant of her child's spirit?

Gleaming chrome countertops supported complex instruments that stood silent sentry; waiting. Waiting for their masters to set them new tasks, new experiments to assess. The air smelled of disinfectant, reminding me sharply of the hospital where we'd spent too much time this last year.

Last year. Her *last* year.

I pushed the thought away. I didn't want to remember her struggling to breathe, eyes filled with pain. I wanted to see her here, working on a theory, her lovely brow furrowed with thought, tapping a pencil against her chin. Remember the joy and excitement in her expression when an experiment had borne out a supposition.

Straightening the notebooks where she'd inscribed her last thoughts on various theories, my fingers lingered over a page of her neat, square handwriting, gloried in the slight indentations left by the pressure her hand had exerted on the pen. Her living fingers had touched that paper. Those words and equations were the final manifestation of the ephemeral, unexplainable phenomena of conscious thought. *Her* conscious thought.

We'd been so lucky. Mother and daughter, scientists, working side by side at the National Laboratory for Temporal and Spatial Research. Her team had specialized in time; mine in the interconnectedness of objects in space.

Now time moved forward without her, and I'd lost my ability, or desire, to connect to the people and objects surrounding me.

2055 had been a hellish year. It had seen my beautiful, brilliant daughter waste away until the wreck of her body could no longer sustain life. And yet...and yet her spirit had remained strong. Her consciousness had still sparkled within its pain-wracked physical shell.

2055 had known her. 2056 never would.

I couldn't face a year without Sophia.

With effort, I pulled my thoughts from their downward spiral and forced myself to concentrate on her journal. To look past the agonizingly familiar handwriting and find meaning in the words she had written.

As understanding penetrated the fog of my grief, I gasped. Weak-kneed with surprise, I stumbled to a chair, clutching the journal to my breast. A few steadying breaths later I was ready to reread the passage.

A slow smile spread across my face, the first in too many months. If I was following the line of her thoughts, and I was sure I was, she'd done it. She'd found her way through the maze of quantum mechanics and various theories of physics into the continuity of the time stream.

My brilliant daughter had solved the riddle of time travel.

And I, her proud mother, would be the first to test the validity of her theorem.

2

I told no one of my discovery. Sophia would receive her credit, but not until I had tested the device. No one would tell me I couldn't turn back time and revel in my precious child's life. No one would tell me I was too emotionally invested, too close to the subject to make reasonable and rational decisions.

2026 held no promise for me, but the past.... My Sophia waited in the past.

Death had stolen our future. The powers-that-be would not steal my ability to visit her in our shared past.

I followed her instructions to the letter. Carefully analyzing and re-analyzing each segment of every equation. This was her area of expertize, not mine. I refused to second guess her. Sophia understood the nuances of the theories she had coaxed and massaged into new and, to me, unbelievable patterns far better than I did.

When my preparations were complete, I stared at the device Sophia's notes had led me to create. It shimmered and gleamed, there and yet not there. The chrome countertop seemed somehow dull, a muddy backdrop for the glimmer of the creation, reminding me of the flash of silvery scales as a barely seen fish darts through dark waters.

I'd built it, coaxed it into being, been involved in every step of its creation, yet now I was loathe to touch it.

What if it didn't work?

What if it destroyed my mind rather than sending me into the time stream?

I straightened my shoulders and reached for the uncanny thing.

What if it did? Sophia was dead. I had no desire to move into a future that didn't include her. I grasped the glimmering headpiece, forced my hand to hold it as it sought to slither through my fingers like the slippery, silvery fish I'd imagined, and placed it upon my brow.

The laboratory melted around me. I could still see the countertops and their instruments, could still make out the boundaries of the room, the walls and floor and ceiling, but they were misty and insubstantial. If I tried, I could see beyond them, through them, past other rooms in the building, past the building itself.

I gasped, cried out, but no sound escaped my lips. No air moved through my lungs. I glanced down and saw that my body had become as insubstantial as the lab. I could still see the outline of my limbs and torso, but I could also see through and beyond myself.

I closed my eyes, if I still had eyes to close, and thought of Sophia. Remembered Christmas of her ninth year. Her delight when she opened her gift from Santa and discovered the chemistry set she'd been dreaming of for the last six months.

My world tilted and the stomach I wasn't sure was still there roiled. I opened my eyes and was inside the memory. I was there.

3

The room smelled of pine and cinnamon and candle wax. The Christmas tree, a real scotch pine that year, stood in pride of place before a picture window revealing a snow-covered suburban neighborhood. Treasured family ornaments hung from the tree's branches, a snowman made from cut crystal, the sleek, stylized reindeer in red and white, a Santa face carved from deer horn — an heirloom from my mother's childhood. And on the floor at its base, garbed in red and white striped pajamas like the sweetest candy cane imaginable, sat my Sophia ripping gold foil gift wrap from a package.

If I'd had knees, they would've buckled. This wasn't a memory. This was real. I was in the room watching my precious girl unwrap the gift that would set her on the course that would lead me back to this very moment.

Another me walked into the room carrying a steaming cup of cocoa. A much younger, much happier me. The me who belonged in this time still had dark hair unstreaked by gray. She was slender and clear-eyed and smiling at Sophia's joy. She moved gracefully across the room, settled on the wide arm of an overstuffed leather sofa, and handing him the cup of cocoa, kissed an unshaven man on the top of his wavy-haired head.

Did I still have a heart? Was it still beating in my chest some-where else? Perhaps in the laboratory? Wherever it was, it had just received a jolt as if from a defibrillator.

Jared.

I'd forgotten Jared would be here at Sophia's ninth Christmas.

Jared. The other half of the equation that had created my bril-liant, beautiful daughter. Her father. The man I had loved more than life itself.

4

I didn't want to see Jared. I had come for Sophia. But the sight of my lost love sent me spiraling forward to a time I didn't want to relive.

I settled into a hospital room not unlike the ones I'd inhabited frequently with Sophia. This one held the pall of death, a unique combination of atmosphere and scent and emotion that can't be adequately described, but can never be forgotten once it's been experienced. I wanted to turn away, to escape, to fly to another time and place, but the scene held me mesmerized.

Jared lay unmoving upon the bed. His head was bandaged and what little flesh was visible bloomed purple and fuchsia with tinges of green. Tubes ran from his arms to hanging bags of IV fluid and monitors beeped quietly in the background. The room smelled of blood and urine and disinfectant.

Two years had passed since the happy Christmas scene. The me of this moment sat hunched in a chair beside Jared, clinging to his limp fingers with one hand while hugging Sophia close with the other.

Sophia.

Pride welled in my nonexistent chest at the sight of my gangly eleven-year-old daughter. Though her cheeks were bloodless and tear-stained, she gazed unflinchingly at her dead father, all the while stroking her bewildered mother's dark hair.

"Don't worry, Mom," she said softly. "We'll be all right. We're strong. Daddy knows we're strong. He knows we can handle this."

The me in the chair raised her head and gazed at our daughter with tear-soaked eyes. "You're right," I/she said, my/her voice thick and choked. "We'll get through this. We can do anything we set our minds to." Then I/she buried my/her head in my/her arms and wailed.

Sophia turned her wan face to the corner where I stood, an unwitting sentinel. She nodded at me, though she couldn't see me — could she? — and repeated her mother's words, "We can do anything we set our minds to."

5

Sophia's somber gaze sent me spiraling forward. Flashes of light and color, images as clear as newly minted pictures swirled past me as I was pulled inexorably forward. Sophia dressed for her first dance; garbed in cap and gown for graduation; with her doctoral stole around her neck; the laboratory, her eye to a microscope; her last Christmas, her frail body wrapped in layers of soft, woolen blankets; the hospital room where she died, not an accident like Jared, but a simple cessation of breath, a relief of anguished pain.

I cried out as I sped past her death, but I didn't stop. The object on my brow drove me forward into the unknown. Into the years where Sophia didn't exist.

And yet, when I stopped at last, there she was.

Sophia held out her hands to me and I took them gladly. She was tall and lithe, her body whole and beautiful once more. Her eyes sparkled with joy and anticipation.

"You built it!" she cried. "Oh, mother, how wonderful. You built it and it works."

I smiled back at her. I couldn't help it, her joy was infectious. Besides, the sight of my living daughter had healed all the wounds of that terrible year. Of course I smiled!

"Yes," I said, "it works. I went back in time and then I came here." I stopped and looked around. We stood in a cozy room much like the living room of the home she'd grown up in. The home Jared and I had built. The one I'd been forced to sell in order to survive that first horrendous year after his death. Light brown leather furniture, dark forest green carpet, an accent wall painted a pale gray-green and a wide picture window looking out over ... an ocean vista.

I frowned. That house had been in Denver, Colorado. Nowhere near an ocean.

"Where are we, Sophia?" I asked. "And how are we together? Am I ... am I dead?"

She laughed, a sound like soft wind chimes, and hugged me tight. "No, Momma. You're not dead, though Dad and I are."

As though her words had conjured him, Jared stepped into the room. I'd forgotten how tall and broad-shouldered my love was. His dark eyes sparkled with mischief as he stepped forward to join our hug.

"You always were amazing, Maggie," he said, and I relished the sound of his baritone voice, "but you've outdone yourself this time." He stepped back and indicated Sophia. "Look what a magnificent job you did raising this beautiful woman. And then to top it off, you built her incredible device."

He beamed, and held his arms out wide. "Two such extraordinary women, and I've been loved by both."

Somewhere, somewhen, my heart jolted, as though an electric shock had run through it.

Before I could ask another question, the scene faded and reality swirled around me. But I heard Sophia's voice call after me, "Remember, Momma...you can do anything you set your mind to!"

6

My fingers tingled and my toes curled. A cool breeze played across my chest, and something hard pressed against my mouth and nose.

Distant voices called my name. "Dr. Janssen. Dr. Janssen, can you hear me?" Fingers tapped my cheek.

I opened my eyes. At least, I tried. My lids seemed to be glued together. Frowning, I concentrated and succeeded in blinking.

Blinding light met my disoriented gaze. The empty lab was now full of people. My white-coated colleagues fluttered around the edges of my vision, while two young men in dark blue uniforms hovered front and center.

Slowly the scene resolved and my brain made sense of the images.

Paramedics.

My shirt was open, my chest bare to the gaze of any who cared to look. A defibrillator lay nearby. The electric jolt had been real. I'd been pulled from wherever Jared and Sophia were by paramedics attempting to restart my heart.

Tears flooded my eyes and my emotions raced.

Grief — I was separated again from the two I loved best in the world.

Joy — wherever they were, they were together and happy.

Determined — I refused to wallow in self-pity. I would make Sophia proud. I would live up to Jared's stellar opinion of me.

2056 no longer held despair for me. As long as I lived, Sophia and Jared lived as well. I had work to do. Sophia deserved recognition for her amazing breakthrough, and I ... well, I wanted to perfect her device. I wanted to revisit the glorious life I had shared with my loved ones, as well as glimpse the joyous reunion that waited in my future.

PART V

SPINNING

DEBBIE MUMFORD

BESTSELLING AUTHOR OF *SORCHA'S HEART*

SPINNING

SPUN YARNS
A Short Story

1

Brett D'Agostino leaned against the roulette table, hands clasped, eyes haunted, as he watched his life careen around a wheel of blurred red and black in the form of a little white ball. How had this happened? How could his entire existence be riding on a wheel of fortune?

He'd always been a solid citizen. The man who rose every morning with the dawn, dressed in a white shirt, dark pants, well-shined shoes, knotted on a conservative tie and, after a sensible breakfast of oatmeal and orange juice, made the commute to his office.

Numbers were his expertise. Accounting his profession. He knew the odds, probably better than anyone at the table other than the croupier, but that hadn't stopped him from placing his chips and calling his bet, "Seventeen to the maximum, with approved override."

Now all he could do was wait. With his heart in his throat, sweat beading his brow, his hands clasped to keep them from shaking. He'd signed his home over to the bank, scraped together every penny he could and then told management he wanted to place one make-or-break wager. Two hundred thousand dollars rode that wheel. When the ball dropped, he'd either be able to book passage to Arcturus Prime, or he'd be penniless, his family homeless.

How could he have been so stupid as to bet his family's future on a spinning ball?

How could he allow his son to die?

He'd cast his lot with the Fates. He would live or die on the vagary of chance ... and so would Jeremy.

2

_____

Life had been good. Predictable, but good. He loved his wife, adored their three children. He had a profession that, though often ridiculed in the media as the ultimate in boredom, both satisfied him and provided a genuine service to his clients. His life had orbited twin suns of home and work; he'd been content.

Now one sun had collapsed into a black hole and was consuming everything else in his universe.

Life had changed a little over a week ago when his fifteen-year-old son had taken Brett's motorcycle for a spin — without license or permission. Not only had Jeremy caused an accident that had earned him a police citation and would send the family's insurance to the moon, but the boy had also been critically injured. If Brett didn't act quickly, the injury would prove fatal.

Hope existed, but it existed in space. Jeremy needed to be transported to the medical colony on Arcturus Prime. Medical science had discovered that injuries such as his responded well to the gravitational spin and ion-rich atmosphere of the newly colonized planet.

But insurance didn't cover intergalactic travel, even if such travel was deemed life-saving by the best medical minds on earth.

Brett needed well over a million dollars, and he needed it now.

3

"Brett! You can't be serious." Despite lack of sleep and a face bloated by tears, Elyn's eyes had flashed. Normally she was a neat and attractive woman, well dressed, with a happy disposition, the wrinkles on her forty-something face from sun and laughter. However, this had been anything but a normal day. Her dark hair had lost its luster; her usually creamy complexion appeared muddy. She radiated misery. "I know you want to save Jeremy. So do I. But not this way, not by sacrificing Jenny and Mike's security and future."

"We'll figure it out," Brett had stormed, taking his wife by the shoulders and gazing into her tear-soaked eyes. "Jenny and Mike have time. We have time. Jeremy doesn't." He released her and paced the impossibly clean floor of the hospital waiting room. "If we lose everything, we'll start over. Your parents will take you and the kids in, see that you're safe, and I'll find a way to rebuild, but Jeremy ..."

He choked. Stopped at the window and, placing his hands on the sill, leaned forward until his forehead rested against the glass. The coolness of the pane soothed the ache behind his eyes. Momentarily. The vision of Jeremy's twisted body swam to the surface, and Brett whipped away from the window and stalked back to Elyn. "Don't you see? This is Jeremy's only hope. If I win, we'll be able to get him to Arcturus Prime and pay for his treatment. If we do nothing, he'll die."

"He'll still die if you lose," she said, but her voice was gentle, little more than a whisper, "and we'll have lost our home." She went to him, leaned into him, face pressed to his chest, arms encircling his waist. "You can't fix everything, Brett. Sometimes you lose."

He hugged her tightly, as if she were the only thing anchoring him to this swiftly spinning planet, laid his cheek against her hair. "I know. I also know the odds are stacked against me ... against Jeremy." He kissed the top of her head before pushing her back so he could look into her eyes. "But I have to try. I understand what I'm risking, what I'll be forcing you and Jenny and Mike to risk, but I have to try. No bank is going to make that kind of loan. We don't have anything to secure it with. Our friends don't have this kind of money. There is no other way. Not in time.

"Either I play with our lives, or Jeremy loses his."

Elyn closed her eyes and moved back into his arms. "I'm not a gambler and neither are you, but I won't fight you on this, and I won't make you choose between Jeremy and the rest of us." She squeezed him with more force than he would have thought possible for his petite wife. "Do what you have to do. We'll live with the consequences."

4

The next few days had been a whirlwind of paper. He'd negotiated with the bank. They agreed to take the house back and give him his equity since he didn't have time to sell. He was grateful. They could have taken the house and given him nothing, but the banker was sympathetic and the house was a good risk.

Liquefying his assets had been gut-wrenching. Everything had taken too long. The minutes and hours he spent dealing with paperwork were minutes and hours Jeremy didn't have. Still, the process was necessary, the time unavoidable. At last he'd gathered his resources, had wired the money to Las Vegas, and booked airfare.

He strode through the hospital, his purpose the only armor against the agony that clawed at his gut. Arriving at his son's room, he stood in the hall for a moment, observing his family, the sum of his universe. Elyn stood at the head of Jeremy's bed, gently stroking the little shock of hair that hadn't been shaved away to tend to his injuries. Twelve-year-old Jenny stood near his feet, her hand resting on the one bit of his foot that wasn't scraped raw. Mike huddled in a chair in the corner. His big brother's bedside obviously terrified the eight-year-old.

Brett straightened, entered the room and went straight to Mike.

Picking the boy up as though he were still a toddler, he hugged him tightly. "How are you doing, buddy?"

Mike wrapped his legs around his dad and buried his face in Brett's neck. "Okay, I guess," he whispered.

Still carrying the child, Brett moved to the bed, paused to smooth Jenny's hair, and then bent to kiss his wife. Setting Mike on his feet, Brett dug some change out of his pocket. "Why don't you take Jenny down the hall and get her a candy bar."

Mike glanced at the money his father handed him.

Brett smiled and ruffled his hair. "I think there's enough there for both of you." He winked at Jenny, and she gave him a sad little smile and allowed her little brother to pull her from the room.

Slipping an arm around Elyn's waist, he turned his gaze on his eldest child. It hurt, God, how it hurt to see him so still, this son who had been in constant motion since birth. Jeremy was never still, even if it was only a toe, some bit of him was always moving. Should be moving now.

Instead he lay still as death. The few pieces of him not covered in bandages were scraped red and raw. But that wasn't the worst. He'd suffered massive internal injuries as well. Tubes ran helter-skelter across his body, crisscrossing with lines and feeds from the machines that monitored and directed other machines that held Jeremy to this life.

Brett longed for him to wake, to see the light in his eyes, to hear him speak. On the other hand, he was grateful the boy was unconscious, as the pain would be intense if he woke. No. Not if. When. When he woke. Once they got him to Arcturus Prime, he would heal. He would wake. Their son would live a long, full life. Brett refused to believe otherwise.

He kissed the top of Elyn's head before resting his chin there. "How is he? Has there been any change."

She shook her head, reached for his hand. "No. Everything is the same as the last time you were here. How are you?"

He turned and pulled her into a full embrace. "Everything is set. When I leave here, I'll go straight to the airport. Wish me luck."

Warm tears soaked through his shirt. "You know I do. Always." She sniffled, pulled away to wipe her eyes on an already sodden handkerchief, and gave him a wavery smile. "I'll keep everything together here. Mom and Dad will be by in an hour or so to take Jenny and Mike home with them. Dr. Ames has arranged for me to use family lodging down the hall. I'll stay close to Jeremy."

Brett nodded. "We'll survive this. We'll *all* survive this."

5

The flight to Las Vegas was interminable. Brett tried to rest, but his mind wouldn't shut down. He'd left his family homeless, dependent on Elyn's parents. Gus and Patrice were heart-broken about Jeremy, but thought what Brett was doing was beyond reckless. Gus had told him so in short, crisp sentences. But they were good people. More, they were family. Having expressed their disapproval of his course of action, they had stepped up and done what they could to help. Gus had even offered to have movers pack the house, but Brett had asked him to wait. The bank had agreed to give Brett and Elyn first right of refusal on their home. It wasn't scheduled to go on the market until well after the Vegas trip.

If all went well, movers wouldn't be necessary.

If all went well. God! He was gambling so much on a game he didn't even understand.

He'd done his homework, had chosen roulette because of the mathematical formulas governing the odds and pay-outs, but good as he was with money and spreadsheets, he was still a novice and his lack of experience terrified him. He wasn't a gambler, wasn't the type to seek thrills. Yes, he loved a challenge, loved problem solving, understood probabilities, but he had always sought security. Risk wasn't part of his nature.

But fate had pushed him to his limit, and he had discovered that some risks were worth the gamble. Jeremy's life was priceless.

At last the plane landed and the slug-slow process of debarkation began. You'd think that with the advent of interstellar travel someone would have figured out how to get people on and off planes more efficiently, but no. A queue of people was still a queue of people.

With no baggage to claim — he wasn't here on a vacation, he headed straight for the curb, hailed and cab and soon found himself at Las Vegas' most prestigious casino, The Galaxy.

He paid the cabbie, shouldered his duffle, and then turned to face the adversary he prayed would become his savior. The building glittered in the late afternoon sun. Lights danced across the entrance in bewitching displays. Glass sparkled, chrome shone, carpets invited him to leave the hot, hard pavement and step onto their cushioned surfaces. Inside voices called, laughter billowed, and more lights glowed from machines designed to excite and entice.

Heart hammering with the sheer gall of what he was about to do, Brett took a firm grasp of his duffle and stepped inside. He had gone only a few paces when a young woman in black slacks, black vest, and white shirt approached him. Her long black hair was slicked back from her face in a high tail and she wore a barely visible earpiece for communication.

"Welcome to The Galaxy. May I be of service?"

Brett steeled himself, met her gaze levelly. "Actually, yes. I'm here to make a high-stakes wager. I believe your manager is expecting me."

She sized him up, noting his typical accountant suit and white-knuckled grip on his duffle. "May I ask your name?"

"Brett D'Agostino."

She stood in silence for a moment before nodding and smiling at Brett. "Of course. Mr. Nguyen will see you now. If you'd follow me, please?"

They rode a private lift to a floor accessible only by palm print. She ushered him down a narrow hallway, one wall of which was glass, revealing their position as a balcony above the casino floor. At the end of the hall an intricately carved, highly polished wood door opened in a slow arc. His guide gestured him inside.

He stepped across the threshold onto glass. Vertigo assailed him and he was forced to close his eyes and concentrate on breathing for a moment.

A soft laugh sounded across the room. "My apologies, Mr. D'Agostino. I sometimes forget how disorienting the view can be. Please, open your eyes. I've darkened the glass."

Brett opened his eyes only to glance involuntarily at his feet. A heartfelt sigh escaped as he saw that the floor was indeed opaque. He glanced up to find a slender young man of Asian descent studying him from behind a massive walnut desk. The wall to his right was a continuation of the hallway's glass, the one to his left a panorama of liquid light. Behind the desk, Brett recognized the surface of an over-large computer touch screen, most likely with holo capabilities.

"Thank you for seeing me, Mr. Nguyen. My apologies for the shaky start."

The man smiled, though the expression didn't quite reach his eyes, which while dark and tilted at an exotic angle maintained an aloof wariness.

"Not at all, as I said, that was an error on my part. Please, sit. Tell me how The Galaxy can be of service."

Brett crossed the room with determined strides. He wouldn't be caught off-guard again by the disappearing floor trick. Somehow he doubted its transparency had been an oversight. He dropped his duffle beside the indicated chair and folded into it.

"As I mentioned in our correspondence, I wish to make a single high-stakes wager on roulette."

"How high are you considering?"

"Two hundred thousand."

"And your wager?"

"Single number, maximum."

"That's well above our usual house limit."

"I understand."

"Tell me why I should allow this."

"I have an urgent need for cash."

"You have two hundred thousand."

"I need well over a million."

"If I allow it, and if you win, you'll have it." Nguyen steepled his fingers and tapped his chin. "Forgive me, Mr. D'Agostino, but you don't strike me as a gambler."

"I'm not."

"Then surely you would prefer to raise this money another way. Go home. Go to your bank. Whatever your need, there are steadier ways to gain capital."

Brett leaned forward, pressed an unsteady hand to his forehead. "I don't have time." He stood, paced, the floor's opacity or lack thereof forgotten. "I'm an accountant. I understand the odds. Believe me, I know they're not in my favor, but my son is in critical condition. If I don't get him to Arcturus Prime, he'll die. This wager is his only hope."

Nguyen stood, walked around his desk, placed a hand on Brett's shoulder. "And if I allow this, if you wager and lose ..."

Brett shuddered, but meet Nguyen's gaze. "Then I'll go home destitute. I'll sit by my boy's side while he dies, but at least I'll know I tried."

Nguyen studied Brett's face a moment longer, and then held out his hand. "I wish you the best, Mr. D'Agostino. I have sons of my own. I'll make the arrangements."

6

Brett leaned against the roulette table, hardly aware of the press of people watching in fascination as the Fates made their life and death decision on the clatter of a little white ball bouncing from slot to slot in a roulette wheel. He held his breath. Surely it would land soon. It couldn't continue to bounce forever.

The revolutions slowed, the ball appeared to land ... on 32.

Brett's head dropped, grief shredded his heart as the crowd exhaled a low moan.

And then, the impossible happened. He heard a click as the ball jumped again. Squeezing his eyes tight shut, he prayed. One space. That was all Jeremy needed, just one little space.

Silence reigned as the wheel spun to a stop. The croupier called, "A winner! Seventeen black!"

The crowd roared with delight, and Brett felt hands thumping his back, his shoulders. Slowly, he raised his head, opened his eyes, and met the croupier's gaze. The man nodded to the wheel. Brett angled his head to see a small white ball lodged firmly in Jeremy's slot.

He bit his lip, fought back tears, as relief flooded his heart. He barely heard the croupier's comment, "The pay-out is with your bet, sir. If you wish to let it ride, I'll need to ask for approval."

"What? No. Hell no! Cash me out. I never want to see another roulette wheel!"

Those who still stood nearby laughed, but Brett didn't care. All he wanted was to gather his winnings, find a quiet corner to call Elyn, and make arrangements to take his family to Arcturus Prime where the gravitational spin was just what the doctor ordered.

PART VI

STARGAZER

DEBBIE MUMFORD

BESTSELLING AUTHOR OF SORCHA'S HEART

Stargazer

1

When I was a child, I dreamed of space. Of marvelous ships that would take me to the moon...and far beyond.

When I was a girl, rockets were being launched on a regular basis as the super powers raced to leave the confines of our familiar planet. Unmanned flights broke through the atmosphere, followed by experimental shots with dogs and chimpanzees as unwilling astronauts.

How we cheered when those creatures returned to us unharmed.

Finally, Yuri Gagarin orbited the earth.

But though we had escaped the atmosphere, we had not yet conquered gravity's pull. And then, in the summer of my fifteenth year, Neil Armstrong took "a giant step for mankind" and set foot upon the moon.

I still dream of space, and though I am no longer young enough to take that journey to the stars myself, I have faith that my descendants will.

Actually, I am blessed with absolute certainty, for I have seen the future ... and it is glorious.

"Glorious?" you ask. I can hear the skepticism dripping from each syllable.

Yes. Glorious.

It's hard to imagine right now when our race is suffering through the mess and pain of a difficult delivery, when the next phase of humanity struggles to emerge from the womb, to take its first breath of air into as yet untried lungs and scream its birth-cry to the stars.

But as women through the ages can tell you, no matter the pain, blood, sweat-drenched physical exhaustion, the child is always worth the effort.

So too will humanity's next iteration be worth the effort when our current travail has passed.

I am part of that next iteration, humanity's next step. I am a stargazer, and though I am doomed to live and die on the surface of only one planet, I have seen my race's diaspora to the stars. I am content.

I have always understood my connection to Mother Earth, have felt the fluctuating pressures of her tectonic plates, understood the moody shifts of her ocean swells, reveled in the rhythmic flow of her molten core. She is my mother, and her steady heartbeat soothes and comforts me.

But my connection to the moon was a revelation.

The moment Neil Armstrong's booted foot touched the airless surface of our nearest neighbor, my senses awoke. They have been expanding outward for nearly fifty years. Some days it's very difficult to tether myself to this frail human body, but my time has not yet come.

My task is not to set plans and programs in motion. Mine is to ensure that the suns, moons, asteroids and planets that we pass will recognize us. That each will give its blessing and speed us on our way.

For each star that I gaze, each bit of the universe that my

consciousness touches, retains a memory of mankind. I spread wonder and joy and the awe of exploration so that when my physical descendants arrive they will be welcomed and acknowledged.

My task is to dream; to imprint the universe. Others will design and engineer and build the means to achieve what I dream.

I am a stargazer, the first of my kind. And when the next of my kin arrives, I will pass on my knowledge, and then ... and then I will untether my soul and fly free among the stars I have dreamed.

PART VII

THE WARBIRDS OF ABSAROKA

THE WARBIRDS OF ABSAROKA

UNIVERSAL STAR LEAGUE
—— FILE ONE ——

DEBBIE MUMFORD

PROLOGUE

John Standing Bear lay upon his deathbed. Though his eyes were closed, he was aware of the fading sunlight streaming through his bedroom window, felt the cool breeze freshen the stale air in a room kept overly warm to comfort a dying man. His lips twitched in a half smile. He had sat death-watch for many a brave warrior. Now his turn had come to be watched.

His body felt oddly light. Perhaps he no longer perceived it properly, perhaps his spirit had already begun to detach itself from his flesh. And yet, an anchor remained. His granddaughter sat beside him, a quiet presence. She remained silent, but gently stroked his right hand, letting him know she was there.

"Granddaughter," he whispered. The word held little substance, like a breath of wind barely stirring the aspen leaves in the high mountain valley of his birth, so long ago on Earth. He had grown to manhood in that valley, had loved it fiercely. But he had chosen to leave Earth behind, had been instrumental in founding the colony on this planet, on his beloved Absaroka.

Brenna squeezed his fingers, bringing him back to the task at hand: dying.

"I am here, Grandfather."

He marshaled his strength for a final act of will. He must pass on his warning, must know that Brenna understood. His people had forgotten the horrors of war with an alien species. He had not. To them, the bug-eyed monsters were merely a cautionary tale written of in history books, but to John, the memories were real. He had served on the *USL Ascension*, had experienced the heart-stopping fear as the ship battled for its life and the lives of humanity. The Bug-Eyes had withdrawn all those years ago, but he knew with a certainty he could never explain that they would return. And when they did, Absaroka must be prepared to defend herself. Brenna must understand.

"Do not," he wheezed, each word an effort, "allow them ... to remain ... complacent." It was difficult to control his breathing, hard to draw enough breath to push out a word. Light sparkled beyond his closed eyes. So beautiful. So free. All he needed was to let go.

Not yet. Not until she acknowledged his words. He must pass the baton to his grandchild. She must keep knowledge of the enemy alive.

"The Bug-Eyes..." More words refused to come. His breath failed; his strength had ebbed.

Brenna stroked his hand again. He focused his remaining attention on her words. "Be at ease, Grandfather," she said, her voice calm and reassuring. "I am on guard, and you have taught me well. I will build a fleet to defend Absaroka."

John tried to nod, but the effort was too much. His work was done. The fate of Absaroka rested in Brenna's hands now. A dry exhalation escaped his lips and he released his spirit to join his ancestors..

1

Brenna Standing Bear waited for her turn to address the Planetary Council. Though her face wore a mask of calm, her stomach roiled, making her wish she had not eaten even her usual light breakfast of tea and buttered toast with honey. Her palms were moist and she longed to rub them dry on her slim black skirt, but she refused to betray her emotions with such a noticeable act. She closed her eyes, exhaled slowly and willed herself to be calm. Feeling more in control, she opened her eyes and surveyed the chamber.

The Longhouse was crowded, the Confederated Nations of Absaroka were well represented. Brenna nodded, pleased. She wanted as many of her people as possible to hear her words, to understand her grandfather's warning.

Unlike the traditional Earth buildings for which it had been named, Absaroka's Longhouse was a gleaming multistory building of glass and plasteel. The seat of government for the Confederated Nations, the edifice held offices for the leaders of each of the one hundred and forty-seven tribes that had chosen to band together to establish this new world more than eighty years before. The central chamber where the Planetary Council now met was designed to hold several thousand onlookers. Rows of tiered seats rose in semi-circular waves around a large central platform where the representatives of each founding nation sat to discuss matters of global significance. The Longhouse also housed several smaller council chambers, miniature versions of the central chamber, for use by smaller groups to consider tribal or regional concerns.

Though Brenna sat on the central platform, she had no official place on the Planetary Council. She was a guest, tolerated because of her grandfather's reputation and influence. She had petitioned to speak before the council, and because John Standing Bear's memory was to be honored at today's meeting, his granddaughter would be indulged.

Councilman Jason Wolfclaw opened the meeting. "The Confederated Nations of Absaroka meet today to honor a great man. John Standing Bear was instrumental in choosing this planet, founding the original colony, and helping Absaroka gain admittance to the Universal Star League. Because of his service, Absaroka is defended by USL ships. Because of his sacrifice, Universal Star League acknowledges the courage and fortitude of Absaroka's warriors and welcomes them into the USL Academy. John Standing Bear's wise counsel will be sorely missed."

Councilwoman Amanda Silverfox rose as Councilman Wolfclaw resumed his seat.

Brenna's stomach jumped and flipped like a fish pulled from clear water. The councilwoman would introduce her. She prayed that the Great Spirit would direct her words, that He would open the ears of the council to heed her grandfather's warning. She sought strength and calm as the councilwoman's words washed over her.

"...John Standing Bear's only surviving descendent. Please give your attention to Sister Brenna Standing Bear."

Her moment had come. Brenna rose to face the council, smoothing her skirt and discreetly tugging her black, military-style jacket into place.

"Thank you, Elder Silverfox." She inclined her head in acknowledgement of the councilwoman. Her eyes swept over the members of the Planetary Council, then she turned to the audience, her people, the ones her grandfather had always sought to protect.

"My grandfather was a great man." Murmurs of assent whispered through the chamber. "He worked tirelessly to protect Absaroka. To protect you." Heads nodded all around her. "Even as he lay dying, his thoughts were of his people. Though he was one hundred and fifteen years old, an age at which most men would have laid down their burdens, Grandfather was still concerned with the safety and viability of this planet. With *your* continued safety."

A quiet mutter of discontent reached her from the council members behind her. She turned to face them, the decision makers. The men and women who held the fate of Absaroka in their hands.

"Grandfather believed passionately in the need to establish a fleet of ships to defend Absaroka, and I agree. We cannot rely utterly on the USL for our defense. We must establish a planetary militia and arm it with a fleet of space worthy vessels. We must be prepared to defend Absaroka."

Quiet murmuring grew to a din a raised voices. Her people voiced their opinions, both for and against her assertions. Brenna stood quietly, aware that her voice would not carry above the swelling roar. She assessed the mood. Many supported her, but as she had expected, just as many disagreed.

When the crescendo of voices reached its peak, Brenna became aware of a gavel pounding on plasteel. She turned again to the council and saw Principal Chief Winona Old Coyote standing and applying the gavel vigorously. Gradually, the chamber quieted.

Principal Chief Old Coyote eyed Brenna thoughtfully. A diminutive, silver-haired woman, Winona Old Coyote exuded authority. She listened attentively and spoke infrequently, but when she did, her words carried weight. The Principal Chief had been a good friend to John Standing Bear for many years. A contemporary of his son, Brenna's father, Winona had grieved with the family when Brenna's parents had died in one of Absaroka's infrequent cyclonic weather disturbances.

But she had never supported John's unshakable belief that humanity's alien enemy, the Bug-Eyes, would return.

"Sister Standing Bear," Principal Chief Old Coyote said, "will you relinquish the floor?"

Brenna nodded. "I will." She resumed her seat, outwardly calm, but fighting a rising panic. Now she would need every bit of skill she could muster to win the council's approval. This wasn't a new petition. They had heard her grandfather's arguments before. But this time Brenna intended to bring ancient memories to the surface. To remind her people of things her grandfather had been unwilling to voice.

"Thank you, Sister." Winona Old Coyote gazed around the central chamber. "Our sister raises an old argument. John Standing Bear often harangued this council to build a planetary fleet." Nods of agreement and more than a few smiles met her statement.

"The Planetary Council is well aware of Sister Standing Bear's family phobia regarding the Bug-Eyes." She turned to Brenna, her expression sorrowful. "We appreciate your grandfather's military service and sympathize with the horrors he experienced aboard the *Ascension* during the Bug-Eye invasion." She paused, granting time for attention to focus on her words.

"But we are also aware," the principal chief continued, "that there has been no further sign of the Bug-Eyes in the ensuing sixty-eight years. This council has not seen fit to expend the resources or manpower necessary to build and man a fleet against a threat that does not exist ... except in the mind of one elderly warrior, who has now joined his ancestors, and the grandchild he indoctrinated quite thoroughly."

A silence so profound it pressed against Brenna's soul descended on the chamber. She inhaled deeply, marshaled her strength, and stood.

"With your permission, Elder?"

Principal Chief Old Coyote nodded and folded into her seat.

"I believe, as did my grandfather, that the Bug-Eyes will return." She paused while a susurrus of whispers flowed around the room. "I also believe," she continued and the chamber quieted, "that we are foolish to place all our trust in the USL."

Councilman Wolfclaw shot to his feet. "What basis do you have for impugning the USL? Why, your own grandfather served with their fleet. He knew them to be an honorable and trustworthy service. He fought for our inclusion in the Universal Star League, and that membership guarantees that the USL will protect this planet from all enemies."

Brenna's heart raced and she raised sweat-damp palms as if to ward off his words.

"Forgive me, Elder," she said. "I did not mean to imply that the USL was untrustworthy..."

"But you said..."

Winona Old Coyote's gavel sounded, bringing them both to silence. "Sister Standing Bear has the floor, Councilman. Please allow her to finish."

Councilman Wolfclaw scowled, but sat down.

"Thank you, Principal Chief." Clasping her hands to control their shaking, Brenna continued. "I agree that the USL is an honorable service and I am not saying that they would intentionally fail us. However," she turned slightly to include the audience, "can you not imagine a scenario where the USL was so besieged by pleas for help that they could not answer all? Though their flex-drive can bring ships to our aid almost instantly, what would happen if multiple worlds were attacked simultaneously? Would they not be forced to triage?"

Brenna paused while council and listeners alike absorbed her words.

"Absaroka is a small planet. Our population is negligible compared to many of the Universal Star League worlds. If faced with more requests than they could handle, would not the USL fleet go where the greatest numbers were at risk?"

The central chamber was so quiet Brenna could hear her own pulse pounding in her ears. They heard her. She must deliver her final blow before they had time to assemble arguments.

"Also," she said, keeping her voice quiet so that her listeners would need to pay close attention to her words, "there is the matter of history. On Earth, when a purely human enemy invaded our land, our ancestors were unprepared. They failed to acknowledge the threat until it was too late, and so were unable to protect our people. Our nations were nearly exterminated, our cultures almost obliterated."

"Now that we have regained our heritage, now that our nations have chosen to abandon Earth and begin again on Absaroka, let us not repeat the mistakes of our fathers. Let us never again fail to protect our people. Especially not from an alien race that destroyed whole worlds in their last incursion. Absaroka escaped the Bug-Eye's notice sixty-eight years ago. We cannot expect to be so lucky again."

Silence reigned. Brenna completed her argument.

"I believe the Universal Star League is a great system. I believe that the USL will do everything they can to protect Absaroka in the event of invasion. I also believe that Absaroka has a duty to be prepared to defend herself. We have a proud and noble heritage. Let us honor the warriors of our past by producing a new breed of warrior: the Warbirds of Absaroka."

A war cry sounded from the audience; it rang through the chamber. Brenna turned toward the sound only to be met by an escalation of yips and ululations.

Her soul calmed. Her people had heard her. She was content.

2

Brenna stood at the viewport, staring intently into the inky blackness of flexed space. Nothing was to be seen while the commercial transport's flex-drive was engaged, but she didn't want to miss the instant of Earth's appearance against the backdrop of infinite space. Her first glimpse of the world that was the Great Mother of all humanity should be a sacred experience.

When the Planetary Council had first charged her with this mission, she had balked.

"Me? Go to Earth and buy a space ship?" she had asked.

"Who else?" Principal Chief Old Coyote had countered. "This is your idea, sister. Your grandfather's dream. You are the perfect choice."

"But I don't know anything about space ships or military tactics," she'd retorted. "I wouldn't know what to look for!"

"Learn," the Principal Chief had commanded.

The ship hummed around her as it prepared to drop out of flex-drive, and Brenna leaned closer to the viewport's transparent surface. With an infinitesimal shudder, the ship dropped into normal space and Earth materialized before Brenna's dazzled eyes. She soaked up the vision of the blue and green globe, of the white clouds that swirled and shifted, shrouding the land masses and oceans alike.

Earth! She was actually staring at the planet that had given birth to them all.

Giddy laughter swelled in her chest, but she contained it, contenting herself with a broad smile. Grandfather had told her so many stories of Earth. She longed to see its majestic mountains, wade in its clear, clean streams, observe its plains teeming with wildlife! In a matter of hours, she, Brenna Standing Bear, would step onto the magical, mystical planet her grandfather had immortalized.

Breathing deeply, Brenna pulled herself from her awed reverie. She wasn't visiting Earth on a spirit quest, she was here on a mission. She had six months to familiarize herself with military history, strategy, and the technical details of the various classes of military space vessels. Before she returned to Absaroka, she intended to purchase the flagship of the fleet they would build.

The enormity of her task overwhelmed her and she breathed a quiet prayer. "Guide me, Grandfather. Don't let me fail our people."

Two hours later, Brenna stepped out of the shuttle and onto Earth. At least, she stepped onto the surface of the commercial transport's shuttle bay in the spaceport at New Atlantis. Far from open sky and grassy plains teeming with animals, she found herself in a multi-story building thronged with thousands of people of every race and nationality.

She'd never seen so many people ... or so vast a structure. Why, the crowd flowing around her could very well be equal to the entire population of Absaroka. Everywhere she looked her sight was assaulted by color and movement. The crowd ebbed and flowed like a river swelled by torrential rainfall. Men, women, and children clad in clothing styles she'd never dreamed of — flowing garments that trailed the wearers like wisps of clouds, form-fitting unitards that left nothing to the imagination, headdresses so elaborate Brenna wondered how the wearers maintained their balance. Reds, purples, greens, oranges, colors she had no words to describe. The variety was endless and overwhelming.

Mechanized voices repeated instructions while conversations buzzed in every tone and timbre imaginable. Loud and soft. Brash and soothing. Demanding and whining. If a human voice could produce it, Brenna heard it among the throng that surrounded her.

And the odors! Hot oil and spices from food carts whose vendors shouted the delights of their wares, rich floral perfumes, and the earthy musk of human bodies packed too closely together.

Her head ached from sensory overload. She wanted nothing more than to run back onto the shuttle and demand to be returned to the peace of Absaroka.

"I'm not here for pleasure," she reminded herself grimly. "My comfort is unimportant. I have a job to do. My people are counting on me."

Settling her pack more comfortably on her shoulders, Brenna joined the queue waiting to be processed through customs.

3

Brenna leaned back in her chair at the reference library at the USL Academy. The carrel in the back of the military history section had become an office of sorts for her during the last five months. She stood, stretched, and noted with satisfaction that her collection of sim-card note files had grown significantly during her tenure in the library. Few reference sources remained that she hadn't at least skimmed. She was particularly proud of the files she had amassed on military vessels.

She now knew the difference between a battleship, a cruiser, a destroyer, a frigate, and a fighter. She understood which methods of propulsion were used in which circumstances: flex-drive to cover interstellar distances in a matter of hours; conventional thrusters for navigating within a solar system. And the armament necessary for the defense of Absaroka: mag-rail guns, nuclear warheads, gigawatt laser canons fitted to specialized turrets, and the fearsome anti-matter weapons.

Brenna's shopping list was long and she knew it would take years to fill, but she had a plan now, and knew what she hoped to purchase before her return to Absaroka next month.

With a smile of satisfaction, she packed the contents of her cubicle for the last time. Her time of study was at an end. Now was the time for action.

She left the reference library and strode to the main administration building of the USL. The white marble and glass edifice glistened in the afternoon sun. Twenty stories tall, the building's footprint covered more ground than any ten buildings on Absaroka — even the imposing Longhouse. Brenna shook her head. She'd never look at her own world with the same eyes again.

Though she would never admit her feelings to another soul, Brenna was disappointed by Earth. The stories her grandfather had told had led her to believe Earth was a paradise. Its waters purer than anywhere else in the universe, its mountains more glorious, and its plains teeming with wildlife. Reality told an entirely different story. Earth certainly had its merits — gleaming cities, both terrestrial and aquatic, and amazing technological research and development stations — but the land itself, the mystical entity that had always been sacred to her people, had been subsumed by the works of men.

No, Brenna would not long for Earth when she left. She was glad to have had the opportunity to visit, but she was content to live out her life on Absaroka. And she was pleased with the care her people lavished on their new home, and proud that she had convinced its leadership to defend it properly.

With that defense in mind, she strode confidently to the main desk of the administration building.

A young woman with elaborately styled hair and wearing a USL uniform smiled and asked, "May I be of service?"

Brenna straightened her shoulders and assumed her most official expression. "I'm here to buy a battleship. With whom should I speak?"

The young woman's eyes widened and her unnaturally pink lips formed a small 'O' of surprise before she caught herself and regained her pleasant, but neutral expression. "Forgive me," she said, "but that's an unusual request. If you'll be seated, I'll contact my superior." She motioned Brenna to an alcove of sleek-lined chairs and tables before turning to a display embedded in a console behind her.

Brenna moved to the alcove, seated herself and reviewed her notes on what she hoped to purchase for Absaroka. The Planetary Council had given her a strict budget. A set amount for her personal use during her stay on Earth, food, lodging, transportation, incidentals, and an enormous amount for the purchase of a military vessel and the hiring of a crew to transport the craft to Absaroka. At least, the amount had seemed enormous to everyone on Absaroka. Now that she'd lived on Earth for five months, Brenna could only hope the budget would be sufficient for their needs.

After what seemed like an eternity, a dark-skinned man with graying hair and an impeccably fitted USL uniform approached her. She recognized the insignia of an admiral on his jacket and stood at once.

"My name is Admiral Jacobs," he said, offering her his hand. "and I understand you're interested in purchasing a battleship?"

"Yes. Thank you," she said, shaking his proffered hand. "I'm Brenna Standing Bear, a representative of the Confederated Nations of Absaroka. We wish to build a fleet for planetary defense."

Admiral Jacobs motioned to the chairs. "Why don't we sit down and discuss this decision. May I ask why your government wishes to go to the expense of building a fleet? Absaroka is a Universal Star League planet, is it not?"

Brenna steeled herself, bringing the old arguments to mind. "Yes. We are a member of Universal Star League, and we appreciate and honor USL's pledge to defend our world," she paused, glanced at her hands and licked her lips.

"But?" the admiral encouraged.

"Well, you see, sir, my grandfather fought in the Bug-Eye War. He was an engineer assigned to the *USL Ascension*, and he ... well, he always felt that the Bug-Eyes would return. That no matter how prepared the USL is, in the case of a catastrophic, coordinated attack, the fleet wouldn't be able to defend everyone." She paused again and then blurted out, "And we're an insignificant planet, with no strategic value."

She raised her eyes and glared at the admiral. "We need to be able to defend ourselves. We *need* a planetary fleet."

Admiral Jacobs nodded, his expression somber. "Your grandfather was a wise man and your government was well-advised to listen to him."

Brenna's jaw dropped. "You're not insulted?" she asked.

He smiled. "Not at all. I only wish more of our member worlds would follow your example." He stood, motioning Brenna to join him. "Let's go to my office and discuss your specific needs and budget. I'm sure we'll be able to work something out."

After discussing terms, Jacobs requested a pilot and shuttle, and took Brenna to the USL supply spaceport where available ships were docked. She was glad of their talk. In addition to the financial negotiation, the admiral had provided invaluable insight into her plans for the fleet.

"I want a battleship as flagship of the fleet," she'd said. "That's what I'm hoping for today. Then, over the next several years, I want to add three destroyers, five cruisers, and at least six fighters."

He had nodded. "That's a good start. But even for a planet of your modest size, I'd recommend at least five destroyers and ten cruisers, twelve if you can swing it. And as for the fighters, you'll want a minimum of three squads, with five fighters in each."

Her eyes had widened. "That's fifteen fighters," she'd whispered. "Over twice what I was dreaming of."

"I know," he said. "You'll have your work cut out for you back home, but if the need ever arises, you'll be glad of the extra birds."

Reviewing that conversation now, Brenna smiled. Birds. Yes. If ... no, *when* she got them, she'd see that the fighters were named after birds of prey.

"Coming up on the spaceport now, Admiral," the pilot said, breaking into Brenna's thoughts. "Do you want me to dock?"

"No, take us on a fly-by of the new *smart-steel* battleships. We'll dock with the *Sequoia* when we're finished."

Jacobs turned to Brenna. "I know you don't have the budget for one of these new ships, but I want you to see what we'll be able to bring to your defense." He smiled tightly. "Hopefully this will be the only time you'll ever see them."

Brenna marveled at the sleek, deadly looking battleships as Jacobs explained the new technology. "The hull plating is comprised of a technologically advanced substance our engineers have dubbed *vari-steel*. It's a newly created semi-metal, designed to be incredibly dense and difficult to penetrate, but without the weight or thickness of traditional tungsten plating."

After docking with the *Sequoia*, Jacobs gave her a tour of the old-style battleship. While not as sleek and shiny as the vari-steel ships, the *Sequoia* appeared to be in good order. Any scars she might have incurred in battle had been lovingly repaired and burnished over.

"She's not new," Jacobs said, guiding Brenna onto the bridge, "but she's in good running order. All her systems have been overhauled and she's ready for deep space."

Brenna nodded, walking the circumference of the bridge, running fingers over control panels and noting the odor of cleaning solvents mixed with fresh oil. Every surface fairly glistened with cleanliness.

"She's Ascension-class, isn't she?" Brenna asked. When the admiral agreed, she said, "How old?"

"She was commissioned at the end of the Bug-Eye War, so roughly sixty-eight years old."

Brenna made her decision. She slapped her hand on the back of the captain's chair, feeling the give of the supple leather. "We'll take her. Now, what can we do about a crew to transport her to Absaroka? And we'll need competent instructors to train our own crews, and to advise us on future purchases as we grow our fleet."

Admiral Jacobs held out his hand and Brenna shook it firmly. He laid his other hand atop their clasped ones. "You've made a good choice. She'll serve you well. Let's return to headquarters and we'll work out a plan for crew and instructors."

"One more thing," she said as they left the bridge, "will we be able to rename her?"

"Of course. I'll see that you have the necessary forms to take back to your planetary government."

4

Warchief Brenna Standing Bear studied the cloud-enshrouded green and blue marble that was her home world, Absaroka. From the viewscreen in her ready room she enjoyed the never-ending swirl of cloud formations across the planet's face as weather patterns built, shifted and broke apart. The Confederated Nations had done well when they chose this planet. Absaroka was not Earth, would never be Earth, but it had mountains and forests, clear blue lakes and rivers, and large continental masses sprinkled among its oceans. And the face it showed to its children orbiting in space was unendingly beautiful.

The seven years since her grandfather's death and her successes with the Planetary Council and the USL Academy had changed Brenna. She was no longer a simple citizen of Absaroka. The principal chief had decided that since she had fought for and hand-picked most of the fleet, she should be prepared to lead it.

Since the purchase of *USL Sequoia*, which the people of Absaroka had re-christened *CNS Thunderbird*, the Planetary Council had rounded out Absaroka's fleet with five destroyers (named for the original Five Civilized Tribes – *CNS Choctaw, Chickasaw, Creek, Seminole,* and *Cherokee*), twelve cruisers (each named for another of the tribes of the Confederated Nations), and fifteen warbirds — fighters in the USL parlance. Each warbird had been named by its pilot for an old Earth bird of prey.

Brenna smiled. Her warriors might be untested in battle, but Absaroka's fleet was well-trained and ready to defend its home world. She prayed that she and her grandfather had been wrong, that the Bug-Eyes would never return and her fleet would never need to do more than keep Absaroka free of criminal factions.

A single bell-like tone broke her reverie. Brenna turned from the splendor of Absaroka to a flashing light on her comm unit. Acknowledging the signal, she asked, "Yes, Mister Sparrow Hawk?"

"Warchief, the fleet awaits your command to begin the readiness exercise."

"Very well. Chief Whitehorse is authorized to assume command. The action will commence at his pleasure; obey him well. Warchief Standing Bear out."

"Understood, Warchief. It shall be done."

The comm unit deactivated and Brenna turned back to her viewscreen. Settling deeper into her command chair, she focused the screen on her fleet. Alex Whitehorse would command the exercise from the fleet command bridge here on their flagship, *CNS Thunderbird*. Alex was a good officer and commanded his destroyer, *CNS Cherokee*, efficiently and effectively, but he lacked experience leading more than a single ship. This exercise would test his ability to see beyond his own ship's maneuverability. Determine if he had what it took to direct a fleet.

Brenna would watch the action from the comfort of her ready room behind *Thunderbird's* main bridge. She would not interfere with her subordinate's decisions, but she would weigh them against her own instincts as well as analyze their outcome. She needed a second in command, and the chiefs of her five destroyers were all being scrutinized to determine their fitness. Each was a fine ship's commander, but it took more than the ability to lead a single crew to make a warchief, and Brenna's second in command would be in line to be her successor.

The war exercise commenced and Brenna watched with interest as her fleet ran through their paces.

5

C hief Alex Whitehorse watched his fleet deploy across the multiple screens of the warchief's console in fleet command, a secondary bridge in a remote and well-protected section of *Thunderbird's* interior. His thought flickered to Warchief Standing Bear, who normally occupied this seat, wondering how she felt about giving him command. He pushed the thought aside as irrelevant. This exercise was as much about training him as it was the fleet. Warchief Standing Bear needed a second in command. This was his chance to show her that he was up to the task.

Alex opened a direct line to his own second, Randy Foxfire, who occupied the captain's chair on *Cherokee's* bridge while Alex commanded the fleet. "Commander Foxfire, report."

"All is in readiness, Chief," Randy said, his tone clear and confident. "We're standing by."

"Acknowledged." Alex opened a line to *Thunderbird's* XO. "Mister Blackcloud, report."

"The first squad of warbirds is ready to launch, Chief," the XO said. "Second squad is standing by."

"Understood." Alex toggled the line to the destroyer *Choctaw*. "Chief Littlebear, begin evasive maneuvers."

"Yes sir," said Amanda Littlebear's calm voice.

Alex switched back to *Thunderbird's* bridge. "Mister Blackcloud, *Choctaw* is your target. Get your birds in flight."

"Acknowledged, sir."

Alex settled back to watch the imitation dance of death. This was simply a training exercise, everyone involved was part of his team, but the purpose was deadly serious. With loaded and unguarded weapons, this dance could turn fatal.

He knew that too many of the young warbird pilots considered this no more than a real-life version of a holostar. A game that aroused the senses and sent adrenaline flowing through their veins. While he prayed that their perception would never need to change, he pushed their training so that their reactions would become instinctual. Muscle memory could save their lives if a real attack ever came.

The *Choctaw*, with warbirds in pursuit, danced around Absaroka's orbit as though its movements had been choreographed. The squads of warbirds flitted in and out of *Thunderbird's* flight decks like hummingbirds, landing, refueling, and darting back into the imagined fray with seeming effortlessness.

All but one.

Alex straightened in his chair, ready to open a line to the Chief of the Deck, when he saw the man signal the pilot out of *Falcon*. Opening his receiver, he listened in on the confrontation.

"Just what do you think you're doing out there, Pilot Leaping Trout?" the COD growled.

"Followin' orders, shir," Caleb Leaping Trout answered with a distinct slur to his words.

"I don't think so, mister," barked the COD. "You've been sluggish answering your hails and sloppy with the formations." He stopped, leaned toward the young man and then backed away quickly. "And you stink of whiskey. That's it. You're grounded, and confined to quarters until Chief Whitehorse has time to deal with you. Dismissed."

"Bu...but..." Caleb sputtered.

"I said, 'Dismissed,' Pilot Leaping Trout. Do you need me to draw you a picture?" The COD leaned close and glared at the younger man.

"No sir ... I mean, yes sir," he said, confused. Not sure what response was required, he stumbled away from the COD and off the flight deck.

The COD waved one of his men over. "Follow Caleb," he said. "Make sure he gets to his quarters and then stand guard until you're relieved."

"Yes sir," he said, saluting and then turning on his heel to follow the impaired pilot.

Alex closed the receiver and turned his attention back to his screens. Too bad. Caleb Leaping Trout had been a promising pilot, but years with the fleet had taught him that early promise was not always realized. He'd have to reward the COD's astute observation and quick action. An impaired pilot was a danger to his entire squad.

The rest of the exercise went flawlessly. Alex moved the fleet's ships into standard formations, textbook patterns that any chief would recognize, then, with his next set of orders, produced a variation of his own devising. Whatever he ordered, his fleet carried out his commands with precision.

He smiled. No one questioned his orders, even on the most obscure formation. His people trusted him. A wave of gratitude washed over him. He'd do everything in his power to be worthy of that trust.

6

Brenna was impressed. No matter what Chief Whitehorse ordered, and some of those formations were completely unorthodox, the fleet obeyed with alacrity. She nodded. Yes. Alex Whitehorse would make a fine second.

She stretched out her hand to hail Alex, wanting to congratulate him on an exemplary exercise, when alarms blared and lights flashed throughout the ship. She whirled to her monitor to discover the source of the problem, and found it immediately. An unknown vessel had materialized just beyond Absaroka's orbit.

"Warchief Standing Bear," Alex's voice sounded through Brenna's comm unit. "An unknown ship is in our space; they're not answering our hails. Do you wish to take command of the fleet?"

Brenna frowned. She'd pushed to standing the instant the vessel appeared on her screens. Her fingers itched for the controls of her chair on the fleet command bridge, but she knew better than to change horses in mid-stream.

"No, Chief Whitehorse. The fleet is responding well to your commands. A change now would disrupt that flow. We need everyone at their best. Carry on. I'll observe and advise from here."

"I hear and obey, Warchief."

Before either of them could react, the strange vessel glowed green and then aimed a fine energy stream at the *Choctaw*. The destroyer imploded. One moment Chief Amanda Littlebear's vessel held its place in the latest formation, and the next it was extinguished in a blinding flare of light.

"Chief Whitehorse," Brenna yelled into the comm unit, "what just happened?"

"My officers are reporting now, Warchief."

As Brenna waited she noted fighters emerging from the enemy carrier. Alex Whitehorse ordered the warbirds out to meet them. Fourteen small, sleek birds of prey launched and zipped around the enemy fighters. Lasers streaked red and blue against interstellar black.

"Warchief, all our readings suggest a singularity event took out the *Choctaw*, and that carrier and its fighters ... their patterns are reading as Bug-Eye vessels." Alex paused for only a fraction of a second. "You were right, Brenna. They've returned."

Brenna slumped back into her chair, then pounded the armrest. "I never believed we had truly defeated them," she said quietly, "but I always hoped." She straightened her spine and narrowed her eyes. "Carry on, Chief Whitehorse. You're in command. This is what we've trained for. This is why our fleet exists. Protect our people."

"Yes, Warchief. It has been my honor to serve with you."

"And mine as well, Alex. May the Great Spirit guide you."

Thunderbird's XO took his orders from Alex, as Brenna had ordered, but Brenna commandeered one of the flagship's top communications officers to assist her in her ready room. Messages flashed between the *Thunderbird* and the Longhouse as Brenna apprised the leaders of her people of their imminent danger.

[Flagship to Planetary Council]: We are under attack. This is not an exercise. Repeat. This is not an exercise.

[Planetary Council to Flagship]: We see the ship, but do not recognize its configuration. Have you identified?

[Flagship to Planetary Council]: Identification confirmed: Bug-Eye. Notify USL via flex-space communication. *Choctaw* destroyed.

All ships engaged. New weapon in play. May threaten whole planet if we fail.

[Planetary Council to Flagship]: Message received and relayed to USL. Godspeed, Warchief. May the Great Spirit guide you. Absaroka out.

Absaroka didn't have the resources to evacuate the planet, and Brenna was all too aware that with a singularity weapon, her fleet was the only thing standing between the Confederated Nations and annihilation.

Even if the tribes could have escaped the planet, they had no idea how many Bug-Eye ships waited just beyond Absaroka's orbit.

Principal Chief Old Coyote had sent the distress call to USL command. Brenna and the fleet had to hold the enemy at bay long enough for their allies to arrive.

Assuming other Universal Star League worlds weren't under attack as well.

Great Spirit! Brenna wished that her long ago arguments had remained hypothetical.

She paced her ready room listening to the shouted messages from *Cherokee* and the other destroyers and cruisers, and watching the decimation of her fleet on the viewscreen. She'd now seen two of her destroyers (*Choctaw* and *Seminole*) and three of her cruisers (*Kiowa*, *Lakota*, and *Ute*) implode. Each time the Swarm carrier hung motionless against the backdrop of space while the deadly green glow built, and each time the fine energy stream touched one of her ships, it disappeared in a blinding flash.

She had to do something. She couldn't just pace this room and wait for *Thunderbird* to implode. Forcing herself to calm, Brenna watched a replay of the destruction of the *Kiowa*. The enemy vessel hung motionless while the green glow built. The enemy fighters were particularly active during the waiting period. Almost ...

Could that be a flaw?

Could the ship be vulnerable while it charged?

What if...?

But no, her fourteen warbirds were already down to nine, they couldn't afford to waste one on an untested theory. But if it were true? Could they afford *not* to try?

Her thoughts circled like birds of prey over a dying animal. She was missing something. Something important. And then the necessary datum clicked into place.

Fourteen. There had been *fourteen* warbirds in the fray. Now there were nine.

Brenna raced from the ready room into her private quarters, stripping as she ran. Without giving herself time to think about consequences or unrealized futures or things left undone, she grabbed her flight suit and pulled it on. She wasn't the pilot those youngsters were, but she could fly and the mission she had in mind didn't require finesse.

Grabbing her helmet she made a mad dash to the flight deck, screaming orders over her wrist comm to the COD as she ran. "Get the *Falcon* ready," she yelled. "I'm going out!"

"But Warchief," the COD cried, "you can't."

"I can and I will, Chief," she answered. "Obey my command."

"Yes, Warchief," the man said crisply.

Panting, Brenna hurtled onto the flight deck, paused to catch her breath, and secured her helmet to the neck of her flight suit. Crew members finished positioning the *Falcon* for take off as Brenna moved forward.

The Chief of the Deck stepped in front of her and saluted. "Warchief Standing Bear, may I ask for your flight plan?"

She gave the man a crooked smile, returned his salute, and shook her helmeted head. "You may not, Chief," she replied. "You may, however, give my regards and utmost thanks to Chief Whitehorse. You stand as witness that he is my designated choice to replace me as Warchief, should any of us survive. Thank you for your service, Chief. It has been an honor to serve our people with you."

The COD's jaw clenched. He nodded and stood at attention as Brenna climbed into the *Falcon*. She jumped the compact little warbird into the void as soon as she was strapped in.

"Pilot Standing Bear, just what the hell do you think you're doing?" Alex Whitehorse's voice was loud and commanding in her ear.

"What happened to the deference due a warchief?" she asked.

"It went out the window when she stopped acting like one," he snapped. "I repeat, what the hell do you think you're doing, Brenna?"

"Something I will not order one of my pilot's to do," she gathered her thoughts for a moment before deciding. The warchief needed as much information as possible. "Listen, Alex," she said overriding him as he started to object. "I have a theory that the Bug-Eye ship may be vulnerable as that green charge builds. I won't risk one of our pilots to test this, but I'm willing to do it myself."

She took a shuddering breath, waiting for a response that didn't come. Really, what could Alex say?

"The fleet is yours, Alex. If this works, I'll buy you some time and provide some much-needed information. If it doesn't, guard Absaroka as best you can until the USL fleet arrives." She snapped off her communications before he could respond. Sometimes, it was good to be alone with one's own thoughts.

You were right, Grandfather, she thought. *The Bug-Eyes have returned. I built the fleet as you wanted, but it wasn't enough.*

She positioned the *Falcon* where she could observe the carrier, trusting Alex to ensure that the other warbirds kept the Bug-Eye's fighters off her tail. She watched the deadly dance of the birds of prey while she waited. At last the carrier paused in its restless movement and the green glow began to build.

Brenna inhaled deeply, pushed the *Falcon* to ramming speed, and thought with love of the blue-green marble that twirled in the atmosphere below. She was proud to have been warchief of her people, proud to have been tasked with the defense of Absaroka. Her grandfather had entrusted this legacy to her, and she had not failed him.

Brenna Standing Bear rammed the Bug-Eye carrier as it hung motionless in space, and imploded with her enemy in a singularity of purpose.

PART VIII

AWAKENING THE WARRIOR

AWAKENING
THE WARRIOR

UNIVERSAL STAR LEAGUE

— FILE TWO —

DEBBIE MUMFORD

PROLOGUE

W arbird Pilot Caleb Leaping Trout stood at attention in the corridor of Absaroka's flagship. He fixed his gaze on the blank wall opposite him, trying not to see the death of his career in its smooth white surface. The Bug-Eye crisis had passed, no thanks to him, and the time had come for him to answer for his foolishness.

He longed to loosen the stranglehold of his dress uniform's collar, but knew better than to relax his formal stance. He was in enough trouble without giving his superior officers additional evidence of his unsuitability to remain a pilot in Absaroka's defense fleet.

Warchief Brenna Standing Bear was dead because of him, and her people, *his* people, mourned her loss, while thanking the Great Spirit for her courage.

He swallowed, tasting bile. He knew he wasn't actually responsible for the warchief's death, but he also knew that if he'd been at the controls of his warbird ... if he'd been sober and flying the *Falcon* in battle as he should have been, she wouldn't have been able to commandeer his ship and sacrifice herself for the defense of Absaroka.

It should have been him.

Warchief Standing Bear should have ordered him to test her

1

"Come on, Caleb," wheedled Jeremy Wolfclaw. "You know you could fly those stupid readiness exercises with one hand tied behind your back."

"Sorry, Jer. My duty..."

"Your *duty* is to your best friend! Bro, I'm getting *married* tomorrow. I need you at my side tonight. You're my, what do you call it? Oh, yeah. You're my *wingman*! You gotta come, Caleb. Tomorrow's too late. Tomorrow night I'll be busy making little Wolfclaws with Simone." Jeremy wiggled his eyebrows suggestively and clapped Caleb on the back. "Come on, man. You can't let a brother down in his hour of need."

Caleb shook his head, then grinned at his best friend. "I don't know how you managed to get a beauty like Simone to agree to marry you, but yeah, I'll celebrate with you tonight." He paused for a moment, studying his friend's honest, but somewhat homely face. Jeremy was a good man, but he didn't understand Caleb's responsibility to the fleet, or the command structure he answered to. Jeremy was a code-cruncher. He sat in a cubicle all day. The worst thing he ever wrestled with was a snarly tangle of bits and bytes.

The two guys might have grown up together, but their adult lives were worlds apart.

But Jeremy was right about one thing: Caleb could fly readiness exercises blindfolded. He could afford to go out drinking with his best friend tonight. After all, the exercises would force him to miss Jeremy's wedding, so this was his only chance to toast his friend's happiness.

Besides, the Bug-Eyes had turned tail and run before either of them had been born. The readiness exercises, hell, the whole planetary defense fleet, was a product of Warchief Standing Bear's family paranoia. Not that he minded. If there wasn't a defense fleet, he wouldn't be a pilot, and the one thing Caleb Leaping Trout knew for sure was that he'd been born to fly a warbird.

2

Caleb woke to a shrill sound drilling a hole in his head. He yanked a pillow over his ears and applied pressure, trying to make sure his skull didn't explode.

"Alarm off!" he yelled into his bedroom's dim light. The noise ceased and he released the pillow and flopped onto his back. Great Spirit! His head throbbed, his eyes were gritty, and his stomach churned. What had happened to him last night?

He lay still, hoping his body would settle, and his bedroom would stop shimmying and shaking. Closing his eyes, he tried to think. Tried to remember what he'd done last night. Flying lug nuts, dredging up memories hurt! He pressed his hands to his eyes to hold his brain in place while he searched for answers.

Jeremy. Drinking. Celebrating. More drinking.

Right. He'd gone out with Jeremy and the two of them had experimented with every intoxicant they could find in Tahlequah's club district. And Absaroka's capital city had a lot of clubs and a galaxy's worth of liquor.

Caleb smiled ruefully. He hoped Jeremy was in better shape than he was. After all, Jer was getting married this morning, and Simone wouldn't be impressed if her groom couldn't stand up for the ceremony.

Awareness came flooding back, and Caleb jerked to sitting. His head swam and his stomach lurched, but he didn't have time to acknowledge the pain. He had readiness exercises this morning. He had to get dressed and get to his warbird. If he failed to show, he'd be in the brig before Jeremy managed to mutter "I do."

Two hours later, Caleb sat strapped into the pilot's seat in the *Falcon*. He'd launched from the *Thunderbird's* flight deck in formation with the rest of his shroud of five warbirds, and now struggled to maintain his position in the intricate drills his shroud leader commanded.

Sweat dripped from the end of his nose, fogging the faceplate of his helmet. This should've been easy. His shroud had practiced these maneuvers until he could manipulate the controls in his sleep. But today his head throbbed, his muscles ached, and he knew his responses were sluggish. He gritted his teeth and wished he could yank off his helmet and wipe the damn faceplate. He had enough trouble focusing his bloodshot eyes without trying to peer through the condensation of his own sweat.

Static crackled over his communication array. "Pilot Leaping Trout," the voice said. Caleb frowned. A man's voice. Not his shroud leader Jenny Lightfoot's clear tones. "This is Chief of the Deck Black Bear. Return to the *Thunderbird*. Now."

"Aye, shir," Caleb said, his words slurring as his stomach gave a queasy roll. "Jush le' me inform…"

"Now, Pilot Leaping Trout," the COD said sharply. "Your shroud leader has already been informed."

"Aye, shir. Returnin' now."

One less than perfect landing later, Caleb climbed unsteadily from the *Falcon* and swayed to attention on the flight deck as the COD approached.

"Just what do you think you were doing out there, Pilot Leaping Trout?" the COD growled.

"Followin' orders, shir," Caleb answered, his words slurring even more now that he was face to face with his superior officer.

"I don't think so, mister," barked the COD. "You've been sluggish answering your hails and sloppy with the formations." He stopped, leaned toward the young pilot and then backed away quickly. "And you stink of whiskey. That's it. You're grounded, and confined to quarters until Chief Whitehorse has time to deal with you. Dismissed."

"Bu...but..." Caleb sputtered.

"I said, 'Dismissed,' Pilot Leaping Trout. Do you need me to draw you a picture?" The COD leaned close and glared at the younger man.

"No shir ... I mean, yesh shir," he said, confused. Not sure what response was required, Caleb saluted, or tried to, and stumbled away from the COD and back to his shipboard quarters.

Great Spirit! What had he done? Why had he allowed himself to drink so much last night? Why hadn't he accompanied Jeremy on his night out, but limited himself to a single toast? Why in the name of all his revered ancestors had he matched Jeremy drink for drink?

If he lost the *Falcon* ... if he was dishonorably discharged .... It didn't bear thinking about.

He reached his quarters and shut himself in, only vaguely aware of the airmen who'd followed him and now stood guard at his door. He was in deep shit. But his head throbbed and every muscle in his body ached. Chief Whitehorse wouldn't have time to discipline him until after the exercises, so he might as well try to sleep it off.

He shrugged out of his boots and flight suit and collapsed on his bunk. Maybe when he woke up he'd discover this was all a bad dream.

3

But it wasn't a dream. It was a nightmare.

Caleb woke to a clear head, calm stomach, and muscle aches that he knew would succumb to a couple of pain tablets, but his world was in turmoil. Code Red lights flashed and shrill sirens drilled into his ears. He raced barefoot to the door, yanked it open and met an armed guard.

"Remain in your quarters, Pilot Leaping Trout," the man said, eyeing him with disgust.

Caleb raised his hands and took a step away from the door. "What's happening? Is this a drill?"

"It is not. We're under attack," the man growled. "Bug-Eyes." His eyes flicked over Caleb. "And I'm stuck guarding a pilot who's too drunk to be of use."

"Bug-Eyes?" Caleb asked in disbelief. "But that can't be right. They disappeared decades ago!"

"They're back," the guard said, and closed the door in Caleb's face.

Stunned, Caleb stood rooted to the deck of *Thunderbird*, marooned in his quarters. Barefoot, wearing only a tee-shirt and shorts. The siren and flashing lights faded from his awareness, his thoughts spiraling. He should be out there. He should be in the cockpit of the *Falcon*, fighting Bug-Eyes with his shroud.

Great Spirit! His shroud! Jenny and John and Anna and David were out there deploying the maneuvers they'd practiced, but they were a man short ... a warbird short. He'd left a hole in their formations. He'd left his shroud at a disadvantage, weakened. He'd failed his people in their hour of need.

And for what? To celebrate with Jeremy?

Jeremy and Simone might not even survive if the Bug-Eyes broke through the fleet's defenses ... and Caleb had weakened those defenses.

He'd failed. He wasn't a warrior. He was a spoiled child who put his own wants above his responsibilities to his shroud ... to his fleet ... to his people.

Caleb Leaping Trout sank onto his bunk, his head in his hands.

If he made it off the *Thunderbird*, if the *Thunderbird* survived the battle, his military career was over, and he'd richly deserve whatever punishment Chief Whitehorse and Warchief Standing Bear doled out.

4

————

The crisis passed. The *Thunderbird*, the fleet's flagship, survived. Two of the fleet's five destroyers, the *Choctaw* and the *Seminole*, did not. The fleet also lost three cruisers, the *Kiowa*, the *Lakota*, and the *Ute*. But most devastating to Caleb was the loss his warbird, the *Falcon*.

His shroud leader, Jenny Lightfoot, took pity on him and visited him in his quarters to bring him up to speed. Jenny and Caleb were the only remaining members of their shroud of five warbirds, and his fighter craft was destroyed as well.

"From what I understand," Jenny said, sitting crossed legged on the floor beside him, "Warchief Standing Bear commandeered the *Falcon* to test a theory. Whatever that weapon was that they were using against us, it simply disintegrated our ships. The *Choctaw* and the *Seminole* didn't stand a chance against it. The beam touched them, and they imploded."

She shook her head. "It was horrible. The Bug-Eye fighters were bad enough, but that weapon ... it was unbeatable."

"But what happened to the warchief," Caleb asked, when what he really meant was, what happened to the *Falcon*?

"Right. Well, the story that's making the rounds is that she noticed that the ship seemed vulnerable while it was recharging, and rather than ordering one of us, one of the remaining warbirds, to ram the ship, she commandeered the *Falcon* and did it herself."

Jenny shook her head. "She timed it perfectly. No pilot could've done better. She waited until the ship was just about to deploy that terrifying energy and then rammed the *Falcon* right down the maw of that weapon. The thing backfired and the Bug-Eye ship and the *Falcon* imploded together."

The two pilots sat in silence, pondering the courage and quick thinking of their warchief. After a moment, Jenny shook herself and continued. "Once the big ship was gone, the rest was just a mop-up exercise. The Bug-Eye fighters had nowhere to go. Our remaining warbirds and cruisers picked them off easily."

She sighed. "We won. Absaroka is safe and the USL has been warned, but..."

"But the cost was high," Caleb said, finishing her thought. "I'm sorry, Jenny. I know that's not enough. Nothing I do will be enough. But I am sorry. I let you and the others down." He drew a shuddering breath. "And John and Anna and David paid with their lives."

Jenny touched his knee. "I'm not condoning what you did," she said quietly, "but don't beat yourself up. Yes, you were wrong and you'll deserve whatever punishment the chief decides is warranted, but you couldn't have known ... none of us could ... it was just supposed to be an exercise. No one was supposed to die."

Caleb swallowed past the lump in this throat and averted his eyes. She was right. He knew she was right. But how was he supposed to live with the guilt?

EPILOGUE

Warbird Pilot Caleb Leaping Trout stood at attention in the corridor outside Warchief Whitehorse's private office. The moment of truth had arrived. He raised his chin, ignoring the itch of the rarely worn dress uniform, the stiffness of the collar that tried to choke him. Whatever came, he deserved. His failure was unforgivable.

The office door opened with a soft "whoosh" and the Warchief's first officer stepped out. His gaze raked Caleb from head to toe before he spoke. "Warchief Whitehorse will see you now."

Caleb saluted crisply. "Aye, sir." He strode into the office to meet his fate, back straight, shoulders square. The door whooshed closed behind him as he saluted his newly appointed warchief.

Alex Whitehorse looked up from the tactical display covering the surface of his desk and said, "At ease, Pilot Leaping Trout."

Caleb released his salute and assumed a parade rest stance, gaze fastened on the wall behind the warchief's head. Though he maintained a stoic facial expression, Caleb was shocked by Whitehorse's appearance. The man looked like he had aged decades in the week since Caleb had last seen him.

"Caleb Leaping Trout, you have been charged with incapacitation of duty due to indulgence. What do you have to say for yourself?"

"Sir. I have no defense. I overindulged the night before our readiness exercises, being fully aware of the importance of the next day's events. Despite a severe hangover, I reported for duty and took my warbird out. The COD was forced to call me in due to my poor performance, leaving my shroud at a disadvantage."

Caleb paused. He closed his eyes and his shoulders slumped. After a moment, he opened his eyes again and met his warchief's gaze. "When I came to in my quarters and realized we were under attack...." He licked his lips. "Sir, I'm deeply ashamed. I don't deserve to be called a warrior. I left my shroud in a weakened state and contributed to the deaths of my fellow pilots. I acknowledge my guilt and accept any consequences you see fit to impose, though nothing will erase my culpability."

Warchief Whitehorse studied Caleb, his gaze seeming to penetrate to the pilot's soul. After a long moment, he spoke.

"I believe you speak honestly, Pilot Leaping Trout. You had no way of knowing that a scheduled exercise would turn into a full-scale battle, though that is exactly what readiness exercises are designed to do: prepare us for battle. Ensure that we're ready for the real thing."

Whitehorse sighed and scrubbed a hand over his face. "We lost a lot of good men and women in that battle," he said wearily. "And frankly, I can't afford to lose an able pilot over what should have been a simple case of drunkenness."

He stood, leaned across his desk, hands splayed on the tactical display. "I want to believe that this experience has awakened you to the importance of your duty, son. Has it?"

Caleb nodded, his jaw tight. With a conscious effort he relaxed enough to answer. "It has, sir. I am awake and aware of my duty to my people. My warbird carried Brenna Standing Bear to her death ... and to the salvation of Absaroka. I will do everything in my power to be worthy of her sacrifice."

Whitehorse nodded. "Very well. You are grounded until the COD releases you for flight. Until that time you will work with the ground crew assuring that all warbirds are fully functional and ready for battle. Are your orders clear?"

Caleb snapped to attention and saluted. "Aye, sir. Thank you, sir."

"You are dismissed, pilot."

Caleb executed a precise military turn and exited the warchief's office. Once he rounded a corner and was out of sight of the door, he slumped against the wall. Closing his eyes, he pictured his fallen friends, and apologizing inwardly, bade each farewell. When he opened his eyes, he shook himself, straightened his shoulders, and went to find the COD and report for ground duty, determined to be the best warrior in the fleet. To be worthy of his warchief's leniency ... and Brenna Standing Bear's sacrifice.

PART IX

INCIDENT ON THE ODYSSEY

INCIDENT
ON THE
ODYSSEY

UNIVERSAL STAR LEAGUE
—— FILE THREE ——

DEBBIE MUMFORD

1

Captain Caren Fielding stood on the bridge of *USL Odyssey*, a Universal Star League deep space exploratory vessel.

Her ship. Her bridge. Her responsibility.

She presented herself to her crew as an exemplary USL officer should: spotless blue and silver uniform, dark hair pulled into a tight knot at the base of her neck, face calm, controlled.

Everything regulation. Everything by the book.

Everything except the phantom stink of blood and human waste.

She controlled a grimace, refused to acknowledge the bile rising in her throat. The odor was a delusion. She knew it. The cleaning bots had worked through the night, removing all trace of the bodies that had exploded on her watch yesterday.

Blake's body.

Momentarily closing her eyes, she drew a deep breath, forcing herself to catalog the room's actual scents. Harsh chemical cleaning compounds stung her nostrils, overlaid with a clean, salty tang someone had named *ocean breeze*. Caren had never been near an ocean — neither had anyone else on this vessel—so she had no idea if the scent was accurate, but at least it wasn't the sweetly rotten melding of burned flesh, blood and feces.

She opened her eyes, observed the immaculately clean surfaces surrounding her people. Spotless white plasteel walls, gleaming chrome work surfaces, structural seating in a deep USL blue. Her crew's uniforms were equally squared away, their blues crisply pressed with polished silver rank insignia.

Clasping her hands behind her back, Caren listened to the familiar sounds of her bridge. The soft murmur of voices, both human and computer sim, set against the deep hum of engines — felt as much as heard — and the nearly inaudible *whoosh* of air cycling through the ventilation system.

Satisfied, she moved from station to station, monitoring her crew's work. Prowling as silently as a cat, nodding to those who made eye contact, murmuring encouragement to those who did not. Quietly evaluating the state of her bridge, the level of distress among her people.

They were a good crew, these eleven officers. Nine of them had been on the bridge with her last night. Only Perkins and Tse had escaped the horror. The night shift — those officers who had relieved her crew after the *incident* — had taken their watch on the auxiliary bridge. Cleaning bots had maintained sole possession of this space over what passed for night on the deep-space ship.

Caren returned to the command position and lowered herself into the captain's chair. Normally the chair molded to her form, suspending her body and enfolding her arms and hands so that her slightest movement registered against the ship's controls. Today she didn't allow it. She sat stiffly, rigidly erect. On guard. She would brook no comfort, no relaxation. Perhaps if she'd been more vigilant, less at ease, Blake would still be beside her, still be her steady right hand. An excellent first officer ... and her perfect mate.

She pushed the thought away. Blake was dead. She should know; she'd been covered in his remains, bathed in his blood.

He hadn't died alone. Ensign Jordan Whittaker had gone down as well. Now Lieutenant Perkins stood at Blake's station and Ensign Tse monitored Whittaker's controls. Life went on. The ship went on. And it was Caren's duty to move on as well.

Blake would expect that of her.

But Blake would never know the courage that seemingly simple task required.

Moving on. It sounded so easy, but it took every atom of her self-discipline not to run screaming from this place. Her bridge, the place she'd felt most competent, most in control, now felt like a tomb; a monument to Blake and Whittaker. No longer an efficient place where life went on and duty was fulfilled.

She stood again and, using her most controlled command voice, addressed the bridge crew. "If I could have your attention." She paused while every officer in the room turned to face her. She made brief eye contact with each one before continuing. "I know you're all distressed by what happened yesterday. I certainly am, but we need to continue to function in an efficient and capable manner. Our engineering crew and our technical programmers assure me that yesterday's *incident*, while regrettable, was a fluke, that we are in no more danger on this bridge than anywhere else on the ship. While we don't yet know what caused the deaths of Commander Larsen and Ensign Whittaker, we do know that we were not attacked — there are no other ships in our vicinity. We also know that none of our own systems malfunctioned."

Caren scanned her crew again, looking for signs of overt fear or distress. She found none. Deep sadness, yes; concern and confusion, yes; but not fear.

"We will continue to study the ... *incident*. We will discover the cause of the deaths. But we can only accomplish this task if everyone is alert and on guard.

"If any of you feel incapable of working in this environment, report to Lieutenant Perkins. He will relieve you, make arrangements for counseling, and arrange for another officer to assume your duties." She glanced at Perkins, who nodded his understanding.

"No one will think less of you for admitting to being traumatized," she said, her voice quieter, a bit less stern. "However, if you choose to remain at your station, you will be expected to function competently and without hesitation. Are there any questions?"

Her question was met with a low chorus of "No, sir."

She nodded. "Very well. You may resume your duties."

As her officers returned to their screens and controls, Caren moved to stand behind her captain's chair, hands resting lightly on its headrest. Catching Perkins' eye, she motioned for him to join her.

When he stood before her, one eyebrow slightly raised in query, she said, "You have the conn. I'll be in my ready room, if you need me. I want to review the techs' findings. Keep me apprised of the crew's state of readiness."

Perkins nodded. "Of course, Captain Fielding."

C aren's ready room had always been a refuge. A place where she could relax, away from the assessing eyes of the crew and the expectations of command. Unlike the cold white and chrome of the bridge, her ready room boasted walls of a soft blue, its plasteel furnishings hidden beneath a veneer that mimicked Old Earth oak. Sinking into the padded desk chair, she relaxed, appreciating the way its perfectly proportioned contours cupped her body, enjoying the comforting familiarity of its tawny faux leather.

She closed her eyes and sighed deeply, allowing herself a moment to feel the fear and trauma of the unexplained deaths. Danger was inherent in space travel, especially aboard an exploratory vessel. She and her crew lived with the unknown. They plumbed its depths on a daily basis.

But an unexplained death ... something that snuffed out life in such a random manner ... without raising an alarm ... something that attacked life in the most secure environment on the ship ... this was intolerable. The *incident* had to be explained! The danger had to be identified, the threat categorized.

Exploring the unknown was acceptable simply because everyone knew that once it was encountered, it would become known.

She opened her eyes and straightened in her chair.

Trauma and grief would have to wait. There was work to be done.

Blake and Whittaker had died. That was unassailable fact. The manner of their death was part of the ship's record. It was up to her to determine the cause. The unknown must become known for the safety and sanity of her crew ... and every other crew that ventured into this region of space.

She activated her work station, and got on with it.

Caren was studying the various reports from the time of the incident when the door to the bridge *whooshed* open and Lieutenant Perkins stepped through.

"Excuse me, Captain, but there have been several more deaths."

Caren froze, then fisted her hands on the simulated oak desk and snapped, "Report!"

Perkins straightened, clasped his hands behind his back, and stared at a spot just beyond Caren's left shoulder.

"The deaths were all identical to Larsen and Whittaker. One in engineering, one in hydroponics, and one in the medical bay."

Caren stood and paced from one end of the room to the other.

"And there are no signs of a ship? Could it be cloaked? Using technology we don't understand?"

"Nothing has been detected, sir." Perkins paused a moment before continuing. "However, Dr. Okeke from research reported an anomaly."

Caren rounded on him. "What anomaly?"

"She's a physicist, sir. Her verbal report ... well, much of it went over my head." He scrunched his shoulders as though trying to protect the deficient part of his anatomy. Evidently admitting his lack of understanding embarrassed the young officer.

Caren skewered him with her best commanding officer gaze, and he straightened and continued.

"My take was that she saw something in the data that supported an Old Earth theory that has never been proved. Something about emissions from a neutron star. I caught a phrase or two, but you're going to need to hear her findings for yourself."

"Very well," Caren said. "Return to the bridge and do what you can to keep the crew calm and functioning. I'll speak to Dr. Okeke."

Lieutenant Perkins executed a precise military turn, strode to the door, which *whooshed* open at his approach, and disappeared onto the bridge.

The instant the door closed, Caren turned to the viewscreen opposite her desk and contacted the research division. A very young, very pallid man wearing a white lab coat appeared on screen.

"This is Captain Fielding," Caren said before the young man could speak. "Get me Dr. Okeke immediately."

The young researcher's jaw dropped open, his eyes widened. He looked in danger of fainting.

"Now!" Caren snapped.

"Sir ... yes, sir," he squeaked.

Caren drummed her fingers on her desk as she watched the young man dodge and weave out of camera range. A few moments (that felt like hours!) later, a very dark skinned woman with high cheekbones and a cap of sleek black hair appeared on the viewscreen.

"Captain Fielding," she said, her voice calm and melodic. "I am Dr. Chi Okeke. I presume this is in regard to the report I gave to your first officer."

"It is. Thank you for speaking to me, Doctor. Lt. Perkins' summary was rather bare bones. What can you tell me?"

Dr. Okeke nodded, her expression serious, but excitement gleamed in her eyes. "I ... we ... noted some anomalous readings in the data from yesterday evening and again this morning. Readings we've never encountered before, but that correspond to theories raised on Earth in the late twentieth century."

She paused, closed her eyes, took a deep breath, and continued. "We believe we've encountered *exotic hadrons*, *hexaquarks* to be exact." Her eyes flew open, shining with elation. "They seem to be emanating from the neutron star we detected two days ago."

Caren nodded. "I can see that you're excited, Dr. Okeke, but does this have anything to do with the unexplained deaths we're experiencing?"

Dr. Okeke frowned. "Our findings are too preliminary to make such an assumption, Captain. We were only asked to report any unusual readings."

Caren sighed and rubbed her temple. "I sympathize with your need for empirical evidence, doctor. But our people are dying and I don't know what's killing them or how to protect them. These *hexaquarks* of yours are the only anomaly we've discovered. Is there any way for you to determine if they are the cause? And if they are, can you find a way to prevent further casualties?"

"We'll do our best, Captain. I'll keep you informed of our progress. Dr. Okeke out."

Caren's viewscreen went blank.

3

The next few hours wreaked havoc on Caren's nerves and on the morale of her crew. Gruesome deaths continued to be reported at odd intervals. There seemed to be no pattern to either their timing or their location on the ship. Everyone was on edge. Not knowing when the person next to you — or you, yourself — might explode was a unique and terrifying experience.

Caren left Lieutenant Perkins in command and made her way to the research lab. She needed answers, and she needed them now. As she strode through the white and chrome corridors, doing her best to exude an air of confident authority, she acknowledged every crew member she passed, whether by name or with a brief nod of the head.

The manner of greeting was irrelevant. The important part was for the crew to see her as in control and moving purposefully. They were understandably rattled by recent events and needed to see their commanding officer behaving in a calm and competent manner. Needed to feel that the situation was being dealt with.

She only hoped that the physicist had actually found the answer. That the *hexaquarks* were indeed the guilty particles.

The doors to the research sector *whooshed* open. The pallid young man she'd spoken to on her viewscreen scrambled to greet her.

"Captain Fielding," he said. "It's an honor to meet you. I'm Research Assistant Second Class Rolf Markham. If you'll follow me, I'll take you to Dr. Okeke."

"Thank you, Markham."

The young man led her through a maze of sterile white counters covered in complex chrome and plasteel equipment. Machines hummed, clicked, and whirred, while white-coated staff spoke in low voices, sometimes into recorders, sometimes to each other. The air smelled of disinfectants, triggering Caren's memory of the too clean bridge and causing bile to rise in her throat. She coughed and choked it back down.

In addition to the white coats, many of the scientists wore safety goggles or face-plated helmets which obscured their features. Her guide stopped behind just such a pair and cleared his throat.

"Dr. Okeke, Dr. Inarsson," he said. "I'm sorry to disturb you, but Captain Fielding is here to see you."

Dr. Okeke turned, but the man, Dr. Inarsson, continued to stare into the viewscreen on the device he held. He straightened, his posture suddenly rigid. Without looking up, he bellowed, "Down! Everyone down!"

Caren dropped to the deck, her training too instinctual to allow for questions, But Markham remained upright. She grabbed for the cuff of his pants to encourage his compliance when his body crumpled. Warm liquid sprayed her face and hands and she closed her eyes. She knew without looking that the young man would never grow old.

The room was silent except for the mechanical sounds of the still working machinery and a steady *drip ... drip ... drip* that Caren didn't want to think about. After what seemed an eternity, Dr. Inarsson called, "All clear!"

As she rose to her feet, Caren noticed that Dr. Okeke and Dr. Inarsson had remained on their feet. Both looked shaken. Dr. Okeke's normally glowing dark cocoa complexion had an ashen tinge, and even Dr. Inarsson's lips were white, but both scientists gazed at the containment canister held between them with an expression of barely suppressed awe.

Dr. Okeke turned to Caren and said quietly, "Dr. Inarsson managed to cobble together a functioning hexaquark detector. That's how he was able to see the particles enter the lab."

The tall blond scientist nodded. "The *hexaquarks* came through on a plane approximately three feet above the deck. That's why I called for everyone to get down. If all life forms were prone, they would be safe." He glanced at Markham's body. "I wish I'd had more time to explain."

"I'm grateful for the warning," Caren said, "And grateful to my early drill sergeants for beating that automatic response into me." She too glanced at Markham's remains, and, accepting a towel from a silent scientist, scrubbed his blood from her hands. "I guess we can now conclude that the *hexaquarks* are the cause of our recent spate of unexplained deaths."

Dr. Okeke nodded. "Yes, though I would have preferred a controlled experiment with a nonhuman subject."

"Agreed. May I ask why neither of you hit the floor," Caren asked, "and what that is that you're holding?"

"I could see their trajectories," Dr. Inarsson explained.

"And this canister holds a containment field that we hoped would capture a *hexaquark* for us to experiment with," Dr. Okeke continued. "Lars, Dr. Inarsson, built it at the same time as the detector."

Lars Inarrson was a tall, rangy man who appeared to be built entirely of angles. Sharp cheekbones, nose and chin. Long thin fingers that looked like they could substitute for scalpels. But the shy smile he wore now softened his angular appearance, allowing Caren to see the child he'd once been.

"It worked," he said quietly, his voice full of wonder. He met Caren's gaze "It was worth the risk, because it worked."

Caren glanced again at what had been Markham. His death brought the body count to twelve, maybe more — Perkins would update her when all decks had reported in — but at least now they knew the cause. Now they had a chance.

"Well done, doctors. I know it's early — you've just captured that particle — but do you have a recommendation?"

Dr. Okeke closed her eyes and drew a deep breath. Her shoulders slumped slightly, but her face regained a bit of its color. When she opened her eyes, she met Caren's gaze without hesitation. "I suggest we move as far as possible from the neutron star that is emitting the *hexaquarks*."

Caren nodded, but remained still, silently encouraging the doctor to continue.

When Dr. Okeke failed to speak, Dr. Inarsson picked up the narrative. "The particles travel in a straight line and, with no friction to interfere with their initial velocity, could continue to infinity. But the further we are from their source, the more distance there will be between their lines of travel. We should be able to reach a point where we can hide in the interstices between them." He met Caren's gaze. "Does that make sense?"

"It does," Caren replied. "Can you supply our navigation team with a detector so we'll know when we've reached a place of safety?"

Dr. Inarrson nodded. "I'll work with engineering to get a prototype wired into the navigational system."

"Very well. Let engineering know that this is a priority. I want this ship moved to safety as quickly as possible."

"Yes, sir," Dr. Inarsson said. "We'll continue our investigations with the contained *hexaquark* once we've reached a position of safety." He paused, then added, "Of presumed safety."

Caren nodded. "Understood. We have no guarantees at this point, but it's good to have a course of action."

4

Once *Odyssey* reached the coordinates Dr. Inarsson's detection device specified, Caren breathed a sigh of relief. Her crew should now be safe while the research sector carried out its investigation. She needed a solution. Something to make *Odyssey,* and every other ship in the fleet, *hexaquark*-proof.

Caren moved to the captain's chair and allowed it to enfold her. She turned to her communications officer and said, "Ensign Schaeffer, open a ship-wide channel."

"Aye, Captain," he said. "Channel open."

"Attention. This is Captain Fielding with an update on our current situation. *Odyssey's* research department has determined the cause of the recent deaths. We encountered uncategorized emissions from a neutron star. *Odyssey* has been bombarded by particles that have been theorized, but never before observed. Unfortunately, these particles are not compatible with human life."

She paused, composing her thoughts. "Fortunately, we have an excellent research team. Dr. Lars Inarsson has been able to build a detection device and we have moved to what we believe is a safe location. Dr. Inarsson and Dr. Chi Okeke have captured and contained a particle for study and are working with the research scientists to develop some form of protection against further incursion from these particles."

Caren glanced around the bridge and was relieved to see her bridge crew's expressions relaxing. The unknown had become known. Now it was just a matter of figuring out a fix. They could deal with that. They were good at that. They had confidence in the abilities of every member of *Odyssey's* crew. Now it was just a matter of time ... and hard work.

"I want to commend every member of this crew for your excellent work ethic under stressful conditions. Well done. Captain Fielding out."

She nodded to Ensign Schaeffer, who cut the transmission.

"Lt. Perkins," she said, catching her first officer's eye. "You have the conn. I'll be in my ready room. USL Command needs an update on our situation."

"Aye, sir."

5

Two days later, Caren again joined Dr. Okeke and Dr. Inarsson in *Odyssey's* research sector. The room remained bright, with light reflecting off the white walls and chrome work surfaces. It still smelled of disinfectant, but this time Caren's mind was calm, more removed from the gruesome deaths that had haunted her last visit. Machines still whirred and clicked and researchers still filled the air with a murmured buzz of conversation, but this time the atmosphere was less tense, the tang of fear was gone.

Dr. Inarsson greeted her at the door. "Captain Fielding. Thank you for coming."

Dr. Okeke moved to join them, once again exuding a calm, capable aura, though her eyes shone with excitement. "Come, sir. We have so much to show you."

The trio moved deeper into the white and chrome labyrinth, finally stopping before a small, glass-encased room.

"We've been running tests round the clock since we captured the *hexaquark*," Dr. Okeke said.

Dr. Inarsson nodded. "Our people have been very engaged. Young Markham was somewhat of a pet. His death touched us all. Brought the real world crashing through our scientific detachment."

"I can appreciate that," Caren said. "It's one thing to know people are dying. It's something else entirely to witness the event ... to be splattered with their blood."

"Yes," agreed Dr. Okeke. "We would've worked diligently regardless, but Markham's death provided a singular focus that has allowed us to move more quickly, with perhaps greater leaps of intuition."

"And what have you discovered?"

The two physicists exchanged a glance. Dr. Inarsson raised an eyebrow, and Dr. Okeke nodded.

"First," Dr. Inarsson began, gesturing toward the enclosed space, "the *hexaquark* remains contained. That is our best news. The field I initially developed and which allowed us to capture the particle has remained stable. The less satisfactory news is that the *hexaquark* passes through every other material we've put it in contact with as though the material didn't exist. Plastisteel, gold, silver, chrome, every material we've managed to get our hands on. Nothing stops it."

"Of course," Dr. Okeke said, "nothing is damaged by it either. It's as though the particle doesn't exist. Which is why we've seen no damage to the ship itself. Only the crew."

"Yes," continued Dr. Inarsson, "the particle has no effect on inanimate objects, no matter their composition. But life forms ... life is another matter entirely."

Dr. Okeke's eyes shone and her hands moved quickly across a virtual keyboard, bringing up a viewscreen with dozens of charts and diagrams. "It doesn't matter what type of life we expose to the particle: a seedling, an insect, even a microscopic bacterium; when a living organism comes in contact with the particle, it..." she moved her fisted hands apart and splayed her fingers, "explodes."

"More study will be required," Dr. Inarsson added, "to determine exactly what the catalyst is, for of course both animate and inanimate objects are ultimately made up of the same atomic particles, but for now, we have our answer."

"And that is?" asked Caren.

The scientists exchanged surprised glances. Evidently they thought they'd already explained it all.

"Why, that the particle is inimical to life," said Dr. Okeke.

"And that we'll need to work with engineering to add the containment field to our shields," said Dr. Inarsson. "But we'll need to reverse the polarity," he glanced at Dr. Okeke, who nodded, "in order to repel the particles rather than capturing them and adhering them to our hull."

"I see," Caren said, and she did. At least the part about repelling instead of adhering. "Let me know when we have a workable shield. Until then, since we've suffered no new deaths, we'll remain where we are."

She stared at the diagrams and charts still displayed on the viewscreen and shook her head. She'd been called something of a tactical genius, but this information left her feeling like a school girl again. Thank the universe (and the fleet and academy she represented) she had a full complement of scientists aboard. She'd have had no idea how to proceed without them.

"Well done, doctors. Between you and the engineers, we'll be able to ensure that no other USL ship ever has to experience the trauma we've endured these last few days."

"Thank you, sir," said Dr. Inarsson.

"We'll let you know as soon as we have a workable shield," Dr. Okeke said.

Caren nodded, and with a *whoosh* of the door, left the scientists to their work.

Returning to her ready room, she collapsed into the tawny faux leather of her padded desk chair and, closing her eyes, allowed herself to mourn. The crisis was past. The *incident* had been explained. Now, at last, she could allow herself to acknowledge her loss.

Blake was dead.

His death had left a whole in the fabric of her life that might never be fully repaired, but she had not fallen apart. She had seen it through, as he would have wanted ... as he would have expected. The cost had been high, fifteen lives had been lost all told, but *Odyssey's* duty as an exploratory vessel had been fulfilled. An Old Earth theory

had been confirmed; a new particle had been catalogued, its proper-
ties recorded. Human knowledge and experience had been
expanded.

And, yes, life went on.

PART X

THE QUEEN'S CAPTIVE

THE
QUEEN'S
CAPTIVE

UNIVERSAL STAR LEAGUE
— FILE FOUR —

DEBBIE MUMFORD

1

I am a worm; the property of the Tse-Tsunxhanaga queen.

My people, the grotesque and rebellious humans of Earth and its feeble colonies, call the noble Tse-Tsunxhanaga hive *Bug-Eyes*. This detestable name came about because the insipid human vocal apparatus is unable to adequately pronounce the sublime clicks, hums, and sub-vocal stops of the elegant Tse-Tsunxhanaga language; also because the hive's superior exoskeleton bears a superficial resemblance to an ancient Earth insect: the cockroach.

My name is Zara. I am a human female. I was taken captive by the hive when my human colony was destroyed by the noble Tse-Tsunxhanaga. I was four earth-years old at the time. I have no idea of my current age, although I believe I have reached sexual maturity. I have not seen the open sky since the day I was taken. I am the property of Queen Tsetseg and am an object of study in her Royal Academy of Science. It is hoped that someday I will be capable of acting as an interpreter for the queen. However, my vulgar and inadequate vocal apparatus render this hope unlikely. While I understand the language of the hive, I am incapable of speaking it in any form fit for presentation to a personage as great and glorious as Queen Tsetseg.

I remain unworthy of her notice.

My body, soft and vulnerable as it is, requires frequent mainte-
nance. Unsightly thread-like protuberances grow from my scalp,
necessitating shaving. Since gaining maturity, these threads also
appear in other places on my body. Removal is often painful. My
keepers, the noble Tsagai, Tsila, and Tserig, despair of ever making
me presentable, for in the process of cleansing, my delicate skin often
turns unsightly shades of blue, green, or purple, and in some cases is
torn, allowing my disgusting red bodily fluids to ooze forth. My
keepers discovered early that if that red fluid should gush rather than
ooze, my pitiful existence would be in danger of being extinguished.
Worse yet, even when healed, the tears leave ugly blemishes upon my
person.

I am covered with such scars.

Tsagai, Tsila, and Tserig, the keepers who have studied me since
my arrival in the hive, often click their pincers in perplexity as to how
such a fragile species could possibly have survived long enough to
attain the knowledge required to build ships and journey to distant
stars. They have often posited that I must be an aberration, a
dysfunctional unit allowed to live for scientific purposes, perhaps to
learn why my anomalies came into being.

Since I have almost no memory of my time among my own kind, I
have been unable to enlighten my noble keepers as to the reason for
my existence. However, as I am currently their only human specimen,
my deformities are catalogued and I continue to be studied.

Recently, something went awry in one of Queen Tsetseg's
campaigns to exterminate the vermin that are my species. I know this
only because my keepers despair of my understanding and so feel
free to discuss hive gossip in my presence.

Two of my keepers, Tsila and Tserig, had taken me to the hexag-
onal cell that served as my training center: a large, sterile white room
with a glass enclosure on one wall where my keepers could seal
themselves safely out of my reach, but still observe my every movement. I sat quietly on the antiseptically clean floor (there being no
furniture in the room) perusing the electronic device my keepers
allowed me to study. The device had been found in my domicile

when my colony was destroyed, and the warriors who captured me brought it along, thinking it might provide clues to my care and feeding.

My keepers found it useless, but allowed me to play with it, thinking that the familiar unit from my home might soothe my early terrors. It was good that they did so, for the device was an educational tool and allowed me to learn to read my native tongue. It also held an encyclopedia of knowledge, which has allowed me to understand my people and their history.

My keepers are unable to read the human language, and I allow them to think the device contains no more than pretty pictures of the planet that gave rise to my species. What they do not know benefits me.

Tsagai, the most senior drone in the triad tasked with my study, entered my training center, his pincers clicking with excitement. "Have you heard?" he asked Tsila and Tserig, who were located in the glass enclosure, working at a long metallic counter piled high with the instruments and devices necessary to their research. The enclosure was not sealed against me; my keepers had long ago judged me incapable of harm. Tsila and Tserig were currently working on an enhancement collar, a device they hoped would allow me to speak intelligibly, but they put down their tools and turned their attention to Tsagai.

Tsila's anterior antennae waved in greeting. "Heard what?"

"The campaign to remove the vermin from CSG-159— the planet the vermin have named *Absaroka*— has failed. Our flagship was destroyed, and the fighters, left without support or retreat, were lost."

All movement in the room stilled as Tsila and Tserig processed this horrifying news.

I sat quietly on the hard, white floor, hardly daring to breathe. I desperately wanted to hear more. I couldn't imagine how humans, weak and fragile as I knew my species to be, could possibly have inflicted great harm on the Tse-Tsunxhanaga hive. Damage a few fighters, perhaps, but to destroy a flagship? Unthinkable! Perhaps my weakness was truly an aberration after all.

"Are you certain of your facts?" Tserig asked, his anterior and lateral antennae vibrating with agitation. "While I do not doubt your word, noble Tsagai, this report seems highly unlikely."

I agreed, but kept still, my eyes on the device in my lap, hardly daring to breathe lest they remember my presence and seal the enclosure, thereby ending my ability to listen.

All of Tsagai's antennae ruffled, then relaxed, proclaiming his authority. "My source is unimpeachable. Champion Tsagadai himself told me of the disaster."

Tsila and Tserig bowed their six-eyed heads and murmured in unison, "Praise be to the One from whom the Jelly flows!"

Silence reigned while my keepers processed this astounding information.

I had learned from my device that, while the hive's exoskeleton resembles a cockroach, their social structure is more like that of the ancient Earth species known as bees. The hive consists of a single Queen, the alpha female, and millions of drones and workers of both genders. Drones, such as my keepers, are intellectuals and warriors. Workers are servants, destined by their DNA to obey the commands of the drones.

While technically a drone, Champion Tsagadai was in a caste by himself. His official title was Queen's Champion, but he was more than her guard and defender. He was her mate. When the time was right, he would sire the egg that would become the next Tse-Tsunx-hanaga queen. For him to have spoken directly to one of my keepers was a distinct honor.

Tserig recovered first and, raising his head, broke the reverent silence. "You bring us great honor, Tsagai. For Champion Tsagadai to speak to one of us..." he paused, waving his anterior antennae, "...it is beyond expectation."

Tsila nodded his great head. "We are merely keepers of a lowly human. We are unworthy of his notice."

Tsagai straightened to his full and considerable height. "It is because of the human that the Champion spoke to me. Her people did what no other species has done: they destroyed one of our flag-

2

I sat alone in an exo-bubble on the surface of a dead moon, far from the home world of the noble Tse-Tsunxhanaga hive. My bubble contained a recycling unit to ensure my supply of breathable air, a food processor, a toilet, atmospheric controls so that I would neither bake in the harsh sunlight nor freeze in the interstellar night, and my educational unit. I wore nothing but the enhancement collar that allowed me to speak intelligibly. The exo-bubble also contained an emergency beacon tuned to a frequency known to be monitored by the vermin who were the species of my birth.

Were I not bait, I would have enjoyed sitting in my bubble under the moon's open sky. The brightness of the stars, not to mention their sheer numbers, enchanted me. But, as always in my captivity with the Tse-Tsunxhanaga, my pleasure or displeasure was not a concern. I was merely a means to an end.

Champion Tsagadai and the queen's war council hoped to lure a human ship to my rescue. They wished to ensnare the ship and its crew in order to learn how my vastly inferior species had managed to destroy their flagship at the Battle for Absaroka.

I prayed that I would die alone on that harsh and lifeless moon, under those beautiful but uncaring stars.

The speaker on my beacon crackled to life, and I heard a human voice for the first time since my captivity began. "This is *USL Odyssey*. We have received your distress signal. Respond if you are able."

My heart sank. The emergency beacon had no microphone. I had no way to speak a warning. I could only observe as the system automatically pinged out a response.

"Confirmation received. A rescue party is on the way."

The trap had been sprung. I could do nothing but wait and observe the outcome of the confrontation between my people and the hive which had raised me.

All too soon, a shuttle craft landed on the barren surface of the dead moon. An exterior portal opened and three beings emerged. I knew from my educational device that they wore exo-suits, skin-tight protective gear that included a helmet designed to provide breathable air while allowing maximum visual and auditory acuity.

I had no such gear.

The three humans approached. The exo-suits molded so closely to their body contours that even I, who had such limited experience with my species, could tell that two were male and one was female.

Unfamiliar emotions roiled through me. I'd read about such feelings on my educational device, but had rarely experienced them. The thunder in my ears and palpitations of my heart told me I was excited to meet others of my kind, while the swooping sensation in my core and the prickles of tears in my eyes spoke of sorrow...and perhaps shame.

I was the bait who unwillingly lured these three, and very likely all of their shipmates, to their doom.

I knelt in my exo-bubble and awaited their fate...as well as my own.

The female approached while her companions held back, scanning the horizon with weapons drawn. She placed a small, black-and-silver device on the surface of my bubble and spoke.

"Do you understand Standard?" she asked. Her voice buzzed slightly, but was pleasant to my ears. Not the harsh clicking and humming of the Tse-Tsunxhanaga language, but soft and melodious.

I stared at her in wonder, longing for her to speak again.

She knelt on the dusty ground, placed her hand on the bubble, and leaned as close to me as her helmet and the exo-bubble would allow. "Can you understand me?"

Her meaning broke through my enchantment with the sound of her voice, and I nodded my head. "I understand."

My own voice sounded creaky and hoarse; disuse and constant practice with the clicks and sub-glottal stops of my captors' language had caused my native tongue to languish.

She smiled, and I was awash in emotion. This female had come to help me. She didn't deserve what was about to happen. My mind raced as I tried to piece together words and phrases from my educational device that would convey her danger.

"Flee," I said, rising upright on my knees. "Leave this place before you are trapped. Ignore me. I am bait."

My voice strengthened with each word I spoke, the pitch rising as my emotions tainted the content.

Before she could answer, or I could explain further, Tse-Tsunxhanaga warriors swarmed from the underground bunker where they kept watch.

My would-be rescuer sprang to her feet, drew her weapon, and shouted a warning to her companions. The two males laid down cover fire as they raced to their shuttle craft. When the shuttle doors closed and its engines fired, the female spoke again.

"Captain Fielding to *Odyssey*. I have activated a force field and am adhered to the subject's exo-bubble. Deploy the tractor beam. We are in imminent danger. Prepare for an emergency jump."

Before I could take a breath to speak, my bubble— and the human attached to it— lifted from the moon's surface. I watched in awe as the Tse-Tsunxhanaga warriors dwindled to mere specks and my rescuer and I flew through the upper atmosphere, into the black clarity of space, where we were drawn toward a vast deep space vessel.

I had never seen an interstellar craft.

I had been caged and taken aboard the Tse-Tsunxhanaga vessel like so much cargo. No one had been concerned with my experience. When we arrived at the desired location, the drones had simply placed my cage in a shuttle craft and then transferred me to the exo-bubble on the surface.

The *Odyssey* was immense, so shiny it sparkled against the back-drop of distant stars.

But a second sparkling craft emerged from what I guessed to be the mouth of a light-speed tunnel. My captors' ship had arrived. My rescue, though sweet, had been too short to be of consequence.

My rescuer and I were drawn into an open aperture on the *Odyssey* and deposited upon a dark metallic deck. As soon as the aperture closed behind the returning shuttle craft, before she even deactivated the force field adhering her to my bubble, the female shouted an order. "Fielding here. Shields up! Jump to light-speed. Now!"

The floor beneath the thin skin of my bubble thrummed with energy. The female joined her companions as they emerged from the shuttle, and all three removed their helmets. They stood at ease, but the edges of my vision darkened and I felt as though my whole body were being squeezed in the pincers of my Tse-Tsunxhanaga keepers. My breath expelled in a *whoosh*...

...and then all returned to normal.

The female stared at me, a small frown wrinkling the skin between her brows. "You're unfamiliar with the jump to light-speed?"

I rose to my full height and returned her stare, noting that her male companions turned their eyes away from my body. "I am unfa-miliar with all things human, including your light-speed engines," I said. "I have been captive to the noble Tse-Tsunxhanaga since I was very young."

"The what?" she asked, confused by the pronunciation my enhancement collar required.

I closed my eyes, imagining Champion Tsagadai's rage at having lost not only the *Odyssey*, but his bait as well. A bubble of...delight?... welled up in my core. For once, my captors had been outwitted. By lowly humans. And I had been part of their failure. I relished the knowledge.

Opening my eyes, I clarified the term for the captain. "You call them *Bug-Eyes.*"

3

Captain Fielding had a young female escort me to the medical bay, where a doctor evaluated my health. When I was released, the female took me to what she described as *my quarters*. I was certain I had misunderstood her intent. The enclosure was far more spacious than my container coupled with the training center where all three of my keepers studied me and conducted their research.

She explained that the three sections were a bedroom (for sleeping), a combination living area and kitchen (for entertaining and eating), and a toilet for relieving myself and ritual cleansing. The bed fascinated me. I'd never had more than a mat on the floor and a thin blanket, a concession to the fragile nature of my pitiful, non-chitinous body.

The female remained, having been instructed to help me clothe myself. She didn't believe I needed assistance, but my complete bafflement as to what to do with the pieces of cloth she provided soon convinced her.

Once I was cleansed, groomed, and suitably clothed, she escorted me to yet another enclosure, this one containing a long white table surrounded by ten fixtures I recognized as chairs. I continued to bless my keepers for allowing me to retain my instructional device. The knowledge I had gleaned over the years was proving invaluable in my new surroundings. The enclosure had white walls and floor (I wondered if they might be the plasteel I had read about), and one long wall contained indentations I thought might be windows, but they were also covered in white.

On one short wall was what I imagined to be a holoscreen showing images of a green and blue planet. I approached it, fascinated. The images shifted from— were those trees?— a forest to mountains—I'd seen mountains on my device—to a planet hanging against the backdrop of interstellar space.

I had never seen such beauty. The size of the holoscreen magnified the grandeur of what I'd experienced on my small handheld device. I couldn't imagine what it would be like to experience those wonders in person.

The door *whooshed* open behind me, and I turned to face Captain Fielding.

She smiled. "Well, you certainly clean up nicely."

I glanced down at myself. I felt... foreign... with my body encased in cloth, but I also felt warm and...protected. My young escort had named each piece as she helped me put it on. I wore soft knit leggings of the color known as navy blue, a long-sleeved tunic, also knit, in russet, and soft leather boots. I believe their color could best be described as *fawn*. She had seemed distressed by the scars on my body, and by my shaved head, but assured me that the soft blue scarf she'd wound around my head accented the color of my eyes.

Silence rang through the room, until my escort nudged me.

Ah. I was expected to respond.

I thought back to the conversational records I'd read on my device, and said, "Thank you."

Captain Fielding nodded. She wore what I now recognized as a uniform, blue and silver. Like my escort, her head had not been shaved. She wore her dark hair in a knot at the base of her skull. She gestured toward the chairs and my escort moved to sit upon one.

I watched how she folded herself into the space, and, licking my lips, made an attempt to do likewise. Soft padding cushioned my buttocks and supported my spine, I glanced sideways and saw that my arms could also be supported by cushioned comfort.

I closed my eyes and relished the...perhaps the word *decadence* applied?

Everything on this ship felt soft to me. How could such creatures have defeated a flagship of the mighty Tse-Tsunxhanaga? I shuddered to think how easily they would have been crushed had the captain not managed to jump to light-speed so expediently.

Captain Fielding's voice pulled me from my thoughts.

"I have your initial medical reports here, Zara. I believe you told Dr. Jansson that was your name. May I call you Zara?"

I opened my eyes and nodded.

"Dr. Jansson finds you malnourished, but otherwise in reasonable health." She paused and swiped forward a few screens on the device she held. "He also commented on the number of scars on your torso. Were you tortured?"

I frowned, trying to place the word in context. "I am unsure of your meaning," I replied. "My keepers discovered that my skin tore easily when they were forced to scrape the unsightly tendrils—I think you call it hair—from my body. They found me fragile and assumed I was defective. They continued to study me since I was their only test subject, but they could not imagine that a species as weak as I could possibly endure the rigors of space exploration."

Captain Fielding's eyebrows rose and the skin on her face flushed an interesting color. "I see." She swallowed, and I watched the play of muscles on her throat. Fascinating. "Do you remember how old you were when you were taken captive?"

I concentrated, accessing the few memories I had of the time before the Tse-Tsunxhanaga. "I was four Earth-years old when the hive invaded my colony. All were destroyed except me."

My guide gasped, and I glanced at her. The expression on her face made my heart pound. Her already pale face was even more pallid, and the expression in her eyes...

I could not interpret its meaning.

Captain Fielding asked, "Do you remember the name of the

colony?" and I turned my attention back to her. The calmness of her tones and her straightforward questions were soothing. Emotions were too new. I did not understand them, did not know what they meant. Questions I could answer; had been answering as long as I had existed.

"I do not know. I have often wondered, once I matured enough to understand that not all places are the same, but I am not sure I ever knew. I was too young to be concerned. It was simply my colony. My home."

"I understand." Captain Fielding looked down at her device. Fleetingly, I wondered if she might be avoiding my gaze. But my experience was too limited to judge.

When she again met my eyes, it was with calm assurance. "When we spoke on that moon, you told me to flee, that you were bait. Why did you say that? Why warn me away? Wouldn't it have been safer to stay silent?"

I lowered my eyes to my hands, where they rested on the soft padding of the chair, and composed my response. "I have dreamed of meeting my people, though my keepers assured me that my species were vermin to be exterminated from the universe.

"When I understood that I was to be used as bait to trap additional humans for continuing study, I wished to die. My existence has been unpleasant. I did not wish anyone else to share it, though I desperately longed for the company of my own kind."

I raised my gaze to hers and held it. "I did not believe you would be able to escape my captors. I never dreamed you would rescue me as well."

Her eyes brightened, seeming to fill with fluid, possibly tears. I had not cried in many years. The exercise was unprofitable, as it would only cause my keepers to do intensive, painful research on my eyes to try to determine the cause of the moisture.

"I thank you, on behalf of myself and my crew. We'll never know if we could've battled our way out, but our experience with the Bug-Eyes argues against it. Can you tell me why they chose to use you now, and not years ago?"

"Years ago they did not consider humans a threat," I answered, "but recently their opinion of you has escalated. Humans destroyed one of their flagships at the Battle of Absaroka."

Her gaze sharpened and she leaned forward in her chair, placing her arms on the table. "How do you know that?"

I shrugged. "My keepers doubted my intelligence."

She frowned, but remained quiet.

"Because my vocal apparatus is unable to produce their language intelligibly, they think me stupid. I understand them perfectly; I simply could not respond well, until recently. Because of that, they often discussed events in my presence. Things they might not have said if they had known I understood."

"What changed recently?"

"They developed the enhancement collar."

"The one you were wearing when we found you?"

"Yes."

"Where is it now?"

"The doctor removed it when he examined me."

She turned her attention to my guide. "Ensign Walker, go to the medical bay and secure that collar."

My guide jumped to her feet and raced to the door. "At once, sir."

When the door *whooshed* closed behind my guide, Captain Fielding rose, walked around the table and sat beside me. I swiveled my chair to face her and met her gaze. She studied my eyes with an intensity I had never experienced, and I struggled to remain still, to not squirm under that scrutiny.

She leaned forward and held out her hand. I frowned at it, sliding my gaze to her face. "Take it," she murmured. "Touch your hand to mine."

I laid my palm on hers, my flesh tingling at the warmth of another human's touch.

"I want you to understand something, Zara," she said, and I raised my eyes from our linked hands to her face. "You are not weak, and you are not stupid. You have survived, alone, on an alien world. That alone speaks of your strength and your intelligence. More than that, you are brave. You showed your courage when you warned me away without concern for your own safety."

She paused and tightened her fingers around mine. My soul glowed with her praise.

"The Bug-Eyes have continually underestimated us. Both you as an individual, and humanity as a whole. They will regret allowing us to take you back."

Her words puzzled me. "But they didn't..."

"They thought to trap us, but they underestimated you. They failed to take your courage and compassion into consideration. They also underestimated us, both our people and the capabilities of our ship. Finally, they failed to understand and value the treasure that you are."

Her meaning escaped me. "I do not see how I can be a treasure."

She grinned and released my hand. "I know you don't. You've been undervalued for as long as you can remember. But, if you will consent to help your people, I can guarantee you will be treated as royalty. You will be a queen among us."

Queen. That was a word I understood.

"I have no wish to rule humans."

"No, you wouldn't, and you won't. What I mean to convey is that you will be valued for your knowledge, for the insight you can provide. You not only understand the Bug-Eye language, you understand their culture. If you will help us, we can find a way to share this universe. Hopefully without extermination on either side."

I cocked my head and studied her. "I have a choice?"

She nodded, her expression grave. "You do. You have been a captive long enough." She stared past my shoulder. "We desperately need your knowledge, but I will not allow you to be forced. If you will explain what you know of the collar and will work with one of our linguists while we travel, I will personally put you ashore on an amenable colony before we reach Earth and I will ensure that no records remain of where you landed."

I stood and walked to the holoscreen, watching the images play while I considered.

"Are all humans like you and the doctor and the ensign?"

"The *Odyssey* has an excellent crew, but no, not all humans are alike. There are good people who are brave and true and strive to do the right, the honorable thing. But there are also bad people, and a lot more who are neither good nor bad, simply doing the best they can with what they have been given."

"I understand." I turned away from the beautiful images and walked back to Captain Fielding. "I have not known you, or any human, long, but I trust you. If you think I can help, then I will."

I held out my hand, and she grasped it firmly.

"I have dreamed of finding my people too long to desert them now."

Without releasing either my hand or my gaze, Captain Fielding activated her comm. "Bridge, this is Captain Fielding. Set our course for Earth, by the fastest route possible."

She laid her free hand on my shoulder and squeezed. "Welcome home, Zara."

My heart sang at her words. I was home!

PART XI

THE LOST COLONY

THE
LOST
COLONY

UNIVERSAL STAR LEAGUE
—— FILE FIVE ——

DEBBIE MUMFORD

1

Lieutenant Nick Adams strode across the carefully trimmed green lawns of the Headquarters of the Universal Star League. Located in the teeming city of New Atlantis on Earth's North American continent, the white marble and glass edifice glistened in the morning sun. Twenty stories tall, the building's footprint was immense, housing as it did the administrative offices of the Fleet, the Academy, and Nick's own service, Military Intelligence.

He jogged up the wide marble steps leading to the main entrance, his leather boots beating a clean, crisp rhythm against the stone. The gleaming glass doors *whooshed* open at his approach and he made his way briskly to the glide that would take him to Lieutenant Commander Popescu's office on the twelfth floor.

His superior officer had a new assignment for him, one she wouldn't trust to the USL's highly secure and very effective communications system. No, he'd been ordered to report in person this morning to receive a briefing on a complex and confidential assignment.

Excitement buzzed in his brain and sizzled through his blood. Adventure was afoot... and he was definitely the man for the job.

Whatever it was.

Nick had graduated top of his class from the Academy a few months earlier. He knew himself to be brilliant, insightful, and diabolically cunning. His academic record proved him to be the most able analyst USL had ever trained. Now it was up to him to prove himself in the field, which he intended to do quickly and efficiently.

After all, he was the best. If Nick Adams couldn't see a pattern or discern a motive, then it didn't exist.

Jumping off the glide, Nick strode across the thick, USL blue carpet, past old-fashioned oak doors set in plasteel walls disguised as dark green painted plaster panels with oak wainscoting. Stopping in front of the door labeled *Lieutenant Commander Elena Popescu, Military Intelligence,* Nick tugged his USL blue uniform jacket straight and brushed imaginary lint from the silver USL insignia and lieutenant's bars.

Satisfied that his appearance was in good order, he tucked his cap under his arm and knocked.

"Enter."

Nick opened the door, stepped through into a small, but neat office, boasting a large desk in front of a floor-to-ceiling view wall, a pair of visitor chairs, and a tall potted plant that might be some form of palm. Closing the door with a satisfying snap, he came to attention and saluted, calling out, "Sir. Lt. Nick Adams, reporting as ordered."

LCdr. Popescu, a petite woman in a neatly pressed uniform with her dark hair drawn into a sleek knot at the nape of her neck, glanced up from the document she was studying on a holoscreen embedded in the surface of her twenty-first century walnut desk. Nick felt sure the piece of furniture was actually made of plasteel. Lieutenant commanders weren't high enough up the food chain to rate real wood... even in Military Intelligence.

"At ease, Lieutenant Adams. Take a seat," she said, indicating one of the two dark wood, padded chairs facing her desk.

"Thank you, Commander." Nick folded himself into the seat, but did not relax his vigilance.

LCdr. Popescu blanked the holoscreen and leaned forward on her forearms, hands clasped. "What I have to tell you is not to be discussed outside this office."

Nick nodded, his pulse rate increasing.

"Captain Caren Fielding of the *USL Odyssey*, a deep space exploratory vessel, has delivered an extraordinary asset to MI." She paused, studying Nick's face. Satisfied with what she saw, she continued. "Vice Admiral Zhou has assigned the asset to our section, though other sections, including linguistics, will have regular access to her."

Nick's interest piqued. A female asset. With information valuable to linguistics. Interesting.

"You will interview the asset, determine her native colony, and, if possible, her identity."

"Excuse me?"

Popescu smiled. "So you haven't heard any scuttlebutt regarding this asset?"

Nick shook his head, frowning. "No, Commander. Should I?"

"No, Lieutenant, you shouldn't," she said, relaxing back into her chair. "But, given your reputation, I thought if anyone had ferreted it out, it would be you."

Nick wasn't sure whether to be complimented or insulted, but he kept his expression carefully neutral, and nodded, waiting for her to give him more information.

LCdr. Popescu continued, "The asset, a young woman known as Zara, has been a captive of the Bug-Eyes since early childhood. As far as she knows, she is the only survivor of a colony that was attacked and destroyed when she was about four years old."

"A Bug-Eye captive?" Nick blurted, his eyes widening, pulse thundering. "Are you sure?" He fought to bring himself under control, schooled his expression, and apologized for his outburst. "Sorry, Sir."

"That's quite all right, Lieutenant. Zara represents a huge question mark to the entire USL, which is why we have been assigned to research and check her story. She was young enough at the time of her capture that she has no idea which colony she belonged to."

Nick's mind whirled with questions. Some he would ask this Zara in his interview, others he would have to discover for himself.

"And Capt. Fielding believed her story?" he asked.

"She found no reason not to," Popescu responded. "The *Odyssey* rescued Zara from a remote moon where she had been placed by the Bug-Eyes." She paused, watching his reaction, and seemingly satisfied, continued. "The young woman was used as bait. Only Zara's warning and Capt. Fielding's fast action saved the *Odyssey*."

Nick frowned, leaning forward. "I've never heard of the Bug-Eyes attempting to take captives before."

"Which is probably why their trap was so deficient."

"But why make the attempt now?"

"According to Zara, the Bug-Eyes are concerned over the loss of their flagship at the Battle for Absaroka. They believed their new weapons would render them invulnerable to our species." She smiled, though the expression was hardly a happy one. "We've risen in their esteem. They want to know more about us and our capabilities."

LCdr. Popescu rose, and Nick followed her lead. Walking around her desk, she extended her hand to him, he clasped it firmly and, after a single brisk shake, released it.

"Good luck, Lt. Adams. My aide will assist you in scheduling your first meeting with Zara. Be discreet, and be careful in your dealings with her. Remember, if what she tells us is true, this young woman has had very little contact with humans. She is unfamiliar with our customs and our history. You may find her very difficult to read."

"Understood, sir," Nick replied. "And, sir?"

"Yes, Lieutenant?"

"Thank you for trusting me with this mission."

LCdr. Popescu nodded and motioned to the door. "You are dismissed, Lt. Adams."

2

Two days later Nick Adams entered one of the posh apartments in the headquarters building that were kept in ready for visiting planetary dignitaries. One had been set aside for the asset's use. When the female ensign assigned to act as her aide ushered him into the living area, he noted appreciatively that Zara had been given one of the best suites. Rose-brown carpet so plush his boots sank into the pile, tasteful furnishings that spoke of old world elegance, actual paintings on the walls instead of the more standard changeable holo-screens, and floor-to-ceiling windows that looked out on the great forested park behind the gleaming edifice.

Someone wanted to ensure this woman's comfort and contentment among her own people.

Nick understood the impulse.

He'd spent the intervening time refreshing his knowledge of the Bug-Eye incursions into human occupied space in general, and the Battle for Absaroka in particular. The enemy had chosen that lightly populated, and to its mind lightly defended, planet to experiment with a new and deadly weapon. Only the intuitive grasp of the situation on the part of the planetary war chief, coupled with her willingness to sacrifice herself for her people had won the day. Absaroka had lost a valiant warrior, but the planet had survived to provide valuable information to USL Command.

That defeat had also led to Zara's recovery, and from the reports Nick had read, her knowledge of the Bug-Eyes and their social systems was unparalleled, and therefore priceless.

He had read Capt. Fielding's report on Zara's rescue and their subsequent interactions. And he had viewed the holograms of her initial intake screening. The young woman had arrived on the *Odyssey* naked, bruised, and scarred. She had also been entirely hairless: her head shaved, her eyebrows and lashes removed, and her pubic ridge denuded.

Nick, who prided himself on his emotional detachment and a certain worldly acceptance of the times he found himself in, had been appalled. Zara might be a spy, brainwashed by the enemy and allowed to be rescued in order to wreak havoc among her own kind, but there was no doubt she'd been captive, poorly treated, and tortured.

Even with advance preparation, Nick failed to stifle a gasp and the automatic reaction of turning his eyes away when she entered the room. Flushing and swearing silently, he mastered himself and came to attention.

"Lt. Nick Adams, ma'am. LCdr. Popescu has asked me to assist you in finding your identity."

Zara smiled, a wistful expression that did nothing to diminish the power of her presence. For even before she uttered a word, the strength of her personality pervaded the room. She was casually dressed in dark leggings, a pale green tunic, and a paisley scarf of muted colors. Her feet were bare. Of average height, perhaps five-six or five-seven, she was slender and lithe and bore herself with dignity.

Nick wondered where the captive had learned that innate self-respect.

Her hair had begun to grow out, honey blonde and perhaps two inches in length, the bones of her facial structure were fine, her eyes a clear blue.

She would have been a beautiful woman were it not for the scars crisscrossing her face and every other portion of exposed skin. Their evidence even carried into her soft hair, causing streaks of premature white amid the honey blonde strands.

"Please be seated, Lt. Adams. I have been briefed on your assignment and am ready to assist in any way I can."

Nick forced his eyes away from his scrutiny of her person and met her gaze. "Thank you, Zara. May I call you Zara?" He selected a comfortable looking padded chair and sat.

"You may," she said quietly, seating herself on a creamy blue sofa across from him. "You may also continue your scrutiny. I am accustomed to being observed."

"Forgive my rudeness," he said, flushing yet again. "I didn't mean to offend."

"No offense was offered," she said, inclining her head, "and none was taken. I have learned that humans find my appearance... disconcerting. I accept that fact."

Nick released the breath he'd been holding and nodded. "You were tortured, then."

She frowned, her newly grown eyebrows drawing together. "Tortured?" she asked. "Not intentionally, no."

Nick's eyes widened in surprise, his own eyebrows shooting toward his hairline. "Then how..."

"Forgive me," she said, thoughtfully. "I am still learning to interpret your meanings, to understand your ways. Perhaps I am mistaken. Does torture not require a certain malice? An intent to do harm to the person undergoing the torture?"

Nick nodded. "Yes. Those things were not present when you were... mistreated?"

Her full, lovely lips curved upward in the smallest of smiles. "No. My keepers, while not precisely concerned with my comfort, were nonetheless making an honest effort to care for me. Being a species with a nearly indestructible exoskeleton, they found my tender skin mystifying."

"Then all the scars on your body..."

"Came from their attempts to cleanse me and make me

presentable. They were horrified by how easily my skin tore, by the dark colors that would appear for no apparent reason."

"For no apparent reason?" Nick echoed, unbelievingly.

She laughed at his confusion. "Certainly for no reason they understood. The taps which caused me to bruise wouldn't even be felt by one of their kind."

Nick closed his eyes. He couldn't imagine a small child enduring the amount of abuse this woman must have borne.

"I am sorry for your suffering, Zara," he said quietly, searching for a question that would move the interview to a new topic. He asked the first thing that occurred. "You speak standard very well for someone who has been away from it so long. May I ask how you kept the language fresh in your mind?"

Her expression brightened. "Of course! It was my educational device." At his blank look, she jumped to her feet, moving quickly away from the sitting area. "Wait. I'll show you."

When she returned a few moments later, she handed Nick a small tablet of the type he himself had used as a child.

"The warrior who captured me found this in my home. He gave it to my keepers thinking it might be of use in determining my care." She gazed fondly at the device, then raised her eyes to meet Nick's. "It was useless to them since they understood neither our writing nor our spoken language, but it was invaluable to me."

"And they allowed you to keep it?" he asked, amazed at the stupidity of a species that the USL considered highly intelligent.

Zara shrugged and resumed her seat. "It calmed me, and they thought it contained no more than nursery songs and pictures of my home world, neither of which threatened them."

"But this unit contains far more than that," Nick objected, studying her intently. "If it's similar to the one I used, it contains a data base and courses of study to prepare a student for university."

"Exactly," she said, her expression shrewd. "But I never allowed my keepers to see it as more than a toy, a reminder of my lost life."

His respect for her intelligence and cunning increased exponentially.

"Capt. Fielding's report stated that you can both understand and speak the Bug-Eye language."

"Not precisely," she said. "I understand their language and can translate it accurately, but I can only speak it intelligibly when wearing the collar my keepers designed for me."

"Of course," he said, remembering the notation in the report. "I believe we have scientists attempting to reverse engineer the device now." She nodded, and he continued, "You're also working with Linguistics to teach our best people to understand and translate."

"Correct, though it is a slow process. They would learn faster through immersion, though I wouldn't wish my captivity on anyone."

He nodded, and felt for the test packet in his pocket. It was time to end this interview, but he needed a DNA sample before he could move to the next phase of his investigation.

"I know the doctor on the *Odyssey* took blood samples, but I'd like to collect a fresh cheek swab to test your DNA." He pulled the packet from his pocket and held it out for her inspection. "Will you permit this?"

She stared at the packet, but didn't take it, frowning slightly, puzzled by the request. "For what purpose?"

"Your DNA will help us identify the colony you came from. All colonists are tested, their DNA recorded. Those records are kept in the administrative offices of the USL's Colonial Bureau. Even if you were born on the colony, your DNA should help us identify your parents, who are undoubtedly listed in the Bureau's records."

"I see," she said, nodding. "This... *swab*... may allow you to tell me who my parents were?"

Nick nodded. "Better than that, it may help us determine if you have any living relatives."

She gasped. "Living relatives?" Her complexion paled, and she closed her eyes. "Forgive me. I never considered that such a thing might be possible.

Crap, Nick thought.

"I'm sorry," he said quickly. "I shouldn't have gotten your hopes up. It's unlikely I'll find anyone in your family still living."

She opened her eyes and laughed, the first truly happy sound he'd heard. "Don't worry, Lt. Adams. It's very hard to disappoint someone who has learned to always expect the worst." She leaned forward. "By all means, take your sample."

3

Nick studied the holoscreen in the research carrel he'd been assigned in the Colonial Bureau's Hall of Records. The carrel was actually a small enclosure with glass walls that could be blanked for privacy. The charcoal gray plasteel work surface gleamed in the soft, even lighting and the ergonomically correct chair supported his body efficiently, if not precisely comfortably.

He'd inserted Zara's DNA profile into computer system, and the vast database now searched for matches, both exact and familial. While the system worked, Nick ran a parallel program searching for colonies that had failed to report for more than a decade. Since regular reports were not a requirement for colonization, he doubted this particular enquiry would be fruitful. Colonies often ignored the Bureau unless a catastrophic event forced them to request USL assistance.

As expected, his search returned dozens of possibilities. He needed more details. Before he left Zara's apartment, he'd examined her educational device, hoping that the manufacturing stamp would provide a clue as to its colony of origin, but that too came up empty. The tablet had been manufactured on Excelsior, like almost all of the Fleet's electronic equipment, and shipped to the Colonial Bureau at

New Atlantis on Earth. From there it had been added to stores and loaded onto a colony ship.

The Bureau kept track of lots and crates, but not of individual units.

The only meaningful information Nick had to go on was Zara's DNA, and that search could run for days.

He'd just decided to take a walk and find the Bureau's cafeteria, when the holoscreen lit and two 3-D images appeared in the air above the work surface. The images revolved slowly to allow viewing from all angles. Nick sat back down, staring at the couple before fingering their data onto a second holoscreen beside their images.

The woman strongly resembled Zara... an unscarred Zara, but the slant of her eyes and the shape of her nose weren't quite right.

Nick glanced at the man. Yes. His eyes and nose matched Zara's more closely.

The woman's hair was platinum blonde; the man's a light chestnut; Zara's honey blonde a blend of the two. Both her parents were young, healthy specimens in their holo-depictions. Vibrant young lives that had been cut far too short.

Satisfied with his visual review of the images, Nick turned to the written report.

Annalise Cole and Holger Martinsen had been married less than a year when they boarded the colony ship *USL Hope's Horizon* bound for Kapteyn 5. Holger, from Earth's Scandinavian region, and Annalise, from Moon Base Alpha, had met in New Atlantis when both completed internship years in the Colonial Bureau's recruitment division. They'd intended to recruit others to colonize, but had decided to take the plunge themselves.

A fatal decision for themselves, and life-changing for their daughter, as it turned out.

Copying the images and data for his report, Nick blanked the holoscreens and began a new search for information about the colony on Kapteyn 5.

Before he left the Hall of Records, Nick recorded every scrap of information available on the USL colony designated Terranova:

population, climate, geophysical characteristics, even a complete analysis of survey data, including soil and mineral compositions. He also found a few records of births (written only, no DNA had been transmitted) that had occurred during the colony's first two years. Including one for a baby girl born to Holger and Annalise Martinsen, Sara Elise Martinsen.

Nick had completed his mission. He knew Zara's identity, Sara Elise Martinsen, and her native colony, Terranova on Kapteyn 5. Having found her birth record, he even knew her age. Zara was twenty-four standard years old. She had spent twenty years in captivity.

But it was what he didn't know that worried him.

Why had the Bug-Eyes destroyed that particular colony? The aggressive aliens had originally invaded USL space more than seventy years ago. The fleet had beaten them back. Barely, and at great cost... but they hadn't been heard from again until the Battle of Absaroka, nearly two years ago.

At least, the USL hadn't been aware of any further incursions.

Now it seemed that the Bug-Eyes had destroyed a human colony twenty years ago, and then retreated into their own region of space.

Why?

What, if anything, had Terranova done to threaten the aliens?

Nick had the feeling that when he reported to LCdr. Popescu tomorrow, his mission parameters would be expanded.

4

Nick arrived at LCdr. Popescu's office promptly at 0900. Her aide ushered him into the commander's office immediately. The door had barely closed behind him before Nick snapped to attention and saluted.

"Sir. Lt. Nick Adams, ready to report."

"At ease, Lieutenant." LCdr. Popescu stood with her back to the room, gazing out of the view wall. She turned, and motioning Nick into one of the visitor chairs, took her own place behind her desk. "That was fast work, Adams. I hadn't expected a report so soon. What have you learned?"

Nick handed her a printed copy of his full report, succinctly summing up his findings verbally.

LCdr. Popescu paged through the print-out as he spoke, nodding at the mention of Zara's name and colony. When he finished, she met his gaze. "And what was your impression of the asset?"

Nick relaxed into the chair. If the commander was asking his opinion, she'd found his report acceptable. "I found Zara compelling and believable," he said. "I'm sure the USL will request a full psychological work-up, but I found no reason not to accept her as what she claims to be... a captive who has been restored to her people."

Popescu nodded. "We are in agreement." She flipped a page in his report before asking, "What do you see as our next step, Lieutenant?"

Brushing a hand through his hair, Nick frowned. "I'd like to follow up on a few items that puzzle me."

"Such as?"

"Why the Bug-Eyes felt the need to destroy that particular colony, and why they felt the need to obtain a specimen for study. Nothing in my research indicates that the colony had any dealings with the aliens, and I didn't find any indication of particularly rich veins of valuable or unusual minerals."

He paused, shifted in his chair, and continued. "And taking captives for study is outside their prior dealings with humanity."

"I agree, those are puzzling points. What else?"

"I'd also like to follow up with a reference I found to a trader from Terranova. He seems to have been off-planet at the time of the attack. If he knew the colony had been eradicated, why didn't he report the loss? Why ignore the deaths of everyone he knew?

LCdr. Popescu frowned. "Excellent questions." She closed her eyes, tapping her lips with an index finger as she pondered. "Yes. Further inquiry is called for. Consider the resolution of these questions your next assignment: why Terranova; why take a captive; and who is this trader and what did he know?"

She stood and nodded toward the door. Nick stood as well, recognizing a dismissal when he saw one. Turning with military precision, he strode to the door.

"Lt. Adams," LCdr. Popescu called.

Nick paused and turned, one eyebrow raised in question. "Sir?"

"Well done."

"Thank you, sir." With a sharp salute, he left the lieutenant commander's office.

5

Nick went straight to his desk in the Office of Analysis and Decryption. His cubicle was neither spacious nor private, but the room was usually quiet as the analysts tended to become immersed in their various projects.

Opening his holoscreen, he moved directly into the information he'd gleaned on the Terranova trader. Soren Ivarrson, captain and sole owner of the registered trading vessel *Brisk Venture*. A quick records search found that the *Venture* had been docked on Optimus V at the estimated time of Zara's capture. Nick was able to trace the movements of Capt. Ivarrson and the *Venture* for another few weeks before both the vessel and the man disappeared.

Undaunted, Nick entered Ivarrson's DNA into the system and searched the Space Registry database (ownership records for all non-fleet spacefaring vessels), the Immigration database (records of change of citizenship from one colony to another), and the Inter-Colonial Crime Detection exchange (ICCD), USL's law enforcement database. If Ivarrson was still living, Nick would find the man.

Scrutinizing the records of Ivarrson's final recorded year, Nick suspected that something had frightened the trader into going underground. The man could change his name and the *Venture's* registration, but he couldn't change his DNA. Fortunately for Ivarrson, DNA records were classified. Only a USL officer with sufficient clearance could access that data.

Nick's hunch proved correct when he found a DNA match to one Mitchell Preston, citizen of Proxima Prime, and captain of the *Lucky Fortune*. A little more digging, and Nick discovered that the *Lucky Fortune* was currently docked Earth-side, with her captain listed as berthing at the Spacefarer's Rest, a cheap lodging house in the space-port district of... New Atlantis!

Grinning, Nick wiped his research and left the administration building. Jogging across the USL campus to his quarters, he breathed in the sweet smell of success along with fresh air scented by the nearby forest and beds of blooming spring flowers. New Atlantis maintained scrupulous standards when it came to scrubbing the air for noxious odors and pollutants. Gone were the bad old days when the atmosphere around major metropolitan cities was polluted with smog and industrial gases.

Breathing easily and excited by his progress, Nick palmed the door to his quarters and stepped inside. Quickly changing from his uniform to casual dark brown slacks, deep burgundy short-sleeved pullover shirt, and a stylish faux leather retro-bomber jacket, Nick reviewed the questions he intended to put to Ivarrson/Preston.

An hour later, Nick stood in the lobby of the Spacefarer's Rest. Accessing one of their intercom units, he buzzed Preston's berth. A bleary-eyed man in his early fifties appeared on the small holoscreen. His salt-and-pepper hair was disheveled and he sported a distinctly scruffy beard shadow.

"Preston," he answered, then peered at his screen. "Do I know you?"

"No, sir," Nick replied. "Sorry to disturb your rest. I was told you might be able to help me with a... well, a delicate proposition. Do you have time for a cup of java and some conversation?"

As Nick had hoped, the man's eyes lit at the mention of a delicate proposition.

"Sure. Just give me a minute to pull myself together."

"No problem. Shall we meet around the corner at the Helios Café?" Nick asked. "I'm buying, of course."

"Of course. I'll join you in a few." Preston ended the transmission.

Whistling tunelessly, Nick pushed his way through streets crowded with travelers and residents in many forms of dress from myriad colonies. He recognized the flowing, brightly colored garb of Cenatuarans, the elaborate, though drably colored, headdresses of Seti, and the distinctive wetsuits (so ill-advised in New Atlantis' warm climate) of the water dwellers of Aquarius. Other interesting, and odd to his eyes, folks mingled with the known, but the crowd moved along easily, people weaving purposefully toward their own destinations.

With little effort, Nick found the Helios Café, secured a two-top table, and ordered two cups of java. Coffee, real coffee brewed from beans grown from actual soil, wasn't available in the dives that served this district, but java was an acceptable alternative. The taste was unremarkable, but drinkable, and the non-alcoholic brew wouldn't dull the senses.

By the time the java was served, Preston had joined Nick. The man looked much better than his holo. He'd shaved, combed his hair, and dressed in a black tunic and pants. His expression, no longer sleep-fogged, was alert and interested.

"Mitch Preston," he said, extending his hand, "and you are?"

Nick shook the offered hand. "Nick Adams. Glad to meet you, Mr. Preston."

Preston nodded and took the seat opposite Nick. "What can I do for you, Adams?"

Nick picked up his cup of java and sipped, studying Preston over the rim. Taking his time, he replaced the cup on the table, and folded his hands.

"You can tell me why you changed your name, Capt. Ivarrson," he said quietly, but firmly, "and what you know about the destruction of Terranova."

The man flinched, the color draining from his face. He made a move to stand, but Nick grabbed his arm, refusing to let go when

Preston tried to shake him off. After a moment, he settled back into his chair. Nick released him.

"Where did you hear that name? Either of those names?" Preston asked, a bit unsteadily.

"I've done my homework," Nick said with a shrug, lifting his cup and drinking again. Giving Preston the illusion of safely.

"Why do you care?"

"Let's just say it's an area of interest." Nick placed his cup back on the table and met the other man's gaze squarely. "Look, I'm not interested in revealing your identity. I just want to know what you know about Terranova... and whether or not what happened to that colony caused you to do a disappearing act."

Preston lowered his gaze, picked up his cup and sipped the steaming liquid. Placing the ceramic cup back on the table, he stared into the dark depths of the java. After a long moment, he nodded, raised his eyes, and met Nick's gaze.

"I was an original colonist on Terranova. Our colony ship carried my trading vessel in pieces in its hold. My trade charter was listed with the Colonial Office. I was just getting my trade runs established when the colony governor called me to her office."

Preston paused, sipped his java, eyes clouded with memory. Nick maintained his silence, unwilling to risk interrupting the flow of the man's thoughts.

"One of the miners had found an unknown ore. A substance not listed in the original survey data. The planetary geologist had also been unable to identify it. The governor gave me a sample and the geologist's preliminary report and asked me to convey the packet to a more established world. The geologist suggested the university on Optimus V. He felt the staff there would have a good chance of telling us what we'd found."

Nick nodded. "I discovered that you'd been on Optimus V at the time we believe the attack was carried out. Were they able to identify the substance."

Preston shook his head. "I never delivered the sample." He swirled the remaining liquid in his cup, watching the motion intently.

"I'd just docked when a distress call came in from Terranova, from the governor's office."

He looked up, his expression angry. "I heard them die. Heard the bugs unholy chittering. Heard her scream of pain, then the crackle of flames."

Nick glanced at his own cup. "You were close to the governor?"

"She was my wife."

Silence engulfed their small corner of the café. Beyond their table, people chatted and laughed, ate and drank. Utensils scraped ceramics, sounds of cooking and frying leaked from the kitchen. Waitstaff bustled between the tables.

Yet Nick and Preston sat enveloped by the ghosts of a long dead colony. A lost colony. One that only Soren Ivarrson, now Mitch Preston, and an asset named Zara had survived.

After an interminable moment, Nick spoke. "What happened to the sample and the report?"

Preston rubbed his eyes, as though he could erase the memory, the image of his wife's death from his mind. "I carried them around for a month or so while I made arrangements to disappear, then I stashed them on a planet and stayed as far away from their hiding place as I could."

"Why didn't you report the attack?"

"What good would it have done?"

A surge of anger thrummed through Nick's veins. He glared at the other man. "You might have saved other colonies. Didn't it occur to you that if the bugs had attacked once, they might attack again?"

Preston glared back. "Did they?" he asked. "Did anyone not of Terranova die?"

Nick's anger deflated. "No," he admitted. "But we might have looked for her sooner."

"What?" Preston's hand jerked, sloshing java onto the table top. "Who? Someone made it out alive?"

Nick silently cursed himself. He hadn't meant to mention Zara to this man.

"It's nothing," he said. "You wouldn't know her. She was just a child at the time."

"Who wouldn't I know?" Preston persisted. "How did she survive? I've seen what the bugs did to Terranova."

"Forget it," Nick said, louder than he'd intended. "Just tell me where that packet is and go back to your new life."

Preston reached across the table and grabbed Nick's jacket. "Listen, asshole! You searched me out. I didn't ask for this. Not for any of it. If you want that packet, you'll tell me who survived and how."

Nick jerked out of Preston's hold. "Come with me," he said, standing and dropping credits on the table to pay for the java. "I don't have the authority to make that call, but I know who does."

Preston's expression was grim, his color high, as he stood and nodded. "Lead on."

6

Soren Ivarrson, also known as Mitch Preston, paled as he and Nick approached the massive USL administrative complex. "You didn't tell me you were with USL."

Nick gave him a sideways glance. "Would you have met me for java if I'd shown up in uniform?"

Preston grimaced. "Probably not."

The pair stopped on the marble steps leading to the main entrance.

"You don't have to go in," Nick said. "You can just give me the information on the sample and go back to your life."

Preston stared up at the marble and glass edifice and shook his head. "You've resurrected the ghosts," he said quietly. "I need to see this through. For Emma's sake."

Emma Preston. The colonial governor of Terranova. Of course. Ivarrson's choice of surname hadn't been random. He'd kept her alive in his name. The ghosts had never been far.

Nick nodded. "Let's get this deal done." He escorted Preston through security and up to the twelfth floor and LCdr. Popescu's office.

"Military intelligence?" Preston whispered as they approached Popescu's aide. Nick gave a curt nod.

Stopping before the aide's desk, he asked, "Is the commander in? I have an asset who'd like to make a request."

The young woman glanced at Nick, smiled, and then turned her attention to Preston. After a moment's study, she activated a voice-only communicator and said, "Commander, Lt. Adams and a civilian request a moment of your time."

Nick couldn't hear the response, but the aide said, "Of course, sir." Clicking the communicator off, the aide rose and escorted the men to LCdr. Popescu's door.

When the door closed behind them, Nick said, "Thank you for seeing us, sir."

Popescu stood behind her desk and waved the men forward. "Please, have a seat. Lieutenant, why are you out of uniform?"

Nick and Preston sat in the visitor chairs, while Popescu resumed her seat behind the desk, hands clasped on its surface.

"It seemed like the best tactic at the time, Commander," Nick said. "I didn't intend to end up in your office again quite so soon."

"Understood. Now, please introduce this gentleman and tell me what I can do for you."

"This is the trader I mentioned earlier. At the time of the incident, he was known as Soren Ivarrson. Now he goes by Mitch Preston."

Popescu quirked an eyebrow, but said mildly, "A pleasure, Mr. Preston."

"Preston, this is Lieutenant Commander Elena Popescu, Military Intelligence."

Preston inclined his head. "Ma'am."

"All right. Now that everyone knows each other, let me tell you what's happened." Nick gave his superior officer an abbreviated report on his research and his discussion with Preston.

When he finished, he added, "My apologies, sir. I had no right to allude to the asset. The comment just slipped out. And now Preston is refusing to cooperate further until I give him the identity of the other survivor."

"And tell me how he or she survived," Preston blurted out.

"I see," said Popescu. "Did your DNA research indicate kinship?"

"That doesn't matter," Preston said before Nick could reply. "We were a small colony. I was married to the governor. I knew everyone. I deserve to know who survived and how."

Nick ground his teeth, but kept silent. This was out of his hands.

Popescu leaned back, studying Preston, one long forefinger tapping her lower lip. After a moment, she activated her communicator and said, "Ensign Rand, please see if Zara is available for company."

"Zara?" Preston asked.

"You would know her as Sara Elise Martinsen," Popescu replied. "Lt. Adams only recently discovered her birth name."

"I don't understand."

"She was taken captive by the aliens," Popescu said, her voice calm and controlled. "One of our exploratory vessels rescued her a few months ago. We've been trying to piece together her history ever since."

Preston turned his attention on Nick. "You mean you didn't know about Terranova? Not until..."

"Not until I started researching Zara," Nick finished, giving Preston a haughty glare. "It would've been nice if you'd told us about it twenty years ago."

"That will do, Lt. Adams," Popescu said sharply. "What's done is done. Right now we need to find our way forward."

———

LCdr. Elena Popescu escorted Lt. Adams and Soren Ivarrson, now known as Mitch Preston, to Zara's quarters. As they neared the door to her rooms, Popescu stopped and fixed Preston with a commanding gaze.

"You will remember, Mr. Preston, that Zara was a captive for twenty years, for very nearly her entire life. You will control yourself. You will not cause her undue distress. You may not be under my command, but I will personally hold you accountable for your actions once we enter her rooms."

He nodded, though he looked a bit queasy. "I understand." Wiping his hands on his trousers and then raking his fingers through his hair, he said, "I'm ready."

Popescu nodded, placed a palm on the door panel, and announced herself. The door *whooshed* open.

When Nick followed the other two inside, he found Zara standing before the view wall, dressed in a gauzy blue lounge robe over deeper blue leggings and an ice white tunic. Her very short hair glowed against the backdrop of the deep green forest beyond the wall. Glancing from one to another of her guests, she appeared calm and relaxed, completely at home.

"LCdr. Popescu. Lt. Adams," she said, warmly. "Welcome. Please be at ease and introduce me to your friend."

Nick moved to the seating area, observing Preston as he did so. The man's face had blanched and his hands had begun to tremble. Nick was about to take his arm and guide him to a seat, when the man shook himself and stepped forward.

"Sara," he said, the hint of a smile curving his lips. "I'd know you anywhere. You look just like your mother." He stepped closer and held out his hand. "No, that's not quite true. I can see traces of Holger in your face as well."

Zara's calm fled. Her face paled and she stepped back a pace. "I'm sorry," she whispered. "Who are you?"

Preston dropped his hand to his side, shaking his head. "No. Of course. I'm the one who should be sorry. You were little more than a baby the last time I saw you. You would've known me as Uncle Soren, but that was a long time ago."

She closed her eyes and lowered herself to the sofa, reaching out and finding the seat by feel. After a moment, she whispered, "Auntie Em." Opening her eyes, she studied the strange man. "Uncle Soren and Auntie Em."

His smile transformed his face, startling Nick with a glimpse of the young man he had once been. "Yes," he said with a laugh. "That's right."

"But how?"

LCdr. Popescu answered, filling the breathless gap. "Lt. Adams' research discovered another survivor of Terranova. Soren Ivarrson was a trader. He was off planet when the attack took place. He just happened to be on Earth for business. Actually, right here in New Atlantis. Lt. Adams was able to make contact today. When he learned of your existence, your uncle asked to see you."

Zara touched her face, her hair, and for the first time, Nick saw a hint of embarrassment about her appearance.

"And... and you recognize me?"

Soren smiled. "I recognize your resemblance to your mother." He glanced at the others, including them in his remarks. "I'm not an uncle by blood, but her mother, Annalise, and my Emma were best friends. They grew up together in the Lunar colony. Moon Base Alpha." He turned his attention back to Zara. "You look just like her, except around the eyes and nose." He grinned. "Those are pure Holger."

Zara rose, tears sparkling in her eyes. Soren rose as well. Cautiously, they moved toward each other, until like two magnets drawn irresistibly together, they were in each other's arms.

"Oh, my baby girl," Soren whispered. "I can't believe you're alive."

"You knew my parents," Zara said, her voice choked with emotion. "You recognize me... and know my name. Even I didn't know my name until a few days ago."

He kissed her very short and oddly streaked hair. "I know you. I know where you came from, and, if you'll let me, I'd like to be a surrogate father for you."

Tears streaked her face. "I don't even know what a father is," she sobbed. "Not really." She stepped out of his embrace and wiped her face. A smile blossomed, watered by her tears. "But I'd like you to help me find out."

Soren laughed. "I've never been a father," he admitted, his expression sobering. "I lost the chance when Emma died with Terranova."

He inhaled deeply, regaining control, and let it out in a quick sigh. Then he smiled at her again. "Shall we figure it out together?"

She rushed back into his arms and buried her face against his tunic. "Deal!"

Popescu tapped Nick's shoulder, pulling his attention away from the drama unfolding before him. She motioned to the door, and he nodded. Standing, he followed her quietly from the room.

EPILOGUE

A week later, armed with the coordinates provided by Soren Ivarrson (for the Terranova trader had once again assumed his original identity), Lt. Nick Adams took a cruiser to recover the lost colony's mysterious ore sample and its attendant report. He hadn't yet discovered why the Bug-Eyes had targeted Terranova for destruction, but with that sample in hand, he felt certain the answer would be within his grasp. It was only a matter of time.

Zara and her colony were no longer lost.

He'd accomplished his mission, and— as always— he'd done it admirably.

PART XII

EREMITE

EREMITE

UNIVERSAL STAR LEAGUE
— FILE SIX —

DEBBIE MUMFORD

1

I am Eremite.

The One Who Sees All has sent me forth from the Mountain to gather data on an intrusion that will soon happen.

My journey has been long. I have been severed from my kin.

I am alone.

And yet, The One Who Sees All is with me. The One receives my data and provides instruction.

I am solitary, but not excluded.

The One Who Sees All chose me to be Eremite. The One saw in me an unusual propensity for movement, a shameful hungering to roll, to explore. Our kind do not enjoy movement. I am unique. Many of my kin say my desires are an abomination. But The One takes advantage of all skills and desires found within the Mountain.

Though I am separated from the Mountain, yet I am of the Mountain. My uniqueness serves The One Who Sees All. The One tells me I am not an abomination; that my shameful desire will be the salvation of the Mountain.

The One sees all; I exist to serve The One.

I have endured scorching days when I was locked to the land, unable to move. I tried to rest, to hibernate as is our way. I endured.

Alone.

Without the shared shielding of my kin. Without the sheltering protection of the Mountain. Awaiting the cool darkness that would free me to roll still further from all that I have known.

I cling to my uniqueness. To the knowledge that my shame will save my kin. The One has spoken. The One knows all.

Never before in the history of our kind has one of us existed alone for so long, separated by time and space. I long for the comfort of my kin's close proximity, surrounding me with insulating cool, with calming dark, with solidarity.

But I persist. I must. I am the only one capable of this great task. The One has told me.

Finally, when I feel my consciousness must be crushed beneath the weight of solitude, The One prepares me.

They come.

D r. Jessamyn Davis stepped from the shuttle craft onto the hard baked soil of the eighth planet of the Keptayn system. Keptayn, a blue hypergiant star, burned so hot that even at this distance the planet was assumed to be dead. Dr. Davis, the astrobiologist assigned to the research vessel *USL Carl Sagan*, hoped to disprove that assumption.

A petite woman in her mid-forties, Dr. Davis had studied the limits of life on Earth's oldest and most sterile desert, the Atacama. She had learned that life could exist in even the harshest environments. Glancing around at the barren, flat landscape, the very soil leached of all color by the blazing sun beating against its surface, her hope faltered. She despaired of finding even microscopic life.

This planet made the Atacama look cool and inviting.

Glancing at the comp read-out attached to the left forearm of her exo-suit, she saw that the temperature gauge read 150 degrees Celsius. A quick calculation put the Fahrenheit equivalent at roughly 300. Hot by anyone's standards. Fortunately, her skin-tight protective gear included a highly effective cooling system; Jess remained cool and comfortable in this inhospitable environment.

Even the helmet of this exo-suit was acceptable. She'd worn some older models where the helmet interfered with her vision and the gloves were so thick she could barely adjust her instruments. These gloves were like a second skin. She could pick up a single flake of stone if needed.

Her two research assistants and the away team assigned by Capt. Shin to protect them clambered out of the shuttle to join her on the desolate ground.

Lieutenant Vic Rosslyn, an eager young officer anxious to excel in this, his first command of an away team, stepped to her side. "How do you want to proceed, Dr. Davis?"

"If you'd have your team set up the temporary shelter, my assistants will be able to put our research station in order." She shaded her eyes with one hand and nodded toward the left horizon. "I want to check out that big boulder over there. See if I can find any clues as to how a single rock, especially one of that size, ended up on an otherwise uniformly flat plain."

"I'll accompany you," Lt. Rosslyn said. "Just give me a minute to get the crew started."

3

Even through the stupor of mid-day heat, I felt their presence. Ephemeral entities that buzzed around me at unthinkable speeds, emitting high-pitched, irritating sound waves that impinged on my light- and heat-induced hibernation.

Only the knowledge that The One Who Sees All had anticipated their coming saved me from madness. I transmitted my impressions to The One, for that was the purpose for which The One had sent me forth. I was to collect the data The One would need in order to determine if these entities, these flitting, screeching *things*, could possibly be sapient.

I doubted the likelihood.

How could anything so insubstantial, anything that moved so fast, be capable of deliberate thought?

Inconceivable.

But The One required data. When darkness fell and cooler temperatures released the bonds binding me to the ground, I would investigate, as was my duty and my privilege, for I am Eremite.

The One called me. The Mountain relies on me. I will not fail in my responsibility.

4

As Jess approached the boulder, Lt. Rosslyn stepped in front of her, laser weapon drawn.

"Really?" she asked, expression incredulous behind her faceplate. "It's a rock, Lieutenant."

Rosslyn glanced at her from the side of his helmet. "You don't know that, Dr. Davis. We're here to determine exactly what it is."

"Fine," she said in a scathing tone. "Protect me from the rock while I take some samples." She reached for the core drill attached to her exo-suit's utility belt, while Lt. Rosslyn stood guard.

5

My hibernation-hazed consciousness took note that two of the entities had ceased their frantic movements and stood quietly before me. Groggily, I transmitted the data to The One.

The One calmed my fears. All would be well. I was an emissary of The One, sent to do the bidding of my Mountain.

Dazed from hibernation and still locked in place by the heat and light of the sun that blazed above me, I failed to notice the strange instrument the incorporeal one held until it was too late. The ephemeral placed the device against my skin. A tortuous buzzing sound grated against my consciousness...

...and pain such as none of my kind had ever imagined jolted me loose from my day-side imprisonment.

I jumped.

I rolled away from the strange bringer of pain.

I screamed aloud to The One, to my Mountain kin...

...and The One answered!

Bestirring the hibernating Mountain, The One caused them all to come to my aid.

They jumped.

They rolled.

The Mountain, which had never done so in the living memory of our kind, moved.

6

Jess switched the core drill off. She'd barely scratched the rock's surface, but something had happened. Something she didn't understand.

"Did you feel that?" she asked Lt. Rosslyn.

"What?"

"A tremor. Like a small earthquake."

He shrugged, keeping his laser weapon trained on the rock. "Nothing noticeable."

She stared at the rock. "And I swear the rock moved," she continued, "like it was trying to roll away from the drill."

He cocked his head, giving her an appraising glance. "Aren't you the one who mocked me for drawing my weapon against a boulder?"

A blush heated her cheeks. "Yes. Well. Maybe your training is correct. Use your laser and draw a line on the ground. Right there... at the edge of the rock."

He pointed the laser down and lowered the setting, aiming where she'd pointed.

"Be careful," she said, her voice tense. "Don't score the rock."

"I know how to mark a line in the sand," he growled, grimacing.

When he finished, he returned the laser to a more powerful setting and resumed his wary stance.

Jess lifted the drill and placed it against the rock's gritty surface.

7

The bringer of pain touched my skin again. This time, I refused to wait to be tortured.

I jumped. I rolled away as far and as fast as I could.

The One bestirred my kin again. This time they not only jumped and rolled as one, they let out a mighty shout.

I was humbled by their care for me... in the middle of day-side... when all should be hibernating. My kin might name me an abomination, but they would not leave me to be tortured if they could save me.

The ephemerals ran from me. So fast that the colors and shapes flowed and blended into a sight of such astounding strangeness that I trembled as I transmitted the data.

8

Jess and Rosslyn each took a few steps back. That time they'd both felt the quake. Cautiously, Jess moved forward again, pointing at the score mark he'd made.

"Look at that," she said, pulling out her calipers and taking a quick measurement. "It definitely moved. A full three inches."

Rosslyn shook his head. "That rock's too heavy for your drill to have exerted enough force to move it."

Jess jotted a note into her arm comp, and nodded. "Regardless, a single boulder moving three inches wouldn't account for that tremor." She paused, eyes glazing in thought. "And yet the timing is too coincidental. I touch the drill to the rock; the rock moves; the ground shakes."

She walked around the boulder, Rosslyn shadowing her so that they remained on the same side of the strange rock.

"I don't believe in coincidences," she said, coming to a halt near the mark Rosslyn had scored on the ground. "Those three things are related."

Just then one of the away team ran up. He stopped, saluted Lt. Rosslyn, and waited for acknowledgement.

"What is it, Ensign Richardson?" Rosslyn asked, returning the salute.

"Sir, ship's telemetry just contacted us. There's a hill or structure or mountain... something roughly pyramidical, about a mile past the horizon line."

Rosslyn nodded. "And?"

"Well, sir, telemetry has been monitoring it since it's the only elevated land mass that's been observed."

Rosslyn scowled. A muscle in his jaw twitched. Jess could almost hear him thinking, *Get to the point!*

The ensign must have noticed his superior's growing irritation, because he suddenly blurted, "It moved!"

Rosslyn and Jess both jumped.

"It *what*?" they asked in near unison.

"Sir, telemetry reports that whatever the mass is, it moved. Twice. Each time, it appeared to rise by a few millimeters and then move in our direction. Only slightly," he paused, licked his lips and continued, "but sir, it moved. Twice."

Jess and Rosslyn glanced at each other, and then turned to stare at the rock.

"Lieutenant," she said quietly. "I believe you were correct to offer me protection from that boulder."

Closing her eyes, she calmed and ordered her thoughts. When she felt ready, she opened her communicator and hailed Capt. Shin.

"Sir," she said, in her most official voice. "Preliminary data indicates we may have discovered a completely alien form of life." She took a deep breath, let it out, and grinned at the captain's holo-image. "We have a lot of work ahead of us... and I can't wait!"

PART XIII

FREIGHTER FAMILIES IN SPACE

FREIGHTER FAMILIES
in
SPACE

UNIVERSAL STAR LEAGUE
FILE SIX

DEBBIE MUMFORD

1

Jim raced through the corridors, boots drumming a staccato beat against the metal floor plates. Sweat plastered the syntho-shirt to his back, his heart pounded louder than the ship's old engines, and his breath came in whistling gasps, but he couldn't stop. Couldn't even slow down. His family's survival depended on the outcome of the next few minutes.

Without breaking stride he leapt across a rusted floor panel and then ducked under a sagging I-beam. The ship was overdue for space-dock and major repairs. Way overdue. But Jim knew every nook and cranny, every buckling joint. He'd grown to manhood on the *Quantum Caravan* and he didn't intend to lose her to space pirates now.

Unerring instinct pulled him to a stop before an entry hatch identical to every other hatch on this level. He hadn't bothered to count panels, hadn't paid attention to corridor sections, he simply *knew* this was the hatch he needed. Just like he knew that his family's last hope lay inside.

Thumbing the concealed panel aside, he quickly entered his access code. A puff of stale air brushed his face as the metal hatch squealed its protest at being asked to open. By the Endless Black Void of Space! How long had it been since anyone had inspected this room?

The metal cried and whined and then fell silent as the mechanism jammed.

"No!" Jim cried, throwing himself against the hatch that had opened a bare finger-width. "Black Void! Why now?"

He threaded his fingers through the narrow gap, wrapped them firmly around the hatch's edge and, biting his lip until he tasted blood, pulled with all his considerable strength. No movement. Not so much as a nano's width. A fully functional mecho-servitor might be able to budge that hatch— and the Void knew nothing on this ship qualified as fully functional— but no single human was going to force entry.

Stepping back, Jim paced the corridor before the jammed hatch. He stopped, leaned back against the cool metal and threaded his hands through sweat-dampened hair. Massaging his temples, he forced himself to take deep, calming breaths. There had to be a way past that hatch. He had to get into the auxiliary control room. Had to lock out the main bridge before the pirates managed to completely subdue the bridge crew.

The scent of his own sweat mingled with the stale, dank air still seeping from the long-unused room. Wait. Why was the air stale? Shouldn't the ventilation shafts be circulating air even though the hatch remained closed?

He straightened away from the wall, heart hammering with renewed purpose. Ventilation shafts! He hadn't been in them since he was a boy, but he'd mapped them then and by the Black Void, he'd remember them now.

2

Callie followed Jaxxom through the air lock and into the freighter ship's cargo bay. The pirate behind her nudged her forward with the butt of his phase-rifle. Gantry was an ass, and she knew without looking that the man was leering as he ogled her backside.

"Move it, Blondie," he growled. "You're here to inform, not dawdle and gawk."

She stumbled forward, but caught her balance before falling against Jaxxom. She hated this. She'd grown up on a family freighter much like this one. Would be there still if these pirates hadn't invaded her ship, stolen its freight, and killed everyone who tried to defend their home. Everyone but Callie.

Callie, with her blonde hair, pretty blue eyes, and nicely curved body, had caught the eye of the pirate leader. Markos had spared her life and made her part of his crew. So far, he hadn't forced her into his bed, but she knew his patience was wearing thin. The arrogant bastard actually expected her to be grateful for his mercy, to give herself to him willingly.

But Callie wasn't grateful. She was angry. She wanted nothing from Markos, or any of his foul crew, but revenge for her murdered family. And now, because she'd grown up on a vessel like this one, the detestable pirate actually expected her to help his crew destroy another freighter family.

Not bloody likely! She'd do everything in her power to help the crew of the *Quantum Caravan* survive, and if Markos and his crew were killed in the process, so much the better.

The only flaw in her plan? She was little more than a captive herself. No weapon, and a crew member at her back with orders to keep her in line.

Still, if an opportunity arose, Callie intended to grab it with both hands.

The pirates moved quickly through the ship heading for the bridge. They knew the layout of the ship and didn't need Callie's input... yet. As the murderous boarding party spread like a cancer, they captured a small boy as he tried to dart away to hide and dragged him along in their wake. But when they reached the bridge, they found the hatch sealed against them.

Jaxxom, Markos' second in command and the leader of the boarding party, rapped the hatch with the butt of his phase-rifle. "Open up," he commanded, glaring into the digital eye monitoring the corridor.

No one responded; the hatch remained sealed. Jaxxom motioned to a crew member. The man nodded and dragged the tow-headed boy to Jaxxom's side. The kid was ten or twelve years old, wide-eyed and silent. His mouth clamped so tightly shut his lips sketched an almost invisible line.

Jaxxom grabbed the boy's hair and jerked his head back, eliciting a quick squeak of pain. Angling the kid's head to the monitor, Jaxxom pulled a knife from his belt and placed it against his captive's throat. "Last chance," he said. "Open the hatch or I'll paint the corridor in this boy's blood."

The hatch slid open.

3

Jim dropped from the ventilation shaft into the auxiliary control room and moved swiftly to the control panel. With deft strokes, he transferred command to his location and locked out the main bridge control panels, then strode to the jammed hatch, closed it fully once again, and sealed it, just in case. Slumping into the padded chair facing the command console, he allowed himself a moment's respite. He needed just a bit of space to catch his breath, to calm his racing heartbeat and clear his mind. He'd succeeded in his first task. Now he needed information. He needed to know what the pirates were doing and where the various members of his family were.

His mother, the head of the family and captain of their cargo freighter, had drilled the youngest members of the family— ten-year-old Jackie and six-year-old Dolly— endlessly on how to respond to emergency claxons. The full crew members, Jim, his father, aunt, uncle, and three adult cousins, were required to recite their orders in the event of attack— stations and alternate stations— until they could repeat them in their sleep.

If the adults had been drilled like the children, Jim would've known the hatch was malfunctioning. If the *Quantum Caravan* survived this assault, he'd make sure his mother knew of the difficulty. He'd also check every damn hatch on the ship personally and enlist his cousin Craig's help in repairing any that didn't open immediately upon receiving a proper access code.

But that was for a future that might not exist. Right now, he needed to account for the whereabouts of his family.

Taking a deep, calming breath, he brought up every monitor on the ship, filling the walls of the small room with views of corridors, cargo bays, common areas, and the main bridge. When the image from the bridge monitor blinked on, Jim groaned. A few quick strokes later and that view enlarged and took the central position, directly in front of his control panel.

He watched as a group of men with shaggy hair, unkempt beards, and faces scarred with laser burns strode onto his mother's bridge, pushing his younger brother in front of them.

"Jackie," Jim whispered, "why aren't you under the floor panel in the mess, like you're supposed to be?"

Jackie stumbled when the pirate pushed him, regained his balance, and walked with childish dignity to his mother's side. Jim saw his brother mouth "sorry" as Mom laid a hand on the boy's shoulder and gently moved him to stand behind her.

No matter. Jim had gotten to the auxiliary control room in time. The pirates might have gained the bridge, but they hadn't gained control of the ship.

Jim scanned the scene on the bridge. Besides his mother and Jackie, his father and uncle were also present. A quick count told him that the boarding party consisted of eight rough-looking men and one young woman. Attention caught, Jim studied her. She was close to his age, very pretty, and visibly miserable. She was also unarmed. In fact, it looked to Jim like one of the men was holding a phase-rifle on her.

Interesting.

He had no idea how many more pirates were waiting for a signal to board his home, but he knew how to prevent it. Switching his main monitor to the cargo hold where the pirates had entered, he made sure that none of his family was present. Then he sealed the bay and blew the dock. The blast forced a wedge of space between the *Quantum Caravan* and the pirate ship. Hopefully the unexpected decompression had caused some damage to the other vessel.

The inhabitants of the bridge stumbled in the wake of the blast. Mom recovered quickly and pushed Jackie into a cubicle beneath the science console. Dad and Uncle Mason kept their footing and lunged for two of the pirates, while the young woman whipped around and wrenched the phase-rifle from her captor's grasp as he grabbed for a console to steady himself.

Jim watched as Mom closed the cubicle hiding Jackie and glanced around to find Dad, Uncle Mason, and the unknown woman in a stand-off with five armed pirates. While Jim held his breath, Mom crept stealthily from console to console, got behind one of the pirates, and stunned him senseless with her pocket taser. Picking up his phase-rifle, she nodded to Dad and said in calm voice, "We seem to be evenly matched, but the rest of my crew will be here shortly. I doubt you'll see any reinforcements since that explosion was undoubtedly caused by the docking port being blown."

Glancing at all of the monitors to make sure there were no additional pirates aboard, Jim sounded the all clear and used the ship-wide intercom to tell his aunt and cousins to head to the bridge. He didn't need to tell them to arm themselves. That was self-evident.

Jim watched as Mom smiled, nodded, and said, "Drop your weapons if you wish to live."

The other four adults in the freighter crew converged on the bridge, and the pirates threw their phase-rifles on the deck. While the other family members restrained the pirates, Mom approached the young woman.

"Who are you, and why are you here?" Mom asked.

"Callie Hartswift. A captive from a similar freighter, the *Bluegrass Traveler*," the woman said quietly, surrendering the phase-rifle she held to Mom and lifting a shaking hand to her brow. "They thought I could help them round up stragglers from hiding places once they had control of the bridge." She straightened and gave Mom a grim smile. "I preferred to help your crew."

Mom nodded. "We're grateful. Can we take you back to your family?"

"No." The young woman shuddered and closed her eyes. "I was the only survivor. I have no family."

Mom placed a gentle hand on her forearm. "You do now. If you want it."

Jim thought he saw tears sparkling on the young woman's lashes as he cleared the screens in the auxiliary control room and returned control to the bridge. He glanced from the hatch to the air vent and sighed. Maybe Craig could get him out of here. He really didn't want to climb back into that ventilation shaft.

4

By the time the *Quantum Caravan* reached Space Station Zeta, the nearest Universal Star League outpost to the sector of space they'd been crossing, Callie was adapting well to her new reality. Captain Gwen Verakov and her crew welcomed Callie into their family quietly, without calling undue attention to her newly bereaved status.

The *Quantum Caravan* hadn't wasted time leaving the scene of the attack. They'd secured their prisoners in an unused hold and warped out of the area without bothering to check the status of the pirate ship. They'd leave that task to the authorities.

Once the *Quantum Caravan* was securely docked at Space Station Zeta, Capt. Verakov requested a security team to come aboard and take custody of the pirates. Jim and Callie accompanied her to meet the team at the airlock.

When the lock irised open, a team of ten uniformed USL members stood at attention.

"Captain," the dark-haired officer said with a curt nod of his head. "I'm Security Chief Li Chou, here to relieve you of your prisoners and take your statements. Permission to come aboard?"

"Granted," Capt. Verakov replied. "We're glad to have made port and happy to have you take these pirates off our ship. Jim will show you where they're being held."

Chief Chou nodded and six of his men followed Jim into the ship. "If you'd show us to an appropriate area, my men and I will begin taking your statements."

"Of course," Capt. Verakov said, and she and Callie led the way to the mess hall. "Your men can set up in here. I thought you might like to use my ready room, Chief."

Chief Chou surveyed the mess, nodded, and gave his three remaining crew members their instructions. They would interview the *Quantum Caravan's* crew, while he dealt with Captain Verakov and her newest crew member, Callie Hartswift.

Callie waited on the bridge while Captain Verakov gave her statement. When the door to the captain's ready room *whooshed* open, she stood and waited to be addressed. Capt. Verakov came to the door and said, "You may come in now, Callie."

Stepping into the ready room, Callie moved to stand beside one of the two chairs that faced the captain's desk, a rather shabby old permaplastic relic that had been modeled to resemble the Old Earth wood known as oak. Security Chief Chou stood behind the desk.

"Would you object to Capt. Verakov remaining for your statement, Ms. Hartswift?"

Callie glanced at Gwen, who gave her no clue as to the expected reply.

"Whatever you and Capt. Verakov think best, sir," she said finally. After all, Gwen already knew her story.

Chief Chou nodded. "Very well. Please be seated and we'll get started. Computer, record on. Interview with Ms. Callie Hartswift. Interviewer, USL Security Chief Li Chou. Also present, Captain Gwen Verakov of the *Quantum Caravan*. Ms. Hartswift, please tell us how you came to be aboard the pirate ship known as the *Galactic Marauder*."

Callie glanced at Gwen, licked her lips, and began her story.

"I was born and raised on my family's freighter, the *Bluegrass Traveler*. Approximately three months before the attack on the *Quantum*

Caravan our freighter was attacked and disabled by the *Marauder*. I can't be exact about the timing because I was kept in a dark cell on the *Marauder* for what felt like an eternity. Markos meant to break my spirit, but I'm stronger than he expected."

She was silent for a moment before continuing.

"The *Traveler* was razed. Everything of value removed; the crew murdered. Some died fighting. Some were executed. The freighter was left derelict in space when the *Marauder* was finished."

Callie closed her eyes and took several deep breaths. When she opened her eyes, she met Chief Chou's gaze squarely. "I only survived because Markos liked my looks."

The chief nodded and asked quietly. "Were you sexually assaulted?"

She shook her head. "No. Markos has a singular ego. He fancies himself irresistible to women. He was waiting for me to come to him. After all, he saved me. He expected gratitude." She almost spat the final word.

"Why did he send you with the boarding party?" Chou asked.

"He knew the general layout of the *Caravan*, but also knew it was very similar to the *Traveler*. He thought I'd be able to find any crew that might have hidden in nooks and crannies."

Chou cocked his head, a puzzled expression on his face. "If he's in the habit of killing crew members, why would he care if some were in hiding? They'd die when he spaced the vessel anyway."

Callie grimaced. "Markos hunts *family* freighters. Those most likely to hide are children. You're probably aware that there are high-paying markets for clean, healthy kids, especially those who haven't reached puberty."

Beside her, Gwen startled. Callie hadn't mentioned that part of her story before.

Chou frowned, but nodded. "I see. I'll make sure that the USL sends an enforcement ship after the *Galactic Marauder*. Now that we know where Markos is operating and what his objectives are, we'll track him down, even if he has managed to limp away from his encounter with the *Quantum Caravan*. Computer, record off."

Chou leaned back in his chair and studied Callie before glancing at Capt. Verakov.

"Thank you for your candor, Ms. Hartswift. The USL is prepared to offer you asylum here at Space Station Zeta and to grant you passage to any planet you wish. We can't begin to compensate you for the loss of your loved ones and your way of life, but we can offer you a new beginning anywhere in USL space."

Callie bowed her head and allowed several heartbeats to pass. When she raised her head, she met Gwen Verakov's gaze and raised an eyebrow.

Gwen gave her a small smile and shrugged.

"Thank you, Chief Chou, but if they'll still have me, I believe I'll stay on the *Quantum Caravan*."

Gwen reached out and squeezed Callie's arm. "Of course we'll still have you. You're family now."

Chou stood and gave a single clap. "Excellent. Now let's see about getting the *Caravan* into dry dock. I believe I heard she's overdue for some repairs."

Callie and Gwen grinned. "Jim will be thrilled to hear that," they said, almost in unison... as family members are wont to do!

PART XIV

REMEMBRANCE

REMEMBRANCE

DEBBIE MUMFORD

BESTSELLING AUTHOR OF *SORCHA'S HEART*

1

WHAT WAS

I am a child of the Cold War. When I imagined humanity's annihilation, I envisioned sinister mushroom clouds blighting the world's landscapes, their deadly concussive waves roiling across the earth like tsunamis of destruction.

But Mother Earth is more subtle than man. The death she sent was imperceptible, so quiet we didn't even realize we'd been struck a fatal blow.

I am dying, as all men must, as humanity itself now will. I have no regrets. I have lived a full life; born healthy children; seen them grow to adulthood; held my grandchildren in my arms. No, my regrets are not for things left undone in my life, but for the generations that will not come after me.

I am surrounded by the familiar: the bed I shared with my beloved husband for nearly seventy years supports me in my decline, the quilt I made for his fortieth birthday comforts me, its colors still jewel bright though my sight is dimming. The room is lit by the soft glow of candles in jars, a whim of my youngest daughter. She hopes the sweet aromas of lavender, jasmine, and chamomile will tempt my soul to stay, but I am not interested in lingering. I know what the future holds and I am ready to relinquish my place in it.

I study the faces of my family. The legacy my beloved and I created together in love. Strong, handsome sons. Beautiful, capable daughters. And the grandchildren, grown to adulthood now, though I will always remember them as infants.

There should be great-grandchildren as well. That is my sorrow. The loss of the precious lives that might have been.

My daughters have known the joys and fears of motherhood; my granddaughters never will. I mourn for the birthright they will never experience.

The exquisite pain of childbirth: sheer physical labor that saps the strength and leaves you panting and begging for relief. The inexpressible joy when it is finished and the soft, warm weight you have carried so long beneath your heart is finally placed in your arms. The wonder of seeing your child's features for the first time: your button nose, his cleft chin, the shape of your mother's ear. Ten tiny fingers clutching your one. Toes curling as delicately as rose petals. Tufts of downy-soft hair and skin so smooth and silky you're afraid your rough fingers will mar its perfection.

And the smell! The glorious, delicious smell of infancy, an indescribable but unmistakable combination of warm skin, soft breath, milk, and primal magic that binds a mother to her child, making it nearly impossible to put your newborn down or allow someone else to take the babe from your arms.

This is what we have lost. This is what will never come again.

I glance at each beloved face and my gaze comes to rest on my youngest granddaughter. Her life will be so very different from mine. She may very well live to see the end of our race. She lifts her eyes and meets my gaze. We mourn for each other.

I close my eyes. My time has come.

2

WHAT WILL BE

G randmama closes her eyes and passes from this life with a sigh. I know she worried about us, about me. I felt it in her final glance. My life will not be what she and my parents hoped for me, but it is the only life I have. The only one I have ever known.

Grandmama mourned that I would never have children, that I might live to see the end of our species, that I might be alone in the world at the end.

But she was wrong. The life I will lead, am leading, was unfathomable to her as it is incomprehensible to my parents. I have joined a group of my fellow end-timers — those of us born in the last year that humanity birthed children — and we are laboring to bring another form of life into existence.

My parents' generation used to speculate on the possibility of a man-machine amalgam known as the singularity. They expected it to be a naturally occurring mutation. Unfortunately, Mother Nature took us down a different, completely unexpected path.

But now my friends and I are working diligently to bring that possibility to fruition.

We don't delude ourselves that our creation will save mankind, but we do hope that our brain-child will preserve a record of our existence, will bear witness to any other intelligent species who might someday discover our planet that once our species lived and dreamed and believed ourselves invincible.

This creation, this artificial intelligence, this brain-child will be my legacy. The legacy of all mankind. This is the final pregnancy we labor to bring to term before my generation joins Grandmama in oblivion and the final nights falls on our species.

I pay my last respects to Grandmama, hug Mother, her youngest daughter, and quietly leave the rest of my family to grieve. I have work to do and only my short life-span to accomplish the task.

I join my team at our laboratory. As more and more people die of natural causes — or take their own lives in despair — work space and equipment become more readily available. Grandmama's generation is nearly gone, Mother and Dad's generation has lost heart. They no longer see the point of climbing corporate ladders or struggling to excel in their chosen careers. Even the artists of their generation have lost their focus. Why create when in a few short years there will be no one to view, read, or listen to their efforts?

My generation is, on the whole, manic. Hedonism has reached new heights. Live for the moment and the pleasure it can bring! Why work or behave in a socially acceptable manner? Our elders have no relevance. They will soon be dead. Yes, we can live full life-spans, but why bother? When we die, it's all over anyway, so why not simply live to experience everything now?

Fatal accidents are rampant. There's no reason not to risk life itself. Death is inevitable and there is no future to plan and work for. What does it matter if we die today, tomorrow, next month, or fifty years from now? The end will still be the end.

My team and I are lucky that so many systems are now auto-mated. Basic utilities will outlive our species. Food is becoming less varied as transportation and distribution systems break down, but several of our group have family farms and parents and siblings willing to support our work with their efforts. Our needs are met, and those who meet them are rewarded with a sense of purpose. Some-thing that has all but disappeared.

We are a world unto ourselves. Our small team of computer experts, mechanical engineers, historians, philosophers, and dreamers. We design, build, program, test. We discover bugs, run up against seemingly insurmountable issues, curse fate and the slowness of technological advances, and return to the design board.

Years pass. Attrition dwindles our family. Mom calls to tell me my cousin, a boy just a year older than me, has died from alcohol poisoning. A dare from a friend. They died within hours of each other. I wonder who won the dare, or whether their final idiocy was a draw?

I express my condolences to my aunt and uncle and return to the laboratory.

The work continues. We celebrate a breakthrough. The latest cerebral interface looks promising. All of the initial tests are positive. What is needed now is a human subject.

I volunteer.

When I visit my family for the final time, Mother and Dad are bemused. They never expected to outlive their only child. Of course, they never expected their world to end, either.

I explain that if the experiment works, I will never die.

Yes, my body will cease to function and decay, but my mind will join the artificial intelligence we have created. I will become one with Omega and my thoughts and memories will live on. Omega will remember Grandmama and everything she ever told me about the joys of motherhood, the precious moments of infancy, the complete captivation that a mother feels for her newborn.

Mother and Dad shake their heads, but hug me and send me forward with their blessing and their fervent hope that these dreams of mine come true.

I walk into the lab on my last day as a human being. My team opens a bottle of champagne and we drink a toast to our success, to my continued awareness.

I step up to the padded lounge, rather like the chair my dentist used to have me sit in before cavities became too trivial to be of concern, and my best friend settles the cerebral interface on my head. I feel like I've been crowned empress of the world.

I smile at each of my team members, as Grandmama smiled at each of her family members before she breathed her last, and I close my eyes.

Jared counts backward from ten.

My last conscious thought is of this final infant which we have labored to bring into existence ...

Omega.

PART XV

AN ALIEN ADVENTURE

AN
ALIEN ADVENTURE

A DEEP SPACE
——— SHORT STORY ———

DEBBIE MUMFORD

1

Neila walked briskly through the gray and white plasteel corridors of the security sector of *The Great Beyond*, the generational ship that had been her only home. Head held high, clutching her midnight blue exo-helmet to her chest, she nodded to those she passed with what she hoped was serene calm.

She felt anything but!

Her belly jumped with excitement, alternating between happy flutters of anticipation and a roiling nausea that threatened to expel the light lunch she'd consumed barely an hour ago.

Her mother had chided her for not eating a more substantial meal, saying that Neila would need energy for the landing, but the mere smell of grilled meat made her queasy. Even the bread and cheese had hit her belly like bricks. No way she could've managed more.

With her mother's help, she'd donned her exo-suit. She'd worn one before, of course. Everyone on *The Great Beyond* was required to get into the skin-tight protective gear at least once a quarter. Captain Atherton, a third generation bridge officer, made sure the inhabitants of her ship were ready for any emergency. Her people wouldn't be laid low by native pathogens should they ever be forced to evacuate.

But this was the first time Neila would *need* an exo-suit. She'd come of age last month and her newly adult status placed her on rotation for planet-side exploration. Today was her day; her first chance to plant her feet on something besides *The Great Beyond*'s plasteel decking. She was going to touch down on a planetary surface!

Heart racing, Neila sucked in a deep, calming breath, and winced at the exo-suit's constraint. It didn't hurt, but it was tight. So very different from the loose tunics and soft leggings she usually wore.

She met a young man's gaze and blushed to the roots of her close-cropped dark hair. Honestly! It was like walking around naked, except nothing jiggled. The exo-suit kept her flesh too constricted for anything as normal as jiggling.

The guy nodded and walked on. Evidently exo-suited females were nothing out of the ordinary for him.

Neila rounded a bend and stopped before the hatch to the shuttle bay. Pushing a fist against her jumpy belly, she willed herself to icy calm. This was it. Her moment to prove herself. She would not vomit in front of the away team. She would behave professionally, with a calm beyond her years.

Palming the access panel, she stepped into the bay.

Captain Atherton glanced up as Neila entered, nodded and clapped her hands. The twenty-or-so exo-suited crew members immediately formed into neat lines, with Neila and two others scrambling to find places.

"Good afternoon, team." The captain met the eyes of each crew member. A short stocky woman, she exuded calm and control. "You have been assigned to explore the surface of G-4873, the planet we are now orbiting. Most of you have been on exploration teams before, but we have three newbies joining the ranks today. We all know that classes can only provide a minimum of preparation. The real learning takes place in the field. So teach the newbies what they need to know and bring them back safely."

She turned to the green exo-suited officer beside her. "Lieutenant Dreeson, you have command. Good hunting."

Lt. Dreeson saluted and waited while the captain exited the shuttle bay.

"All right, team. Let's get to work. Corporals Hoskins, Song, and Lomidze, take charge of your assigned newbies. The rest of you, let's get the gear on the shuttle."

Neila watched in confusion as the team erupted into action. She briefly considered moving to stand near the other two midnight-blue suited team members, the only other people looking as bewildered as she felt, but before she could move a green-suited woman approached her.

"Citizen Neila Spiros?" When Neila nodded, the woman continued. "I'm Corporal Ginny Song. Welcome to the exploration team."

Neila nodded, her mouth too dry to attempt speech.

Cpl. Song took Neila's elbow and guided her out of the bustle of activity.

"A few basics. Notice the different colors of exo-suits. Military crew wear green." She indicated her own exo-suit. "We're the most highly trained for combat and provide security for the rest of the team. Once you've passed your field tests, you'll be issued a side-arm, but you'll still rely on the greenies for optimal protection."

Neila swallowed, but nodded. "Got it. Green for guards."

Song smiled. "Exactly. The white suits are scientists; the blue are grunts." She cocked her head when Neila startled. "That is, regular citizens with no particular aptitude for planet-side duty. Those of you in the really dark blue are newbies. Once you pass your field tests, you'll be issued a new suit in the proper color."

"I'm studying biology," Neila said, "specializing in botany, though I'm taking a few courses in zoology. But even when I complete my coursework, I won't qualify as a scientist. At least, not for years."

Song nodded. "Then you'll be issued a yellow suit. Botany is considered a necessary planet-side skill, and our techs wear yellow."

"No techs today?"

"Correct. The make-up of our away team fluctuates depending on who's available and what the head science officer expects us to encounter." Song glanced around. "Looks like we're about ready to leave. Remember, when we get to the surface, stick to me. Don't go wandering off on your own."

"Yes, sir."

Song grinned. "That's the spirit, but I'm not an officer. You can call me Song."

Neila relaxed enough to smile. "Thank you, Song."

2

———

Neila's eyes widened when she stepped off the shuttle. She'd seen pictures of planets, of course. Everything from sand dunes to oceans to craggy mountains, but the experience of stepping onto a springy surface of leaf litter and loam was just... unreal.

Her exo-suit and helmet protected her from the environment, but still she could almost smell the life around her. The shuttle had landed in a long, narrow valley edged by tall plants that could only be described as purple trees. Their trunks, an unexpected lilac shade, rose high above the shuttle before branching out into an interlocking canopy of deep purple. The vegetation growing around their bases was quite varied. Some 'bushes' were deep green with what appeared to be thick, fleshy leaves, and some were shades of rose with delicate, feathery fronds.

All were fascinating and Neila's fingers itched for a sketch pad. But she wasn't here to take notes on botanical specimens, she was here to learn from Cpl. Song.

"Close your mouth, citizen," Song said, tapping Neila's shoulder, "and follow me."

During the shuttle ride Lt. Dreeson had given the team assignments for their explorations. Song and Neila were assigned to assist a white-suited geologist, Dr. Ambrogi.

"I want soil samples," Dr. Ambrogi said. "We'll take the first here in the landing meadow." He pulled a long narrow metallic tube from his pack and handed it to Song. "You take the first one; show the newbie how it's done."

"My name is Neila, Doctor."

He cocked his head at her, then continued pulling equipment from his pack. "Fine. Show *Neila* how it's done, Corporal."

Song turned away from Ambrogi to hide her grin and motioned Neila down beside her in the dirt. "Nothing hard about this. Just stick the tube in the ground and depress the button on the top. You'll feel it vibrate. When it stops, pull it out and give it back to the doc."

Neila watched the process, noting that Ambrogi held the tube to his scanner and typed in a few notes before settling it into a fitted slot in a special compartment of his pack.

They repeated the sampling several times when they reached the tree line. Ambrogi required samples from beneath each species of 'tree' and 'bush,' though he seemed uninterested in the vegetation itself.

After an hour of slowly moving into the dense foliage, they lost sight of the other members of the team. Neila glanced up. The deep purple canopy was so thick she couldn't see the mauve sky, though a few shafts of greenish sunlight did pierce the vegetation.

Wait! What was that?

A flicker of movement caught her eye and she used the zoom feature of her exo-helmet's screen. Something glittered in a shaft of sunlight. Something flying.

She zoomed in again, noting the display's estimation of distance.

Whatever it was, it was sizable. She shouldn't have been able to pick it out from the ground without the zoom. Not when it was nearly 100 meters above her.

She shook her head. According to the display, the canopy of the purple trees was 150 meters up. Unbelievable. Especially when her textbooks said that the canopy of the giant redwood trees back on earth had only been about 30 or 40 meters off the ground. These tree-things were massive.

Just as she was about to apprise Song of her discovery, the creature dove for the forest floor. Right at Neila!

"Incoming!" She closed her eyes, ducked, and covered her head.

"Neila?" Song's voice echoed through her helmet. "What's wrong?"

Before she could answer, strong talons gripped her shoulders and yanked her upward.

3

Neila opened her eyes and closed them again quickly, her stomach heaving. The ground was so far below that Song and Ambrogi looked like ants. She fought to control both fear and nausea. Vomiting in an exo-helmet was so not a good idea!

Whatever this creature was, she sure hoped it didn't plan to drop her. Even with the protective shielding on her suit, Neila knew she'd splat like a raw egg if she hit the ground from this height.

She'd been briefed on how to respond if approached by an alien species, but not on what to do if snatched from the surface and hauled into an unbelievably high canopy.

What was this creature doing? Was she about to become dinner for a gang of its hungry young?

"Neila! Can you hear me?" Song called, her voice sounding even more tinny than usual through the suit's speakers. "Answer me, newbie!"

"I-I'm alive, Song. Wh-whatever this creature is, we're still flying." She opened her eyes again... and swallowed bile. "W-we're really high up. I sure hope this thing is friendly!"

"Friendly," echoed Song. "Yeah. Friendly would be good. Hang in there, Neila. Lt. Dreeson is on the way and *The Great Beyond* has been notified."

Like that's going to do me a lot of good! Neila closed her eyes against the nausea and allowed herself to go limp in the alien's claws.

A moment later the claws released her.

Vertigo hit hard as she fell, undoubtedly to her doom.

But the sensation only lasted an instant before she landed on something solid.

Neila's eyes popped open and she found herself sitting on a branch. A smooth, level branch as wide as a ship's corridor, and she was surrounded by...

...dragons?

She frowned and shook her head, but the creatures still looked like miniature dragons. About as long as she was tall, scaly, with crocodilian heads, leathery wings, two taloned feet, and long spiky tails.

Sun and stars she hoped they were...

"Friendly!"

She turned to face the one that she thought had brought her here. Had that dragon... creature... thing... just screeched the word *friendly*?

"Did you say something?"

"Friendly," it repeated, cocking its head and gazing into her eyes.

Neila stared back... and saw intelligence sparkling in those deep, dark amber pools.

Seriously, could these things be sapient? Could she, Neila Spiros, total newbie, be making first contact with an intelligent alien species?

Yes, said a melodic voice in her mind. *Welcome, Neila Spiros, total newbie, to Omneth. We are the People of the Quarnath, what you think of as 'purple trees.'*

H-How can I understand you? she wondered, staring wildly around at the five dragons surrounding her. One was reddish purple, another dusky gray, the third was greenish gold, the fourth was a deep ocher, and the one that had snatched her from the ground and flown her to wherever the hell they were was the deep purple-black of a bad bruise. Only shiny. And sparkly where the sun touched its scales.

Qunum heard your words as you flew, one of them said, though she still had no idea which. *When your souls connected, our thoughts linked.*

Neila shook her head and said aloud, "Our *souls* connected? What the... heck... does that mean?"

The ocher dragon shuffled its feet and Neila turned to face it.

You... looked into Qunum's eyes. You saw him. He saw you. Your souls connected.

"But I didn't look into your eyes, and you're talking to me."

The bruise-colored dragon shuffled, and she turned back to him. Qunum, she supposed.

We are the People of the Quarnath, he said. *What one knows, all know. Is this not true of your people?*

Her eyes widened and her jaw dropped. She shook her head snapped her mouth shut. After a moment, she answered. "Definitely not."

"Citizen Neila Spiros," said a new voice through Neila's helmet speaker. "This is Captain Atherton. Are you well?"

Neila breathed a sigh of relief before responding. "I'm fine, Captain. I'm somewhere in the canopy having a nice chat with a few representatives of the People of the Quarnath." She glanced at Qunum. "I don't think they mean to harm me. They're friendly."

"That's good to know, Citizen. Ask if they will return you to the surface. We'll have a delegation ready to meet with them. Since we're guests on their planet, we need to establish a few rules."

Neila nodded, though the captain couldn't see her. "Understood, Captain. I'm sure they'll be amenable."

After a moment's silence, Capt. Atherton said, "Well done, Neila. You've had quite the experience for your first away team mission."

"Sir. It's been an adventure," she replied, glancing around at the small dragon-like creatures surrounding her, "and I wouldn't have missed it for the world!"

ABOUT DEB LOGAN

Deb Logan specializes in tales for the young – and the young at heart! Author of the popular Faery Chronicles series, Deb loves the unknown, whether it's the lure of space or earthbound mythology. She writes about demon hunters, thunderbirds, and everyday life on a space station for tweens, teens, and anyone who enjoys young adult fiction. Her work has been published in multiple volumes of *Fiction River*, as well as in *2017 Young Explorer's Adventure Guide*, *Feyland Tales*, and other popular anthologies.

Sign up for Deb's newsletter and receive a FREE story!

To learn more, visit Deb at:
debloganwrites.com
Or send her an email at:
debloganwrites@gmail.com

ALSO BY DEB LOGAN

Children's Stories and Chapter Books:

Cinnamon Chou Files:

- THE CASE OF THE MISSING INARIAN
- THE CASE OF THE GLITTERING HOARD
- THE CASE OF THE RECREATIONAL THIEF
- THE CASE OF THE VANISHING PUPPY

Prentiss Twins Novels:

- THUNDERBIRD
- COYOTE
- WHITE BUFFALO
- THE TWELVE DAYS OF TRICKSTERS (SHORT STORY)
- A TRICKSTER HALLOWEEN (SHORT STORY)

"Read-to-Me" Stories:

- CHATTERMASTER
- DEIRDRE'S DRAGON
- THE FOX AND THE FLEAS
- MOM'S HELPER
- READ-TO-ME STORIES (COLLECTION)

Short Story Collections:

- GALACTIC CADETS: KIDS IN SPACE
- READ-TO-ME STORIES

Short Stories:

- ANGELIC VOICES
- LILAH'S GHOST

Young Adult Stories and Novels:

Dani Erickson Stories:

- DEMON DAZE
- SCHOOL DAZE
- FAMILY DAZE
- CHALLENGING DAZE
- DANGEROUS DAZE
- DANI'S DEMONS (COLLECTION)

Faery Chronicles:

- FAERY UNEXPECTED (NOVEL)
- FAERY BEAUTIFUL (SHORT STORY)
- FAERY UNPREDICTABLE (NOVELETTE)
- LEXIE'S CHOICE (SHORT STORY)
- OF DRAGONS AND CENTAURS (SHORT STORY)
- FAERY COLLECTIBLE (COLLECTION)

Feyland Tie-Ins:

- EMMA: A FEYLAND DRYAD
- ON GUARD: A FEYLAND STORY

Seer Chronicles:

- THE SEER CHRONICLES: VOLUME I (COLLECTION)
- TERRORS (SHORT STORY)
- TO HAVE...AND TO HOLD (SHORT STORY)
- SELKIES IN PARADISE (SHORT STORY)
- THE JOURNAL (SHORT STORY)
- PALADIN SHIELD (SHORT STORY)

Siren Tales:

- SALT WATER
- SIREN SURF

Short Story Collections:

- GHOSTS AND GHOULIES
- MORE GHOSTS AND GHOULIES

Short Fiction:

- AMELIA FOX: SPY IN TRAINING
- BEAUTY OR BUTTERFACE?
- FLUTTERBIES AND FRENCH TOAST
- RUSH!
- THAT LAKE HOUSE SUMMER

"WDM Presents" Anthologies:

- TALES OF MYSTERY & MAYHEM
- 2016: A YEAR OF SHORT FICTION
- 2017: A YEAR OF SHORT FICTION
- WDM PRESENTS: SHORT FICTION FROM 2018
- WDM PRESENTS: SHORT FICTION FROM 2019
- WDM PRESENTS: SHORT FICTION FROM 2020
- WDM PRESENTS: SHORT FICTION FROM 2021

ABOUT DEBBIE MUMFORD

Debbie Mumford specializes in speculative fiction (fantasy, paranormal romance, and science fiction) as well as mystery and historical fiction. Author of the popular *Sorcha's Children* series, Debbie loves the unknown, whether it's the lure of space or earthbound mythology. Her work has been published in multiple volumes of *Fiction River*, as well as in *Heart's Kiss Magazine*, *Amazing Monster Tales*, and many other popular anthologies. She writes about dragon-shifters, time-traveling lovers, and detectives—whether amateur or professional—for adults as Debbie Mumford, and science fiction and fantasy for tweens and young adults as Deb Logan.

Join Debbie's special announcement newsletter list and receive a FREE story!

To learn more, visit Debbie at:
debbiemumford.com/
Or send her an email at:
deborah.mumford@gmail.com

f facebook.com/DebbieMumfordWrites
a amazon.com/author/debbiemumford
BB bookbub.com/authors/debbie-mumford
twitter.com/deborah_mumford

ALSO BY DEBBIE MUMFORD

Kristi Lundrigan Mysteries:

- Delectable Mountain Quilting (Novel)
- In A Pickle (Novel)
- Fool's Puzzle (Short Story)
- Wildfire! (Short Story)

Gus and Ghost Short Story Series:

- Seventh
- Seventh: First Fruits
- Death of an Alchemist (Uncollected Anthology)
- Seventh: The Samhain Dilemma
- Dark of the Moon (Uncollected Anthology)

Logans of Lastalrig Series:

- Her Highland Laird (Novella)
- Her Highland Yule (Short Story)

Red's Series:

- Red's Magick (Short Story Collection)
- Seeing Red (Short Story)

Signs of the Prophecy Novels:

- Youngest
- Seeker
- Chosen (Coming Soon!)

Sorcha's Children Series:

- SORCHA'S CHILDREN (OMNIBUS EDITION)
- SORCHA'S HEART (NOVELLA)
- DRAGONS' CHOICE (NOVEL)
- DRAGONS' FLIGHT (NOVEL)
- DRAGONS' DESIRE (NOVEL)
- DRAGONS' DESTINY (NOVEL)

Supernatural Yellowstone Short Story Series:

- REALITY BITES
- THE CAT LADY OF YELLOWSTONE

Uncollected Anthology Short Stories:

- DEATH OF AN ALCHEMIST (UA ALCHEMY)
- THE WEDDING CAKE (UA MAGICAL ARTS)
- DARK OF THE MOON (UA PARANORMAL PIRATES)
- IN THE BANYAN COPSE (UA UNEXPECTED HISTORIES)
- OLD ONE (UA MAGICAL QUESTS)

Universal Star League Short Story Series:

- VOYAGES INTO THE BLACK (COLLECTION)
- THE WARBIRDS OF ABSAROKA
- AWAKENING THE WARRIOR
- INCIDENT ON THE ODYSSEY
- THE QUEEN'S CAPTIVE
- THE LOST COLONY
- FREIGHTER FAMILIES IN SPACE

Witchling Short Story Series:

- WITCHLING

- THE SOLITARY SORCERESS
- TO PROTECT A PRINCESS

Stand Alone Novels:

- SECOND SIGHT

Historical Fiction:

- HER HIGHLAND LAIRD (NOVELLA)
- HER HIGHLAND YULE
- INCIDENT ON THE HIGH LINE
- MISS BAINBRIDGE'S SUMMER ADVENTURE
- MISS BAINBRIDGE'S CHRISTMAS PARTY
- SISTERS IN SUFFRAGE
- THE TRAIL WHERE WE CRIED
- THE WHITE DRAGON AND THE RED

Short Story Collections:

- LOVE IN A FLASH
- TALES OF BYGONE DAYS
- TALES OF LOVE & MAGICK
- TALES OF THE UNEXPECTED
- TALES OF TOMORROW
- TALES OF DISASTROUS DEEDS

Short Fiction:

- A GROVE OF MOUNTAIN ASH
- A WALK WITH GEORGIA
- ASTROMANCER
- BECAUSE OF THE CHRISTMAS STROLL
- BENEATH AND BEYOND
- DEEP DREAMING

"WDM Presents" Anthologies:

www.ingramcontent.com/pod-product-compliance
Lightning Source LLC
Chambersburg PA
CBHW031033030726
47497CB00004B/1119